Praise for A. K. Arenz

"A. K. Arenz has done it again. In *The Case of the Mystified M.D.*, Glory Harper finds another body part and gives a helping 'hand' to solve a crime. A rolicking good read. You'll smile as you turn the pages."
—Cynthia Hickey, author of *Candy-Coated Secrets*

"I was delighted to see the return of one of my favorite older (and active) sleuths, Glory Harper. *The Case of the Mystified M.D.* weaves together a complex mystery, humor, and appreciation for small town life and the importance of family."
—Sharon Dunn, author of the Bargain Hunter mysteries

"Enmeshed in murder yet again, Glory Harper must tap her Grandma grit and wit to solve her latest extreme investigation. Nicely written with plenty of comic relief, *The Case of the Mystified M.D.* is a punny, page-turning puzzle that will charm readers of every age."
—Cathy Elliott, author, *A Vase of Mistaken Identity*

"Welcome back, Glory Harper! In the second installment in this series, Glory gives the police a hand—quite literally! . . . Another excellent mystery from Arenz. I hope there are many more to come!"
—Christy Barritt, author of the Squeaky Clean mysteries

"Glory's back! The bouncing grandma finds herself neck-deep in another delightful romp as she works with a mischievous puppy to solve a murder plopped right at her doorstep. Arenz' sharply drawn characters and surprising plot keep the reader guessing if the gutsy heroine 'of a cer-

tain age' can discover the murderer before the murderer takes revenge on Glory and her family. A humorous and touching read with an uplifting theme—laugh-aloud fun!"
—Amy Deardon, author, *A Lever Long Enough*

"Delightful grandmother Glory Harper strains at the leash to corral her new puppy and her curiosity when the dog locates a severed hand on a jogging trail. Obnoxious Professor Wallace has been murdered. Glory's penchant for solving mysteries has brought her to Detective Rick Spencer's attention and a special bond has formed between the two. Despite his interest, he warns Glory to stay out of his investigation. Glory tries. But at every turn, the people she's known in her small town reveal secrets. Secrets which could be murder motives. Even a secret her sister holds.

"A. K. Arenz has brought the reader a story of murder and mayhem in small town America, set against a backdrop of God's forgiveness and healing. Bouncy Grandma Glory has succeeded in capturing the heart once again!"
—Eileen Key, author of *Dog Gone*

"A must-read novel: page-turning suspense in a town well-peopled with distinctive characters."
—Donn Taylor, author of *Rhapsody in Red*

"The Bouncing Grandma is back . . . with a vengance. *The Case of the Mystified M.D.* will make you laugh and touch your heart as Glory Harper struggles to solve yet another mystery and protect her family."
—Kassy Paris of the writing team of Kasandra Elaine, authors of The Lazy M Ranch Series

The Case of the
Mystified M.D.

OTHER BOOKS
BY A. K. ARENZ

The Case of the Bouncing Grandma

Acknowledgements

Big THANK YOUs go to Sergeant David Todd of Maryville Public Safety and Maryville Fire Lieutenant Phil Rickabaugh. I truly appreciate the time you both took out of your busy schedules to talk with me. Any mistakes—and I hope there aren't any!—are mine.

A big thank you to my dear friends—Connie Kruppstadt for answering all my insurance questions, and Peg Phifer for Las Vegas info.

I would like to thank members of the following groups: Naners, Grace Marketing, ACFW, and ACFW Prayer loops. To each of you who supported me with prayers, down home sayings, and your friendship, God bless you all!

There were times when I couldn't find my way, and trying to write through it didn't work very well. My daughter Kelly kept me true to the characters and the story. She's the best first editor I could have. Thanks, honey.

Thank you goes to my husband Chris, who saw my anguish on the hard days and elation on the good ones—and didn't run screaming into the night!

Thank you, Randi, daughter number two, for reading those first 150 pages and saying, "Don't stop, Mama. I want more!" A person can never have too many encouragers.

To my grandchildren Madison, Connor, Chloe, and the newest addition, Camden, and sons-in-law, Greg and Gary, you are the glue that holds me together.

There are so many, many people who are involved in day-to-day support and encouragement: my brothers Jim and Ken, sisters Linda and Sandra, sister-in-law Joyce, brother-in-law Bill, and the various nieces, nephews, and greats. Just knowing you're all here for me means a lot.

Thank you Sheaf House and my editor and publisher Joan M. Shoup—your faith in me is inspiring.

A writer's journey may sometimes seem lonely, but we are never alone. To all those I've forgotten to name—THANK YOU. And to the One who constantly reminds me that it is only through Him that I continue along this path . . . You are my Rock upon which all else is built. Thank You for my many blessings.

The Case of the
Mystified M.D.

A. K. Arenz

Charlotte, Tennessee 37036

Dedication

For my husband Chris
and daughters Kelly and Randi

The Case of the
Mystified M.D.

Chapter **1**

I inhaled and almost choked from the heat as it seared my throat and lungs. The air was more than humid, it actually fit the meteorologist's most recent terminology of juicy. The deep blue of the late afternoon sky was so hazy it seemed a bit out of focus. Or maybe that was just the sweat pouring down my forehead.

As I turned toward the sound of a tractor in the nearby field, an enormous horsefly dive-bombed, landing smack between my eyes. Batting at it only seemed to make it angrier. The more I tried to dodge its attempt to take out one of my eyes, the more determined it was to harass me.

All the activity increased the excitement of the puppy at my side. Misty took my strange gyrations to discourage the ardent bug as a new form of play and began barking. But it was her jumping around and tugging on the leash that nearly landed me on the asphalt walkway.

"Janie!" I called out to my sister who was a good fifteen feet in front of me. "You want to come get Misty before she yanks both of my shoulders out of joint?"

Jane didn't break her stride—which was more of a jog than a walk—just turned and headed back to me. When the puppy realized Jane was returning, she became even more anxious, wagging her tail and wiggling so her entire body shook. It was further evidence that this beautiful five-month-old Golden Retriever should belong to my sister instead of me.

"What's wrong Misty-girl?" Jane knelt in front of the ecstatic puppy and allowed the thick pink tongue to lick her hands and face in greeting. "Is Glory still too slow for you?"

"If you didn't insist on running in this heat—"

"I'm not running, Glory," she said as Misty slathered her face with more doggy kisses. "If you walk any slower you won't be moving at all."

"I'm doing the best I can." My protest received a roll of the eyes—from both woman and dog. "Between the heat, Misty, and my leg not being up to snuff, it's a wonder I'm doing this well."

I tried to unwind Misty's leash from between my legs, hers, and Jane's. The more I unwound it, the more the puppy seemed to reweave the thing. Seeing I wasn't having any luck, Jane took the leash and straightened it without a problem. She rubbed Misty's neck and grinned up at me.

"Think you can make it around the field at least once? We've only gone about a quarter mile."

I gazed out across the sea of green in front of me then looked behind us to where my car was rapidly becoming a mere speck in the parking lot. As much as the car and air-conditioner beckoned, I knew I should press onward— and not having to fight with Misty would make the going easier.

"Since you'll tell my doctor if I don't walk, what choice do I have?"

Jane stuck out her tongue. It wasn't a response you'd expect from a mature fifty-five-year-old first-grade teacher. It was, however, perfectly in character for my sister.

"You've been walking without the crutches for several weeks now, Glory, and you know what Steven said." As usual, the mention of her fiancé—and my orthopedist—Dr. Steven Acklin, sent a rush of color to her face. "Your PT reports have all come back fine. You've the strength, and now you have to build up the stamina. Take it at your own pace, okay? I'll go on ahead and give Misty a chance to work off some of her energy."

Jane left, going at a slow jog with Misty happily keeping pace beside her. There was no doubt in my mind that the puppy should belong to her. From the day she and Dr. Dreamboat had presented me with the wriggling mass of fur, I'd recognized which of us was Misty's preferred human, which was perfectly fine by me.

The lively puppy was adorable, loving, and a terrific companion for Jane—especially after a house fire had her taking up permanent residence with me. I figured Misty was the upside to the tragedy. She kept Jane from brooding about a situation that couldn't be changed and also diverted my sister's attention from me.

A sudden breeze teased the perspiration coating my arms. Rather than bringing the freshness of the newly mown field of clover or the scent of the surrounding woods, an odd, unpleasant odor drifted past. A part of me knew the smell, though I couldn't immediately place it. I sniffed again, but it seemed to disappear along with the breeze.

From the corner of my eye, I saw the tractor mower turn in my direction. I caught the tail end of Olav Cawley's wave before he circled back around the way he'd come. At eighty-two, Ollie still farmed the property where he'd been born. And to further prove that age didn't matter, he'd recently set his sights on winning the hand of my former fifth-grade teacher Gracie Naner. All that robust energy from two octogenarians, and here I was, fifty-two and squawking about having to walk a mile!

Taking it slow, I stepped carefully along the recently poured asphalt that made up Tarryton's newest acquisition. The land that would one day have a swimming pool and tennis courts currently consisted of a mile-long walking trail around the perimeter. Situated at the edge of town between Ollie's farm and the college, the area had once been overrun with partying college students. In an effort to curtail the drinking and debauchery—Ollie's words—he had donated the land to the city with a detailed design for Fitness Park.

Ollie got things started by arranging for the walking trail and bulldozing it himself. He then hired his grandson to lay the asphalt. I'd no idea how many people were using the area, but Jane and I found it relaxing with the woods on two sides, the fragrant clover and wildflowers in the field, and the perfect view of Tarryton from atop the hillside.

I looked up to find Jane stopped just a little way in front of me. Misty was nowhere to be seen, her leash disappearing into the brush.

"If she gets dirty, you get to bathe her this time," I shouted, hoping she'd hear me over the mower.

Jane waved, then turned back to the little pathway into the grove of trees. As I neared her, another breeze trickled past, rustling the leaves and sending that unpleasant odor to attack my olfactory senses again.

"What *is* that?" Jane turned to me, her hand covering her nose and mouth.

"Probably something a coyote killed."

"Ah, come on, Glory. There are no coy—"

"That's where you're wrong. Ollie says they go after his barn cats when they can't get anything else."

Jane looked around the area and shivered. Turning her back to me, she tugged on Misty's leash.

"Come on, Misty, that's enough exploring. Misty, come here, girl."

The puppy appeared a moment later, her back low, her head down, and her tail barely swishing the ground between her legs. I'd never seen this kind of posture before and worried she might have gotten hurt. I picked up my pace.

"Oh my! Oh!"

"Janie, what is it? Is she hurt? Do you need a hand?" I came up to where my sister knelt with the puppy, her back blocking my view.

"Um . . . I . . . well, it seems we've more than enough hands at the moment." Jane turned back to me, her face deathly pale. "You want to take her leash? I—I think I'm going to throw up."

I grabbed at the leash as Jane dashed away from the trail to the field inside the perimeter. While she was retching, I bent down to see what Misty held in her mouth.

"Misty, release," I told her firmly.

It didn't help. Instead of dropping her prize, she laid down and tried to hide the object between her paws while keeping it in her mouth. As I bent down to get a closer look, my breath caught in my throat.

"Um . . . uh, Janie, when you're done barfing, you want to call 911?"

"I didn't . . . the phone's . . . in the car. Don't you have yours?"

I dug my cell phone out of my pocket and held it out for her. I quickly realized she wouldn't be making the call—not when she was still puking.

Taking a deep breath that almost caused me to lose the contents of my stomach, I punched in the one touch dial for Tarryton Public Safety.

"Yeah, hi Janet. It's Glory Harper. No. No foot this time." How long would it take for me to live that down? "Janet, we have kind of a situation here. You might want to send Detective Spencer, maybe a full team up to the walking trail."

I covered my mouth with my free hand and drew in a deep breath. "My puppy's just found a hand. And if I'm not mistaken, it belongs to our missing professor."

Chapter 2

B efore the cavalry arrived, I managed to get Misty to release her prize. Convincing her to leave it on the path and join Jane in the field just about cost me both shoulders and elbows. Misty's struggle was going to send me to a chiropractor for sure.

"Is it . . . I mean, is it . . . real?" Jane's face was devoid of color.

I handed her the leash, but when Misty leapt up to give Jane her normal kisses, my sister drew away and started to dry heave.

"Main reason I'm very particular about having a dog lick my face. You never know what's been in their mouth." I patted my sister on the back. "You going to be okay?"

"Are you going to tell me what that thing is?"

"Exactly what you thought it was. A hand. If I'm right, and I'm pretty sure I am, it's Dr. Wallace's right hand. I recognized his ring."

"You recognized—" Jane collapsed on the ground and though she allowed Misty to plop into her lap, she made sure the puppy didn't share any wet doggy kisses. "*You examined it?*"

"Not exactly. I mean, after I got Misty to release it, I looked, and—"

"I've gotta stop hanging around you."

"Huh?"

"First a foot, now a hand. I shudder to think what's next." She leaned down and placed her face into her hands.

Misty, thinking Jane was playing some kind of game, tried to press her nose between Jane's fingers. My sister's ordinary reaction would have been to play along—but not today. She knew where that nose had been.

"Look at the bright side. This time everyone will know I'm telling the truth." My comment didn't appear to reassure my sister in the least. I tried to think of something that would get her mind off her gruesome discovery or make her laugh, but with Zeke Wallace's right hand lying about ten feet away, I didn't feel too funny.

Professor Wallace taught in the Department of Sociology, Psychology, and Human Studies at Tarryton Valley College. Though his expertise was in anthropology, I'd determined his real specialty was causing trouble. In the two years since he signed with the college, he'd managed to get most of the faculty and staff angry with his radical thinking and attempts to eliminate all traces of Christianity from the campus. His more recent assault on the town, threatening to bring in the CCR—the Coalition for Civil Rights, an organization that claimed to be similar to the ACLU but was far more radical—hadn't gained him any fans.

The screech of brakes and the slamming of doors signaled the arrival of the cavalry. Two cars—you couldn't say they didn't know me.

Officers Bradley and Roberts seemed unable to decide whether they should continue to guard the body part, set up a perimeter, or question us. I was familiar with the look Bradley threw in my direction. His stern "Just the facts, ma'am," *Dragnet* attitude had me wishing he'd stand by the hand and send Roberts over for our statements.

I should be so lucky.

Roberts stood staring after his cohort with a hand covering his nose and mouth. I couldn't tell for certain from where I was, but I had the impression the younger man wished he could dash into the field to throw up.

Yep, there it was, the humping back, the twisted body, and he was off to make a deposit among the clover.

Bradley was close enough for me to hear him expel a heavy sigh. He was still rolling his eyes when he reached us.

"Is he back to stand guard yet?"

I peered around Bradley's somewhat rotund form and watched as Roberts slumped forward with another spasm. I shook my head.

"I tried to warn dispatch," I told him. "I thought they'd send someone a little more, um, seasoned."

"Seasoned?" Bradley rolled his eyes again. "The kid came here straight out of training. Tarryton's not the kind of place you expect this sort of thing."

While I had to agree with him on the one hand, on the other, it had only been a little over two months since I'd seen a foot dangling out the back of a rolled carpet. The report hadn't been taken seriously at first—not even by my own family. I think it had something to do with my run-away skateboard and the three-car-pile-up it caused. I was finally vindicated, however, and the police department eventually caught the murderer.

Before that, there hadn't been a suspicious death or murder in our small community since before I was born. I'd call fifty-two years quite a record—for the absence of violent crime, that is, not for my age.

Bradley glanced over his shoulder and shook his head.

"He *is* trying," I volunteered. "In between bouts, he heads back to the path, but the moment he looks down, he loses it. It's probably the ring. Makes it more real. Know what I mean?"

"Can't say I do." Bradley pulled out a notebook and pen, stretched his stubby neck, and took *the position.* "Okay, Mrs. Harper, you wanna tell me how you happened to find the hand."

Gruff voice, stern expression, hard eyes, and a wince every time his partner retched. Yep, this would be a piece of cake.

Ew . . . not the best thing to think of considering . . .

Back to the business at hand . . . again not the best terminology.

"Actually, my sister was the first to see it."

Jane looked up at me through red-streaked, accusing eyes. Though she hadn't gotten sick again, she was still shaking. I went to stand behind her and put my hand on her shoulder for support.

"Mrs. Calvin?"

"We were walking. Misty—the puppy—started acting funny, so I figured she needed a potty break. I stopped where that little path leads into the brush and gave her plenty of leash so she could do her business."

"You're doing great, Mrs. Calvin," Bradley encouraged with a smile.

A smile—I've never seen the man with more than a hint of a smirk on his face. How did she rate a full-blown smile?

It could have something to do with the fact that she's not on the 911 frequent flyer plan. Not that I could help all those times I'd had to call. There was a perfectly logical explanation for every one of them.

"Glory was worried about Misty getting dirty, so I called for her to come out of the brush. When she did, I . . . well, I wasn't positive about what she had in her mouth, but maybe that was just denial."

"So, you got her to release it—"

"No, I, um, I had to . . ."

Jane's face flushed—good, she wasn't so pale—and she lowered her eyes to her lap. Misty gazed up at my sister in ecstasy, her rich brown eyes studying her best buddy. When the puppy nosed her way toward Jane's face, she pulled back so sharply it startled the dog.

I reached down a reassuring hand and patted Misty's head. It might have softened the blow of Jane's rejection, but not by much.

"I guess that brings us to you." Bradley met my eyes, obviously not thrilled I'd be involved in the telling of this story.

Keeping my past mistakes in trying to handle this particular gentleman in mind, I didn't smile, didn't try to make my delivery of the facts any more animated than the monotone he affected.

"I got Misty to release the hand, called 911 and told them what we'd found, then requested they send Detective Spencer and a crime team to work the area."

While Bradley regarded me with his mouth hanging open, I became aware of what sounded like several pairs of feet shuffling through the grass and up the hillside behind me. I twisted around and gazed into the incredible blue eyes of Detective Rick Spencer—Blue Eyes, as I liked to refer to him. He flashed me one of his heart-stopping smiles, reminding me again of how much he resembled Harrison Ford. He then got down to business.

"Hey, Gus, why don't you go relieve Chris before he compromises the scene? We're getting the entire area cordoned off and will need everyone's cooperation until we can get the techs up from St. Joe."

"You're pulling in more muscle?" Ah, so Bradley had more range than his flat monotone standard.

"I think a severed hand warrants it." Blue Eyes looked off in the general direction of Ollie and his tractor mower. "And you need to stop Mr. Cawley from mowing the rest of the field. We don't want evidence further contaminated."

After Bradley headed across the field in pursuit of Ollie, Blue Eyes turned to Jane and me. "How're you girls holding up?"

"I'd like to go home." Another shiver overtook Jane's body.

"Did you give them your statement?"

"Short and sweet, just like *Dragnet* likes them."

I gave my sister a hug and relieved her of Misty's leash. The puppy was so excited by all the company that Jane was having a tough time controlling her. Blue Eyes placed a gentle hand on Misty's head, and the puppy instantly calmed.

He has that affect on humans too.

"Are we free to go, or do you want us to hang around a while." I could have bitten my tongue for even suggesting we leave. But a glance at my sister told me it was the right thing to do—even if the curiosity would kill me.

"I think you'd better take Jane home for now." That was Rick talking, not the detective part of him. "I know where to find you."

"Are you sure? I really don't mind staying."

Oops. My response got me a glare from Jane.

"We've got it covered, Glory," he said, the detective part of him taking charge. "You need to see to your sister." He reached down and helped Jane to her feet. "This place is going to be crawling with officers and techs in a little while."

"So you can locate the rest of the body, right?"

"Oh, Glory!" Jane stumbled off, gagging, as visions of the TV series Bones flitted through my mind. Of course, it was unlikely they'd need the expertise of an anthropologist like Dr. Temperance Brennan. And no matter how good looking and efficient her cohort, Special Agent Seeley Booth, might be, he wasn't our very own Detective Blue Eyes, Rick Spencer.

Staring after my sister, I felt a little guilty. When I glanced up at Blue Eyes, I felt even worse.

"I know your insatiable curiosity—"

"But you'd rather I kept my big nose out of it," I finished for him.

He reached out a gentle finger and ran it down the bridge of my nose. "It's not so big. But it tends to poke into things it shouldn't."

It would be useless to argue with him. In the few short months we'd known each other, I'd proved his point on several occasions.

"Glory-girl?" Olav Cawley tramped toward me, Officer Bradley trailing behind. "What's goin' on? You and Janie all right?"

He passed quickly by me and went straight for Jane. As he leaned over my sister, his arm went protectively around her shoulders.

Bradley finally reached us, breathing heavily. "He said he saw us over here with the ladies."

Blue Eyes nodded. "Thanks, Gus. Go ahead and help the others. I'll take his statement."

Still out of breath, Bradley trudged back toward the path where Roberts stood guard over the hand.

"Sir, I need to ask you a few questions." Rick pulled out a pen and pad of paper, spread his legs slightly, and prepared to take notes.

"Sir?" Ollie frowned up at the detective. "This ain't the military, son. We're all friends here." He turned back to my sister. "You doin' all right there, Janie? You're lookin' a might peaked. The heat get to you?"

"I'm better now, Ollie." Jane gulped down a breath, wrinkling her nose as the acrid odor of decaying flesh breezed by. I didn't think it was my imagination that it was worse now than earlier.

Noting Jane's reaction, Ollie nodded and gazed out across the field. "Been smellin' that all afternoon. Coyotes must've taken down somethin' big."

The statement was enough to send Jane back into the clover once again. The look of concern on the old gentleman's face was typical of Ollie. He had a heart as big as the outdoors he loved so much.

"Mr. Cawley?"

I was torn between going to comfort my sister and staying put so I could listen in on Blue Eyes's questions. The choice was simple. Though I wished it wasn't. As Ollie turned back to the detective, I started for Jane.

I made my way over to where she crouched in the field of clover, straining my ears to see if I could hear even a smidgen of the conversation going on behind me. Couldn't fault a girl for trying to stay informed.

The closer we got, the more excited Misty became. I finally had to rein in the puppy to keep her from knocking my sister over. When I put my hand on Jane's shoulder to offer her comfort, I was surprised Misty didn't try to nose her way between us. Instead, she sat next to me and watched Jane with obvious concern.

"How am I going to host the committee meeting tonight when I feel like this?" Jane moaned. "I'm far from ready."

In all the excitement, I'd completely forgotten about the HEC—Holiday Events Committee—meeting and that it was our turn to host it. Actually it was Jane's turn, but with her own place burned almost beyond recognition. . .

"There's always Randi's Dandies," I told her, picturing Tarryton's awesome little bakery, a place where even window shopping added to your daily calorie intake.

"Oh, Glory!" Jane turned away, her body shuddering. Obviously thinking about the shop's decadent goodies wasn't a smart idea for her right now.

She glanced at her watch, squared her shoulders, and stood. "Andi should be at the house by now."

My daughter and seven-year-old grandson Seth were bringing over extra chairs to accommodate the committee. The additional ten people in my small living room would be a tight fit, and I was glad we'd made other arrangements for next Monday's Bible study. I couldn't imagine having thirty women jammed in there.

Jane relieved me of the puppy's leash and headed back toward Blue Eyes and Ollie, with Misty eagerly lolloping by her side.

It didn't take me long to catch up.

Ollie was shaking his head, a pensive look on his face. He gazed out across the field, flashed Jane and me a brief smile, then turned back to Rick.

When he finally spoke, Ollie's tone was harsher than I'd ever heard it. "That man has made more enemies than Carter's has pills. So if it's him, I guarantee there ain't a person in town who'll shed a tear."

With that said, Olav Cawley turned and walked away.

Chapter 3

Jane didn't stand around making small talk. After a warning from Blue Eyes not to talk about what we'd found, we were on our way home. I didn't even have the opportunity to discover what had happened between him and Ollie.

It was true there was no love lost between the good citizens of Tarryton and Professor Zeke Wallace; his penchant for making enemies was notorious. I just never expected one of the nicest people I'd ever known to express this quite so candidly.

I pictured Wallace in my mind's eye, the way he swaggered instead of walked, the unruly dark hair that never appeared to have been combed in the first place, piercing grey eyes, and squared jaw. I'd thought him a good-looking man until I actually met him. It hadn't taken long to realize what hid beneath that charming smile was an abrasive personality determined to undermine every good thing our town stood for.

Like HEC.

Tarryton's Holiday Events Committee was renowned for its attention to detail and coordination of holiday festivities in town. Committee members consisted of representatives from the city council, the schools, the college, the synagogue, and each of the community churches. Starting with Thanksgiving and going through New Year's Eve, HEC helped in arranging and scheduling events to optimize attendance to all. From Hanukkah celebrations to the pre-school and kindergarten Christmas Extravaganza to Tarryton Valley College's special Christmas concert, HEC was relied upon to keep events from crowding together, making it less likely someone would have to miss out on one of the celebrations.

"Stop brooding." Jane kept her eyes on the road, but her tone said she knew exactly what I was thinking.

Misty responded to the break in silence with a soft woof. She poked her nose between the seats, her tongue lolling out the side of her mouth.

"I'm contemplating. There's a difference," I told her as I gently pushed the puppy's muzzle aside. My reward was a handful of gooey slobber.

Jane shook her head, then spared me half a glance.

"Brooding." She said with finality. "And that brooding better not include me standing lookout while you do something stupid."

That hurt.

The best way to handle this situation—at least for me—was to ignore my sister's comments. As much as I love and respect Jane, over the years I've become quite adept at choosing when, or even if, I needed to heed her advice.

And despite her warning, trying to discover what happened to Zeke Wallace was definitely on my agenda.

But first things first.

"The Kelly's truck is gone," I commented as we skirted Andi's car and drove into the garage. "I hope that means they've finished with the jungle gym."

"Jungle gym? That monstrosity looks more like the entire set of playground equipment at Centerview Park!"

Now it was my turn to stick out my tongue. I'd looked long and hard at the different swing-sets and jungle gyms available in Kelly's Garden and Landscaping catalogs until

I'd found exactly what Seth and I wanted. Maybe I had gone a bit overboard. That's a grandma's prerogative.

The moment the car doors opened, we were greeted by a luscious aroma seeping in from the kitchen.

"I know your deep dish apple pie when I smell it. I thought you said you weren't ready for HEC."

"After what we've just gone through, I'm not certain I am. As for the pie, Andi put it in for me." Jane slid through the kitchen door and went directly to the oven—Misty trotting along at her side.

Jane pushed the inquisitive puppy's nose out of the way and opened the oven door. Along with the delectable scent of baked apples, cinnamon, and savory crust wafting through the air, a wall of heat slammed into the already hot kitchen. My sister backed up a step, then quickly shut the door.

"Maybe baking wasn't a good idea on such a hot day." She turned toward me, her formerly pale face pinkened from the 425° oven setting. As if in response to her statement, the air conditioner kicked on.

"That's why there's Randi's," I muttered, heading to the back door.

"For once you might be right." Jane sighed. "There's a first time for everything."

There was a wicked gleam in her eyes when I turned to glare at her.

I wrinkled my nose. "Nice to see you're back to normal. I thought I might have to call Dr. Dreamboat for a house call."

As I reached for the knob on the back door, something soft hit my back, then drifted with a gentle plop to the floor. I didn't have to look down to know it was one of the potholders that had been lying next to the stove.

"You better get it out of your system now, Janie. You're back to school in a week. Wouldn't be a good idea for the teacher to be sent to the principal's office for disorderly conduct."

Her answer was a snort that wasn't any more lady-like than her tossing the potholder. Which was probably one of the reasons she got along so well with her first-graders. Her lack of pretension and knowing just how to communicate with a bunch of six and seven-year-olds won the kids' hearts and attention every year. I know it's why she and I get along so well.

"Looks like Kelly's got your new playground set up." Jane commented.

A glance out the window to the backyard showed my daughter watching nearby as Seth climbed a rope ladder to the upper platform on the jungle gym. The supports for a two-man tent were in place, its bony appendages looking like the remains of a small dinosaur. Other than the missing tent, it appeared Jane was right.

Once on the platform, Seth turned toward the house and waved. Andi threw a look over her shoulder, then started toward us. Jane and I met her on the patio.

"Hey, Bouncy, Bouncy!" Seth hollered. "This is so cool." He swung out onto a trapeze bar, flipped himself over with a grace I'm sure I never possessed, then hung upside down by his knees.

"Not excessive, eh?"

I refused to take the bait in Jane's challenging tone. Instead I wrapped my daughter in a tight hug.

"It is a little much, Mama." Andi said, pulling out of the embrace. She patted my arm to soften the accusation. "But it's a grandparent's right to spoil their grandbabies." She smiled. "I'm just thankful you had it erected here instead of in my backyard."

"Yours isn't big enough. Besides, I wanted something here for the kids." I gave her tummy a gentle pat and was rewarded with a kick from the little one inside.

Jane was about to make another disparaging comment when Andi stopped her with a quick hug.

"It's ever so much better than climbing trees. Wouldn't you agree, Aunt Jane?"

We all knew Andi's aversion to that. She'd been even more wary of the activity since Seth got caught on a branch of my oak tree and she was forced to climb up to free him.

"Before I forget," my daughter continued, "Will Garrett called a few minutes ago. He was actually polite for once." Andi held out the cordless phone. "What's up with that?"

Will Garrett is a reporter for the *Tarryton Tribune.* To be more accurate, he's the only reporter. He's so pushy and obnoxious that I'm sure he wouldn't even have the position if his parents didn't own and operate the paper. As for him being polite, maybe he'd finally figured out neither Jane nor I would cooperate with him if he didn't show at least a modicum of the good manners we knew he'd been taught.

Which also meant he must have a police scanner and consequently have some idea of what we'd found at the walking trail.

"Thanks for getting those pies in, sweetie." Jane grabbed the phone and successfully changed the subject in one fell swoop.

"Pies?" Which would indicate more than one. And Jane said she wasn't ready. I should have known better.

"We're expecting a pretty big turnout tonight to kick off the season," my sister went on, ignoring me.

The season? In the middle of August, with the heat index near a hundred, it was difficult for me to think of this as the season for anything other than searing heat and the upcoming school year. And I have an excellent imagination.

"Seth and I brought the chairs over like you asked," Andi was saying. "I borrowed some from Mindy, so that makes eight."

"With the eight from the dining room and the four from the kitchen—"

"And just exactly where do you plan to put all those chairs?" My 12' x 14' living room already held about as much furniture as it could and still leave room to walk.

"We'll move the coffee table out, clear the things from the entryway, and move the dining room table—" Jane continued, ignoring me yet again. She was about as good at that as I was.

"Where do you plan to put everything—everybody, for that matter?"

"The den, the bedrooms, we've got it covered." Jane tossed the comment over her shoulder before returning to her discussion with Andi.

"Huh?" Had I missed something? "How can you have people in all the rooms and still have a meeting? You're not making sense. Besides, I thought this was just going to be the executive board. Ten people." A terrifying thought suddenly occurred to me. "Are you saying it's the entire HEC committee? That's what—thirty, forty people? You plan on stacking them on top of one another?"

"Glory."

"It's a valid concern, Janie. Even if we put someone in every room of the house it would be a tight fit. And I really don't think any of them want to share their lap. Except maybe Joe Finley, but that's another story."

My attempt at humor was lost on both of them. Joe was one of the quietest, most innocuous people I'd ever met. In complete contrast to his wife, and my boss, Hannah.

"Relax, Mama. We're moving the furniture to the other rooms to open up more space. With a little rearranging, there's a straight shot from the entryway clear through to the dining room. You'll be surprised how big it really is."

Panic took hold as the implication of the sudden invasion of my private sanctuary set in.

"I haven't vacuumed in days, and God only knows the last time I dusted. And the bathrooms . . . " I dashed for the kitchen door. A few moments ago I wouldn't have thought anything could top finding Zeke Wallace's hand, but the idea of having a bunch of people in my home when I hadn't been cleaning for a solid week in preparation scared me to death.

Visions of Marla Hobbs's *Stepford Wives* perfectionism was bad enough, but just thinking about the gossip that would follow a visit from Tarryton's information broker extraordinaire, Elsie Wilkes, had me running.

I threw open the door and was nearly bowled over by an excited Misty, anxious to get outside to greet her second favorite person—Seth. While I clumsily tried righting myself on the narrow steps, Jane and Andi called out to me.

"Chill, little sister." Jane grabbed my arm to steady me. "Andi and I took care of everything while you were at work today. Except the heavier pieces of furniture. I figured you and I could handle those."

"The cleaning—"

"Done. And I'm sure it'll pass Elsie's white glove test." Andi grinned. "I can't guarantee anything where Marla is concerned."

Excited yips followed by giggles had us looking back to the jungle gym. While Seth swung upside down, Misty ran back and forth just outside the range of his hands. Each time he reached for her, the puppy yipped again, then darted away.

"Now there's where Misty really belongs." I said. "With Seth."

Andi wrinkled her nose. "We'll be taking her home with us for an overnight, but . . . "

Seth flipped over and landed inches from the puppy. Within seconds his arms were wrapped around her with his face burrowed into her fur.

"Don't let her lick you!" Jane was off across the yard in a flash.

"It's not a problem—" Andi started.

"Today it is." I told her. "Trust me."

While Jane gently pulled boy and dog apart, I quickly related what we'd come across in the park. Andi turned a little green, then hustled out into the yard and grabbed her son.

"Is there any way you can, um, clean out her mouth or something?" Andi asked after dispatching Seth to the bathroom to wash the moment we entered the house. "There's no way I can keep the two of them apart tonight."

"Dental bones and rawhide." Jane dug one of the bones from the box and waited until Misty finished slurping her water before holding it out for her. The puppy snatched it up and swallowed it whole.

"That worked well. Maybe you should try some mouthwash."

Jane made a face at me, then turned back to the sink to wash her hands.

"I can't believe this has happened again." Andi sent me a nervous glance. "I know it's not the same . . . "

"But you can't help wondering if she's become some sort of murder magnet," Jane finished. "If I believed in Karma, I'd be questioning what she'd done in a previous life to deserve this."

"Then it's a good thing you don't believe in such things. Besides, sister dear, if you'll recall, it wasn't me who discovered the hand."

"She's your dog," Jane retorted.

"She'd rather be yours."

Misty yelped once, then trotted to stand between Jane and me.

"Atta girl." Andi grinned. "Looks like she's the perfect referee for you two." She sidled over to the dinette and picked up an envelope. "Before I forget, Sally Hawkins brought this by."

Sally's been our insurance agent since our former neighbor, Rex Stout, decided it was more fun to spend our money on himself than to submit it to the company he represented. The town was still recovering from that little fiasco.

Jane took the proffered envelope. "Must be a check from the insurance company."

"Have they finished their investigation?" Andi lowered herself onto a stool on the other side of the counter bar.

"Rick said it was more of a formality than an investigation. There's no question it was an accident." I turned to my sister and found her frowning at the message she held.

"That's odd." Jane shook her head.

"What? What's it say?"

"It's a check for living expenses and a note on the initial findings." Jane glanced up, then quickly lowered her eyes back to the letter. "Sally says that I need to be more responsible when storing flammables, especially spray paint. It seems the heat from the water heater caused them to explode, triggering the fire."

"Oh my!" Andi's startled expression mirrored mine, making me determined to check what unsuspecting fire hazards lurked in my own basement.

"That's what's so odd," Jane said, her gaze shifting between the two of us, "I've never had a can of spray paint in my house."

Chapter 4

Mysteries. I thrive on the intricacies involved in discovering the unknown, while my sister and daughter prefer a more normal, everyday existence. The thrill of the chase—even if only through a book, movie, or TV—invigorates me. Especially when I successfully solve the puzzle.

Jane accuses me of seeing a conspiracy in everything—even the way leaves fall in autumn. While I see ambiguity in the simplest things and wonder what I might be missing, she and Andi look for the more staid and logical explanation. When I'm observant and question events or the actions of others, they think I'm being nosy, bordering on obsessive. I figure it's all in the way you chose to look at it.

I enjoy allowing my curiosity and imagination to run free—maybe too free at times—but at least Seth appreciates this aspect of my personality. We've had a lot of adventures in the past, discovering new things to do and interesting ways to play together. We never *just* go to the park; we embark on an African safari or prepare to climb Mt. Everest.

It's true that my determination to be a fun grandmother has gotten me into a bit of trouble now and then. Just ask Tarryton Public Safety. I'm in the final stages of recovering from one of the last adventures: the skateboarding accident that caused a three-car pile-up and left me in a wheelchair for six weeks. The up side to that little fiasco was meeting Blue Eyes and uncovering a murder.

Jane and Andi were still recovering from that incident.

While we moved furniture and prepared for the HEC invasion, I chewed over the information regarding Jane's fire. I knew my sister well enough to know she was telling the truth about the spray paint. If Jane said she hadn't used any at her house in the four years she'd been back in Tarryton, then that was that.

She'd kept her basement almost as clean and organized as the main living area—something she was attempting to do here as well, though she'd about decided she was fighting a losing battle. Still, I'm sure she was capable of rattling off everything she'd had in her home, right down to the smallest, most insignificant detail. I knew she'd been able to come up with a list, pictures, and serial numbers for the insurance company after the fire—all information she'd kept tucked away at the bank in a safety deposit box.

I, on the other hand, had a basement filled with bits and pieces of everything under the sun. Partially filled cans of spray paint included. Ike and I had tried taking the initiative to list what we owned, but when he'd gotten sick, I dropped the ball. Since Jane's fire, I've learned the value of being prepared with this information. And now, with the latest news regarding the cause of the fire, I could see a date with a broom and garbage can looming in my near future.

Bottom line, those cans of spray paint had been found in her house. If she hadn't brought them in, how had they gotten there? The implication was obvious to me. Whether she realized it or not, we had ourselves another mystery.

But now wasn't the time to mention this fact. The pinched look on her face and sweaty brow said she already had enough to handle with everything else going on today.

After rearranging the furniture and placing the folding chairs and others in what Jane and Andi felt were strategic locations, we gathered up Misty's food, dishes, and a few of her toys, then loaded the lot into Andi's car. It was like getting things together for a baby, all the little necessities for the puppy's comfort on her overnight stay.

With the house ready and Misty out of the way, Jane and I sat down for a quick bite to eat—toasted ham and cheese sandwiches with tall glasses of iced tea. I munched away while Jane picked at her sandwich, barely nibbling it. Between our grisly discovery on the walking trail and the news about her fire, she seemed to have lost her appetite.

"You really should eat something, Janie. You need your energy for HEC."

She pinched off a corner of the toasted sourdough and raised it to her mouth. "What do you think they'll do when I tell them?"

I knew immediately what she was referring to. We'd been mentally in sync since we were kids. Though I knew for a fact there were times we'd both wished to be less in tune with each other.

"Investigate." I reached out and gave her arm a reassuring squeeze. "Blue Eyes will know what to do."

She gave me a funny look, then shook her head. "Why do you call him that? No," she shook her head again when I opened my mouth to answer her. "No, don't bother to explain. I already have a headache."

"All you have to do is look at him, Janie." Picturing Rick's incredible, dark blue eyes, I couldn't help but sigh.

"If you're not careful, little sister—"

"Bite your tongue."

Jane winked and snickered. "It's not a bad thing."

"For you and Dr. Dreamboat it's perfect. For me," I shrugged, "I'm still trying to adjust."

My husband Ike had died three years earlier after a long, hard battle with cancer. Losing Ike and moving forward with my life has been a struggle eased only with the love and support of my family and my faith in God. It hadn't been until my foot-in-the-rug mystery and meeting Detective Rick Spencer that I'd realized I was capable of having a relationship with another man.

Going out with Rick—I still had trouble with the word dating—was one thing. Being prepared to get serious about him or anyone else was a whole other animal.

"Adjust, my foot. From the way the two of you look at each other—"

"Don't go there."

"—you and Rick will be heading down the aisle soon after Steven and me."

I sat back on the stool, straightened my shoulders and glared at her. "I'm an expert at looking and not touching. Just ask Randi. She says I'm the only one in town who comes into the bakery just to window shop."

"While you've been window shopping, Glory-girl, Rick's been preparing to buy." Jane rose from the counter and began gathering the detritus of our meal.

I considered her statement, thought about Blue Eyes's lopsided smile and Harrison Ford good looks, and melted. A rush of heat spread throughout my body, likely bringing with it a full blown blush, and I knew it would be useless to attempt countering her claim.

As my sister placed our dirty dishes into the dishwasher, her eyes strayed to where I still sat at the counter. She flashed me a triumphant grin, then continued her task. I tried to pretend I hadn't noticed, hadn't allowed her statement to get me thinking about the handsome detective.

I'm pretty sure it didn't fool her.

I collected the plates and napkins Jane intended to set out on the dining room table and carted them into that room. She had the pies on cooling racks in the kitchen, their tantalizing scent tempting my taste buds. One bite of that delectable concoction would ruin my diet and my determination to lose the remaining five pounds I gained during my time in the wheelchair. Guess I'd just have to prove to Jane how good my will power really was.

About forty-five minutes later members of the HEC committee began to arrive. Marla Hobbs, Tarryton's number one hostess with the mostess and HEC vice-president, was the first, followed by a steady stream of individuals. It didn't give Marla much of a chance to check out the house, for which I was grateful. As much as I like her and all the good things she does for our church and community, Marla can come across as a bit of a snob—especially when it comes to housekeeping.

And cooking.

And hosting anything.

Next to Jane and Randi Gregar, owner of the fabulous Randi's Dandies, Marla Hobbs was one of the best cooks/bakers in town. Tonight she came equipped with a cake that looked as though it came straight from the pages of a Betty Crocker cookbook. Each curly-cue, every rosebud were drawn with perfection, even putting some of Randi's awesome creations to shame.

Still, I'd sooner eat something from the bakery than one of Marla's delicacies any day; Randi's looked as real and delectable as they tasted. Marla's goodies gave me the impression she'd used shellac to fix everything in place and give it just the right sheen. No one else seemed to have this problem when it came to chowing down on Marla's treats, so I guess it was just me.

The noise level rose with each new arrival. So did the heat. I'd just headed down the hall to readjust the air conditioner when the doorbell rang. I turned to see Jane usher in Elsie Wilkes.

True to form, Elsie had a smile plastered on her face, though it was considerably tighter when she looked at my sister. They'd gone through school together and been what I've always called friendly enemies. Though they remained friendly to an outside observer, anyone who knew the two would notice the barely perceptible coolness, the carefully held restraint. I knew there had been a time when the two were the best of friends and always wondered what created the rift. As close as Jane and I are, this was not something I could ask her about. I liked living way too much.

Though we've never been best friends, Elsie and I have gotten along quite well. As Tarryton's premier real estate agent, Elsie makes it her business to know everything going on in town. She has her finger on the pulse of the community and her ear to the ground. If it's worth knowing, Elsie Wilkes has the information. Often before anyone else—including the person the info pertained to. I found this ability of hers fascinating. And, at times, quite useful.

Elsie's love of gathering information was only equaled by her eagerness to share what she'd learned. Of course, there was usually a price to pay. Elsie's rambling and elaboration was in the form of a master storyteller with all the bends, turns, and roundabouts that could sometimes make your head spin. But if you were willing to let her relate her tales at her own pace, and managed to figure out how to follow along without getting lost, you were sure to be entertained.

Okay. Yes, it's wrong to gossip, but sometimes I just can't help myself. Besides, I really don't tell tales out of school or pass along what I've heard. I only listen. That's different, right?

I caught Elsie's eye and waved. Instead of reciprocating, she pressed her right hand protectively to her left shoulder before she turned on her heel and went on into the living room.

Guess that meant she still blamed me for her getting shot. Not that I had anything to do with it. I don't even own a gun.

After setting the air to seventy, I slipped back down the hall and took one of the chairs angled between the entryway and living room. Though I wasn't an official member of HEC, I frequently attended the meetings to assist Jane with the refreshments. It gave me an early insight into what events were planned and made me feel involved, if only in a small way.

The meeting was called to order, and while Jane waited for everyone to settle down, I scanned the faces of those present. I did a quick tally in my head and realized everyone was accounted for with one notable exception: Lizzie Cawley, Ollie's granddaughter.

Lizzie works full time as the secretary at our church and has held the office of HEC secretary since the committee's formation six years ago. She's not only efficient and personable, both admirable and necessary traits, but she also possesses a near photographic memory, something that comes in handy when dealing with so many people with a variety of personalities. Her sunny disposition makes her a natural for her dual positions.

She's also the only one in Tarryton who believed there was more to Zeke Wallace than his chosen role of provocateur. Which didn't sit well with anyone.

recognized and stood. I'd heard people snicker when they learned her name. But they sang a different tune when they met her.

A tall, statuesque redhead with flashing green eyes, Kelly was the picture of health and vitality—and could hold her own with any scoffer. Now she waited until everyone had quieted down before speaking.

"I know we don't usually start the coordination of events before Thanksgiving, but I'd like to propose a change this year to include Halloween."

There was a bit of dissention in the ranks, but Kelly held her ground.

"Wallace's objections center around our faith and the interaction of the secular and religious branches of our community. We've never seen the need to separate the two because that's who we are, what we believe in. No one has objected—until now."

"What's that got to do with our discussion or with Halloween?" Albert Donovan cast a wary glance toward Kelly. "Are you suggesting we attempt to placate this troublemaker by organizing a city-sponsored Halloween celebration?"

The mumbling grew until they were no longer whispers but outright discussions without consideration for the recognized speaker. Rumors of the increase in vandalism and the belief that Wallace and Renée Brent had more to do with it than Tarryton's small cache of juvenile delinquents were those voiced loudest.

I knew firsthand of one young man who'd been involved with the few Goths in the area—he lived right down the street from me. Nick Pearson owned a hot red Mustang convertible that he liked to drive at breakneck speeds up around the cul-de-sac every night like clockwork. At least he did until he and the other Halloween-painted kids he hangs with got in trouble with the cops.

After his last run-in with Blue Eyes, Nick's parents relieved him of the keys to his sports car and made him wash the deathly black and white paint off his face. It was my hope that Rick managed to scare the young man straight.

Jane cleared her throat, coughed, and asked for order. It was Kelly Greene who held the floor, however, and her strong, clear voice took back control of the meeting.

"This may not seem like part of the same discussion or even a solution, but if you'll just hear me out, you'll see it's both." Kelly flipped her long, auburn ponytail over her shoulder, looked toward her best friend Randi Gregar, then continued.

"Every year, the Chamber's Safe Treats for Tots tries to involve all of Tarryton's businesses and encourages participating owners to stay open a little later on Halloween so the kids can do their trick-or-treating in a safe environment. We work together with the churches who organize activities for the older kids to keep mischief down to a minimum. Even the college arranges special events to involve the students in an attempt to keep them off the streets and out of trouble. By combining HEC *and* the Chamber's efforts, we could make this a city-wide event that would benefit everyone—kids and adults alike." She took a deep breath and gazed out across the room.

"We'll set up a maze out at the nursery again this fall," Kelly continued. "We're going to expand our participation to include hayrides each weekend in October, with a pumpkin carving contest the Saturday before Halloween."

Randi rose, nodding in agreement, her tiny frame seeming to quake with each nod. To look at her, it was hard to believe she earned her living by baking delicacies filled with more calories than a person should eat in a week, let alone a single sitting.

Chapter 5

Refreshments were served with help from Marla and Elsie. Jane's pies and Marla's cake received rave reviews, with some of the men hanging around the table waiting for seconds. I made sure there was plenty of ice, coffee, lemonade, and tea available. The job kept me hopping from the dining room to the kitchen and ensured I stayed far away from the deep dish apple pie and temptation.

It also gave me an excuse to duck out of sight every time Hazel Garrett, Will's mother and owner of the *Tarryton Tribune*, made a beeline for me. My luck finally ran out.

"I know when someone's deliberately avoiding me." Hazel sidled over to the counter with an amused glint in her blue-grey eyes. "You didn't return Will's call."

"So much to do and so little time." I measured out the instant tea with far more care than was necessary.

"So?"

I didn't answer. Just continued making the tea.

"Glory, you know we'll get the details eventually, so why not tell me now?"

One quart of tap water, one from the PUR water pitcher in the fridge.

Hazel released an exaggerated sigh. When I reached for the long-handled spoon to stir the tea, she grabbed it first.

"Glory—"

"Hazel." I smiled.

"Why did the cops go to the walking trail today?"

"They needed the exercise?" I pulled another spoon from the drawer, grinned, and set to stirring the tea.

"You called it in."

Tap the spoon on the side of the pitcher, rinse it in the sink, put it in the dishwasher.

And do your best to ignore Hazel.

It always helps to list things when I'm backed into a corner.

"Glory Harper, whose body did you find this time?"

Hazel wasn't so amused now. She stood before me frowning, hands on her ample hips.

"Body? I didn't find a body." A true statement. "You must not have heard the call correctly."

It's logical the paper would have a police scanner. Far less logical for Elsie to own one, which I knew from experience she did.

Elsie.

I was more afraid of what she could do with the information—and me—than anything Will or Hazel might write.

"Having second thoughts?"

And third and fourth. But there was nothing I could do. Nothing I wanted to do, for that matter.

"I made a call to the station." Voice steady, my eyes met hers. "That's all I can tell you." When she started to protest, I shook my head. "You'll have to get your intel from Public Safety, Hazel. Sorry."

I grabbed up the pitcher and slid past her into the dining room. Hazel wasn't as persistent or nearly as obnoxious as her son. Will was like a battering ram when he was after something. The way he picked, picked at a person, I'm surprised he hasn't had his head handed to him by now.

Or at the very least been arrested for stalking. I knew our police officers didn't care for his tactics.

Hazel followed closely on my heels but didn't pester me. Neither did she go after Jane to see if she'd break. Instead, Hazel mingled with other HEC members, gradually drifting into the living room without a glance back at me. Very classy. Wish she could have taught that to her son.

As I weaved in and out of the small groups gathered throughout the living and dining room areas, I couldn't help but hear snippets of various conversations. Several people commented on Lizzie Cawley's absence, stating this was the first HEC meeting she'd ever missed. I knew she hadn't called Jane to let her know she wouldn't be here and, from the sound of it, she hadn't called anyone else either.

While offering Joe Finley and Albert Donovan refills on coffee, I discovered that someone had once again flattened the tires on Albert's caddy—something that had become an almost weekly event.

"It was right after a 'visit' from that CCR woman. She has the audacity to come into the store and stand there staring at me and everyone who comes in." Albert held his cup out for a refill and nodded at me. "She doesn't do or say a thing, just stays long enough to make me uncomfortable. Public Safety can't do anything about it either since she hasn't actually caused any trouble. At least not that she's been caught at."

"Hannah believes she and Wallace are in cahoots over more than just what's on the surface," Joe said after declining the proffered coffee. He gave me a slight smile, then turned back to his companion. "I just wish the professor would contact Hannah. She's frantic to get his grades."

Trying to be less obtrusive, I stood slightly back, but not so far that I wouldn't be able to hear more. It wasn't really eavesdropping. Hannah Finley's the chair of the department I work for. What concerns her ultimately concerns me. Sort of.

Eventually.

At least it was a good excuse.

While I was busy trying to convince myself that I was justified listening in, the men's conversation continued in the background. By the time I realized that arguing with myself would make me miss something, Joe and Albert had moved on.

That's when I noticed Elsie Wilkes watching them—and me. She held a pitcher of iced tea and had a curious expression on her face. It was too late to pretend I hadn't been eavesdropping. She wouldn't have bought it anyway.

Especially when it was just as obvious she'd been doing the same thing.

I was about to speak to her when Jane passed between us on the way to the front door, escorting several HEC members. Her strained look said she'd be happy to have the meeting over. That was one motion I'd be thrilled to second. After nearly two hours of non-stop chatter, I was more than ready for a more peaceful atmosphere.

As the rooms cleared out and Jane said her last good-byes, Marla and Elsie helped me gather dirty dishes and glasses and cart them into the kitchen.

"I'll load the dishwasher and clean up in here," Marla offered.

To my amazement she retrieved a pair of vinyl gloves from her over-large purse. I knew Marla prided herself on being prepared—isn't that the Boy Scouts' motto?—but this went beyond my overactive imagination. Even Elsie seemed stunned.

Still, the only thing totally out of character for the meticulous Marla was the errant lock of platinum hair that slipped from her perfectly coifed do and into her eye. She lifted the strand in obvious surprise, and hastily tucked it into place along the side of her head.

"You girls go ahead and clean up the mess in the dining room. I swear I've never seen so many people unable to keep crumbs on their plates." She shoved that same stray lock of hair behind an ear with more than a little irritation, then bestowed one of her magnanimous smiles upon Elsie and me.

"Thanks, Marla. I appreciate it." Whatever else I might say about Marla, the one thing she is above all else is willing to help and serve. And those are qualities I admire.

After grabbing a clean dishcloth from a drawer near the sink, I followed Elsie back into the dining room.

I hadn't seen much of Elsie since that fateful day last May when she was shot. Even when we attended Bible study and church events, she'd kept her distance from both Jane and me. With Jane, that was pretty much the norm, but not when it came to me. I was her primary source for what was happening between Jane and Steven Acklin—something I knew interested her a great deal.

"How's your shoulder, Elsie?"

Perhaps not the best ice breaker, considering. But I couldn't help but notice the way she'd winced when she picked up the trash can.

Besides, I couldn't very well just ask what she'd heard of Joe and Albert's conversation.

"Coming along." She inched her way through the room, picking up discarded napkins and sweeping crumbs into the small trash can she carried. "Your leg?"

"Fine." With such stimulating conversational style, was it any wonder I was so popular?

Facetious, Glory. Thinking like that will get you nowhere.

Not that I was making headway in the first place.

"Are you still going out with Detective Spencer?" Elsie stopped what she was doing and turned toward me.

"Um." Yet another brilliant answer. This conversation thing was a lot harder than it should be.

Elsie nodded and went back to work. "He asked to see his grandparents' old house. It just went on the market the other day," she said without looking up.

"Oh?" He hadn't mentioned that. Guess he was getting tired of apartment living.

"It's still in wonderful condition."

Elsie flashed me a sly smile, knowing she'd caught me off-guard with this bit of information. She appeared ready to share a little more until forced to side-step Jane, who was showing the last committee member out the door. Instead, Elsie watched my sister with the usual cross between interest and aversion.

Aversion wasn't quite the right word. It was difficult to convey the varying degrees of emotion that ran the gamut of expressions on Elsie's and my sister's faces whenever they regarded each other. Someday I needed to get the skinny on what happened between these two.

"It's sweet of you to stay and help clean up, Elsie." Jane's smile was genuine, though perhaps a little tight. "But I think Glory and I can handle it from here." She held her hand out for the trash can.

This was the point where they would usually exchange carefully worded phrases barbed with dual meanings. But Elsie Wilkes surprised us both. She handed Jane the trash can and rubbed her hands briskly together.

"If you're sure." Elsie pressed one hand over her mouth to cover a yawn. "I really don't mind helping."

Her glance around the room with her nose wrinkled in distaste spoke volumes. I was afraid she would verbalize what she was thinking, thereby causing a row that none of us needed to deal with right now.

The only thing that saved the situation was Marla coming in from the kitchen, the strap of her massive purse slung over her shoulder. The side of her head with the errant strand of hair now looked like World War III had raged there. From the looks of it, Marla lost.

"The first load is running, ladies. I don't believe in overloading, so you'll have to run the rest later. My, wasn't that a good meeting?"

Jane took advantage of the reprieve, tucked her arm through Marla's, and steered her carefully away from Elsie and me. Seeing her opening, Elsie grabbed up her purse and headed for the front door. Like a good hostess, I followed.

"Thanks again for all your help, Elsie. I really appreciate it."

She waved away my comment with a quick backward glance, then hustled out the door, nearly running into Blue Eyes, who'd just stepped onto the porch.

Elsie emitted a startled "oof" as Blue Eyes steadied her. She muttered a quick apology, then hastened down the steps.

"She's in a bit of a hurry."

Rick stared after Elsie a moment before turning his gaze to me. He raised a single eyebrow in question—a feat I marveled at every time I saw it.

"Don't ask me. We were getting along just fine until she found herself face to face with Jane." I ushered him inside and slammed the door before any more of our precious air-conditioning was lost to the blast furnace outside.

Rick caught Jane's eye, and she was soon ushering Marla out the door. I motioned for him to take a seat, then gladly did so myself. My feet hurt so badly I didn't think I'd be able to take another step. But one look at the trail of crumbs leading from the dining room through the living room told me that after Blue Eyes was gone, we'd continue trying to set the house in order. There was still a lot of work to be done, and with Jane around it was unlikely to be put off until tomorrow.

"So how are you girls holding up?"

"Exhausted and exhilarated." Jane sank onto the sofa. "We had a good meeting."

"HEC." I explained. "How are things going at the park?" Okay, that wasn't subtle in the least.

"Have either of you thought of anything you'd like to add to your report?"

The solicitous expression he bestowed on my sister was more Rick than his detective counterpart. The warning in his eyes to mind my own business came equally from both halves of his persona.

"There's nothing more to tell." Jane gave him an apologetic smile. "Misty found the hand and Glory called it in." She swallowed hard. "There is something I'd like to speak with you about, however."

Blue Eyes leaned forward. "Shoot."

"I got back a report on my fire. And, well, it's a little disturbing." Jane closed her eyes, gently rubbed them with her fingertips, then squeezed the bridge of her nose.

Rick glanced at me before returning his attention to my sister. "Disturbing in what way?"

"Well, it's the cans, you see."

Again Rick turned to me then back to Jane. "Cans?"

"Of spray paint. I've thought a lot about this, and there seems to be only one explanation, though it doesn't make any sense." Jane straightened, splayed her fingers across her knees, and stared directly into Rick's awesome blue eyes. "I—I think someone tried to kill me."

Chapter 6

Jane's words hung in the air between us. One look at her face spoke volumes—she wasn't trying to make a joke; she was perfectly serious. That's what made it all the more frightening.

Blue Eyes's expression was one of concern and confusion—maybe a few more things thrown in. He inched closer to the edge of the overstuffed chair and leaned slightly toward Jane, all the while managing to keep his back board straight.

"What makes you think someone tried to kill you?" His tone was solemn and sincere, which said he was taking her seriously.

If I'd made the same statement, laughter would immediately erupt, and they'd call in someone to measure me for a straitjacket. All the sincerity in the world would have failed to convince them. A sad statement, but all too true.

I don't think I've ever done anything to warrant such treatment. Despite my sister's claim I was on Public Safety's "frequent flyer" program, I could defend every time I'd been in contact with them. It's not like I was Chunk from *The Goonies*; I didn't make a habit of calling in false reports just for the fun of it. My calls were valid and important.

Except, perhaps, when I had Seth call because I got caught in the springs of his trampoline.

"The cans of spray paint they found weren't mine," Jane was saying. "The only time I've even used the stuff was when Glory, Andi, and I tried to rejuvenate some old outdoor furniture. That was last summer. Right?"

"My furniture." I nodded. "We worked on the patio because of the fumes."

"You have any of the paint left?"

"I believe so," I told him. "I know there are several cans in the basement. I'm always reluctant to throw away what's left after finishing a project, you know, in case I might need it again."

"Have you ever taken any to Jane's?"

"No." My sister and I answered in unison.

"You're both pretty emphatic about that."

"I can't abide the stuff." Jane wrinkled her nose and patted her chest. "Even with a mask, the fumes play havoc with my lungs. And as for the cans Glory thinks she has in the basement, she's wrong. I threw them away while I was staying here a couple months back."

"You did?"

Jane gave me a firm nod. "Several were rusted and looked pretty nasty. I didn't figure you'd miss them."

Which I hadn't. Scratch that job off the to-do list.

Blue Eyes watched the exchange with patience—another of the many traits that endeared the man to my heart. Of course, his professional training was part of it, handling people who got off track and all. But I'd figured out how to distinguish between man and cop—though in the end, it was the entire package that made him so special.

His incredible dark blue eyes and Harrison Ford good looks were just icing on the cake.

"Have you notified Lieutenant Holmes of your suspicions?"

"I just got the report from the insurance company," Jane explained. "The moment I read about the cans, I knew something was wrong. Then, during the HEC meeting, people were talking about all the trouble we've had because of Zeke Wallace and the CCR rep he brought to town. That made me remember the awful confrontation I had with the professor right before the fire, and . . . well, it fits."

Now I was the one sitting at attention. Was I wrong or had Jane just given herself up as a person of interest in the demise of Zeke Wallace?

"So you think one of them had something to do with the fire?"

"I do."

"Um . . . uh . . . Janie?"

How could I get her to stop incriminating herself without Detective Spencer catching on? And right now, he *was* Detective Spencer.

They both turned toward me, Jane looking a little peeved I'd interrupted her. To give Blue Eyes credit, he regarded me with what I interpreted as thoughtful consideration. He was probably hoping I'd be able to shed some light on Jane's statements and concerns.

"Glory?"

"Huh? Oh, yeah, sorry. It's just that it's getting late and maybe this isn't the time to—"

I stopped when Jane rolled her eyes and glared at me. If she was bound and determined to implicate herself in Wallace's death, I wouldn't be able to stop her.

It wasn't the first cryptic exchange Blue Eyes had witnessed, and it certainly wouldn't be the last if he stuck around. He took it in stride, turning his attention back to my sister.

"You were saying?"

Jane flashed me a warning glare. I tucked myself as far back in the chair as possible, which wasn't much. My dining room chairs were attractive and comfortable to a degree, but they weren't designed for hiding.

"Wallace stopped me outside the grocery store and told me I should resign as HEC president."

This was news to me.

"Go on." Rick said in his most encouraging detective voice.

"I was carrying ice cream, and I didn't have the patience to deal with his attempt to intimidate me. So I wasn't sociable; I just marched on past him to the car." Jane wrung her hands in her lap, her eyes trained on Rick. "He followed me anyway, telling me that it could be unpleasant for me when everyone learned about the deep, dark secret Steven's been hiding. Of course, I didn't give him the time of day. Just got in my car and drove on home."

That was it? That was the big argument? I wasn't even sure it constituted an argument, especially since she hadn't responded. Of course, it's not necessary to have more than one person participating to have a fight. I've had plenty with myself.

But what was that about some secret regarding Dr. Steven? It definitely wasn't a secret that he'd been in love with my sister since they went to high school together eons ago. The very fact he'd never married attested to his devotion big time.

"And?" Blue Eyes prompted.

"He was there when I got home. Parked right in front of my house as big as you please."

Huh? Had I missed something or was Jane telling this story in some convoluted fashion?

More like me.

"How's that possible, Janie?"

"I dropped the ice cream off at the church for Potluck 'n Praise. Gracie Naner and I talked for just a minute, but it was enough time for Wallace to beat me home." She shook her head as her hands continued to twist and shake. "He followed my car into the garage, and then wouldn't leave. He—he kept alluding to some secret Steven is hiding from me, from everyone. He said that when the news came out, people would know that our faith was just a sham."

As Jane reached for the box of tissues on a nearby end table, I joined her on the couch.

"Did he give you any idea what this secret was?" Rick asked gently.

She shook her head. "He said that if I chose to remain with Steven once the news was out, that I'd prove just how much of a hypocrite I was as well. He—he smiled then, and I thought . . . how could someone with such a pleasant smile be so evil? That's when I noticed his eyes." She looked down a moment, a shiver running through her thin body. "There was the answer. I dropped the sack I was holding and slapped him."

Rick and I drew in a startled breath. We both knew this was uncharacteristic of my sister.

"Then what happened?" Rick asked.

"He laughed." The amazement she still felt etched her voice. "He picked up the sack, handed it to me, and left. Three days later, my house burned down."

"And shortly after that, Wallace went missing," I added.

"Let's not get ahead of ourselves, okay?" Blue Eyes reached out and took one of Jane's hands in his. "The first thing you need to do is contact Jack Holmes, tell him what you've told me about the spray cans. Jack wouldn't have signed off on the fire if he'd seen anything suspicious. He wouldn't have known the paint wasn't yours."

"So he'll investigate?"

"I'm sure he'll go back through his notes with this new information in mind."

"It proves it wasn't an accident, that someone set the fire deliberately." Jane's tone of desperation tugged at my soul.

"He'll contact the fire marshal and we'll go from there. I'm not really involved in that end of things, so I don't feel comfortable telling you how they'll proceed. However, if it turns out the way we're assuming it will, a joint investigation will follow." He released Jane's hand and stood. "In the meantime, I want you to relax. The more you do, the better the chance you'll remember something else about the encounter that might be helpful."

"I'll call the lieutenant first thing in the morning."

"Good girl. Now I need to get back to work." He bent down and kissed my sister's forehead—definitely not part of his formal police training, but a nice, reassuring touch for a friend.

As I accompanied him to the door, there were so many things I wanted to ask him—about the body in the park, whether they had uncovered more of it and made a positive ID, how the individual was killed, and what Rick thought about Jane's allegations. Instead, I found myself completely wrapped up in contemplating the way his fingers intertwined with mine.

"How's it going at work? Have you managed to straighten things out with Dr. Finley?" His fingers gently squeezed mine. "Glory?"

Heat ran through my veins and more than likely burned in my cheeks by the time I tore my eyes from his hand and gazed up at him.

"She's not going to cut back her sister's hours, which means no more for me." I gulped in a quick breath. "She claims I'm more of a yo-yo than an employee. She brought up how the former department chair relaxed my hours during Ike's illness and how she herself bent over backwards for me when I broke my leg in the spring."

"That seems a little harsh, doesn't it?"

"Ridiculous, considering Lila's the biggest screw-up and airhead I've ever met."

Not nice, but true. Lila Samson's only qualification for her position—my former job—was being the department chair's youngest sister. Lila was a year or so older than Andi, but unlike my daughter, who held a BS in elementary education and was going for her masters, Lila had barely finished high school and left the two year administrative assistant program at the college before the end of the first semester.

We stepped out onto the front porch and were immediately hit by the heat, which had failed to go down with the setting sun.

"Hannah—*Dr. Finley*—has never really liked me, though I've no idea why. Unless it's the way Dr. Jensen favored me. He was chair for years and a good friend of Ike's. Come to think of it, Hannah never got along with Dr. Jensen either." I shrugged. "I've got my app in for the next admin position that opens up. Until then, I'm the department floater."

Blue Eyes winced. "I wish you'd use a different term. The image—"

"Ah . . . 'cause that's what you call a drowning victim." Things took on completely different meanings when you went out with a cop.

He nodded, then bent down and brushed his lips against mine. More of a tease than a kiss.

"You constantly surprise me, Glory Harper," He said, his lips still dangerously close to mine. "I'm proud of you." He backed up and winked before heading for the steps.

"Why? Because I didn't bug you for information?"

My voice squeaked a little more than normal. Might be all the air rushing into my lungs once I stopped holding my breath.

He skipped down the steps with a chuckle, briefly turned and saluted, then climbed into his car.

I didn't have any more information than before he'd arrived, but I did have something to think about while we finished cleaning up.

Back inside, I found Jane still on the sofa. Her hands were folded and resting on her lap, her head lowered as if she studied them.

"You all right, Janie?"

Other than a slight shake of her head, she didn't move. I sank into the overstuffed chair Rick recently vacated, leaned forward, and laid a hand atop my sister's.

"We'll get this all straightened out, Janie, you'll see. Lieutenant Holmes will know what to do." When she didn't respond, I thought of another sure-fire tactic to pull her out of the doldrums. "You should go give Dr. Dreamboat a call. I imagine he's out of his meetings by now and missing you like crazy—"

"What if he was right, Glory?" Jane's voice was barely a croak. "What if Wallace knew something about Steven?"

"How could he? He was just trying to get to you, upset you."

"This sudden trip to St. Louis isn't for a conference. I don't know what it's for." Jane raised her head, and I could see she was crying. "Family business. That's what Steven said. And when he told me his parents were accompanying him, I didn't question it. But now . . . "

I scooted over to the couch and sat next to my sister. "Right now you're exhausted." I pulled her into my arms. "You've been through a crazy day, finding the hand."

Jane shuddered and I pulled her closer. "Then the HEC meeting and all this talk about your fire not being an accident. You just need to get some rest. I'll clean up in here—" an impossible task if ever there was one, "—and you go shower, then snuggle in bed while you talk to Dr. Dreamboat."

Jane returned my hug, then slowly pulled back. "Just leave the rest till morning. I'll take care of it then." She stood and headed toward the hallway. "You need to relax. After all, you have to go to work in the morning, and I don't."

I was about to thank her for the reprieve but stopped as she turned back to me.

"I hate to say this about another human being, and it's not at all Christian, but Zeke Wallace was—is a slime ball. I don't know what the man was alluding to, what he professed to know, or whether it has anything to do with Steven's trip to St. Louis or not." A single tear rolled off the end of Jane's nose. "But I have this strange conviction in my heart that whatever's happening with Steven right now will change our lives forever."

Chapter 7

Jane didn't protest my suggestion about taking a shower and getting into bed early. Whether she made her call to Dr. Dreamboat, I didn't know. And didn't want to ask. Her startling revelation that she felt something might be wrong, that their relationship would change as a result of his St. Louis trip, really got to me. After all, my sister is a regular Rock of Gibraltar, staunch and strong in her faith in God and mankind. I hoped for all our sakes that this tiny fracture didn't become a crevasse.

While Jane showered, I found myself carting the kitchen and dining room chairs back to their respective places, stacking all the extras Andi had brought and putting them into the garage, and loading the last of the dirty dishes into the dishwasher. I guess some of Jane's clean genes were rubbing off on me.

Now, as I lay in bed trying to find a comfortable position, a film of the day's events ran through my mind. First I flashed on Misty trying to conceal the hand, next to Gus Bradley's "Just the facts, ma'am" questioning.

Of course, thinking about the police brought to mind my own special officer, his incredible dark blue eyes, and wonderfully soft mouth.

Not the best direction to take here, Glory, if you want to get to sleep.

But even chiding myself didn't work.

I flipped over onto my right side, took a deep breath, and snuggled down against my pillow.

Discovering that Jane's fire may not have been an accident was quite a shock. The moment she told Andi and me about the cans of spray paint, I'd known she was a victim of arson. It was a surprise when she came to the same conclusion—without any prompting from me. But the question remained: Who could possibly want to hurt my sister?

Her description of the run-in she'd had with Wallace might point to him or his CCR buddy, but would either of them have stooped so low? And what motive could they possibly have? True, Jane's the president of HEC, but that hardly gives her any power in the city as a whole. It didn't even give her authority over the committee. She was more a mediator than a policy-maker.

So who could have booby trapped her house?

And how could anyone possibly know that putting old cans of spray paint on top of a water heater could cause such destruction?

Besides, everyone loves my sister. With the exception of Elsie Wilkes, of course. But not even Elsie would go to such drastic measures over some slight from the past.

Now, if this had happened to me . . . well . . . that would be a totally different story. It's hard to admit that you've actually made people frustrated enough—oh, okay—*angry* enough that they might want to get back at you.

But most of those people are in jail.

At least, I hope they are.

"Stop thinking!" *Oh, please let me stop thinking and get to sleep!*

I rolled onto my back, adjusted the sheet atop my chest, and closed my eyes once again.

Zeke Wallace really was a slime ball of monumental proportions. He'd never been one of my favorite people to work with, always fussing over the way his correspondence was handled or how I wrote up his messages. Then there were the snide remarks and innuendo, all of which were sexist and more than a little off color. It was nothing like the teasing from the other guys in the department.

It had all come to a head one day about six months ago when I found Wallace sitting in my desk chair. When I asked him to vacate it, he grabbed my arm and tried to pull me onto his lap. Hannah Finley had come in just as I managed to extricate myself from his clutches. The look they'd exchanged was more than a little barbed and seemed to crackle with electricity. He broke it off first, shoved out of my chair, then sauntered out of the office.

If I had to pinpoint the exact moment when my relationship with Hannah changed for the worse, that would be it. From then on, she was civil but cold. We'd never been friendly, but now it felt like I was being frozen out—of everything.

It didn't make sense why she reacted that way. I mean, it was obvious I hadn't done anything to provoke the incident. I'd even asked her to help me file a sexual harassment form.

But out of respect for her position as chair, I allowed Hannah to change my mind with her promise that Wallace wouldn't bother me again.

He was back to taunting me the very next day, however. He even tried to threaten me, claiming he could uncover secrets that would make me come around to his way of thinking. That made me laugh. I'm pretty sure I haven't done a thing in my entire life that someone, friends, family, or cops, didn't already know about.

But not long after that encounter, he quit bugging me. Whether it was Hannah's influence or my indifference to his threats, I'll never know.

Frustrated, I reached over to the nightstand and grabbed the TV remote. Flipping through the channels didn't calm my overactive brain. It only added a sound-track.

I turned the TV off and rolled onto my left side.

What would it be like at work tomorrow? Since returning to the college after sick leave for my broken leg, I'd come to feel more like a work-study student employee than like the administrative assistant I'd been for the last twenty years—the last ten in this particular department. I'd always loved my job, and the faculty, students, and other support staff were like a second family. I still hear from many of the kids I've had for work study over the years—long after they've graduated.

Things just weren't the same anymore.

I sat up, punched my pillow, and rolled onto my right side.

"Please, God, please help me get some sleep."

Thoughts of arson, murder, and mayhem washed over me, threatening to rev up my system and take over with a new onslaught of retrospection. Then a sudden sense of peace descended like a protective blanket, and the last thing I remembered was the feel of Rick's lips brushing against mine.

Chapter 8

I jumped out of bed like some deranged jack-in-a-box, punched off the alarm, but continued to hear the incessant beep-beep-beep piercing my sleepy brain. A quick shower followed by my first mirror encounter for the day revealed that my under eye bags had bags. With a moan, I slathered on eye cream and hoped the small amount of make-up I used would hide the rest.

It didn't.

I finished dressing in record time—forty-five minutes from the time the alarm rang till I was ready to go out the door.

Jane hates the way I rush my morning routine. Frowns upon my skipping breakfast even more. But this morning I didn't have her peering over my shoulder, remonstrating at my lack of nutritional awareness, and cutting short that all-important communion with the morning.

No matter how many times I tell her that sleeping an extra twenty minutes or so is more important to me than taking time to eat something I don't want or lingering over a cup of coffee I don't like anyway, she doesn't seem to get it. Not everyone's like her, hopping out of bed at the same time every morning with a smile on her face. Some of us just aren't morning people.

Like me.

But it was a little odd for her not to be in the kitchen taking her time over coffee and her favorite western omelet. Jane never sleeps in. For this very reason, I backtracked to her room and peered in through the two-inch crack she always leaves between door and jamb. A gentle snore assured me she was fine but didn't explain this aberration to her schedule.

I left her sleeping, knowing the extra rest would be good for her after yesterday.

As usual, I was the first one in the office. Even though Lila Samson is now the full-time admin of the department, she uses the fact that she's Dr. Finley's sister to get away with—

I was going to say murder, but since my recent encounters with the real-life subject, it doesn't feel apropos. The bottom line is that Lila manages to get away with whatever she chooses to do without consequences. Guess that's how it goes when your boss is also your sister.

Though I'm sure it wouldn't work that way for me if Jane was my boss.

The in basket was full, which made me wonder if Lila had actually done anything after I left yesterday afternoon, aside from reading her romance novel. I began dividing things up into three stacks—one for the student workers, one for Lila, and one for me.

As I neared the bottom of the basket, I found confirmation that Lila spent the afternoon reading instead of working. Now I'd have to reprioritize items to make sure those left over from yesterday were the first to be done today. That's when I remembered we wouldn't have student workers during the two week break.

With a heavy sigh, I went back through the student stack and interspersed those items throughout my own. It would be useless to expect Lila to take on a little extra responsibility. She's just there to delegate.

The shuffle of feet in the hallway outside the office brought me to attention. It wasn't even eight-thirty yet, so I knew it couldn't be Lila or Hannah. I looked up to find David Quinn standing in the doorway with a sheepish grin on his face.

David's been one of the department's most reliable work-study employees for the last three years. After a recent disagreement with Lila, however, he requested a transfer to a different department for his senior year. A real shame. I'd miss his quiet efficiency.

Tall and lanky, with John Lennon glasses and curly brown hair, David—never Dave— reminded me of a bespectacled Greg Brady of *The Brady Bunch* during his Afro period—only not quite as "hip." Always more at ease in front of a computer than communicating with humans, the computer science major never was much of a conversationalist. But his willingness to work and get things done right made him one of my favorite employees of all time.

"Hey, Mrs. H, what's up?" He stepped into the office, pushing his glasses up his nose.

"Morning, David. I figured you'd be home for break."

He shook his head. "My parents aren't going to be around. Besides, I didn't want to leave 'cause of my part-time job."

I'd forgotten he'd started working for one of the local trash haulers—er, waste management firms, in modern jargon.

He lowered himself into an office chair. "Hey, did you hear the news this morning?"

"No."

Another of my morning quirks was not turning on a TV or radio. After being blasted by the alarm clock, my brain needs time to assimilate before adding more noise and distractions.

"I just ask because I know you and your sister walk at Fitness Park every afternoon."

Now he had my full attention.

"They found a body up there. They said a couple of women discovered it and contacted the cops—it *was* you, wasn't it?"

There was no way to deny it, not after I'd reacted by nearly falling over. I reached for the desk to steady myself.

"What else was in the report?"

At least my voice was calm. With all I've been through in the past, you'd think I'd have handled this better.

Of course, I didn't expect to be hit by it quite like this either.

"They didn't release a name, if that's what you're wondering." He eyed me speculatively. "You know, though, don't you?"

"I want to see you in my office right now, Glory." Dr. Hannah Finley breezed into the room, passing on into the inner office without a glance at David or me.

I was never more thankful to see her than I was right then. I grabbed a steno pad and pen, flashed an apologetic glance at David, and followed my boss.

"You know the situation we're in because Dr. Wallace failed to record his grades with the registrar." Hannah threw her purse onto the desktop and tossed me a look of disdain. "It's a gross misconduct that has gotten the entire college in an uproar. Lila and I have searched his office, and IT has checked his computer, all to no avail. We've left messages on his cell and home phones with no response. We cannot wait any longer."

She opened the center desk drawer and removed a key hanging from a garish tag advertising a local used car dealership. "Zeke hasn't any family, so he gave me the key to his house in case there was an emergency. I'd say this constitutes one." She came around the desk and thrust the key ring into my hands. "I want you to go to his home and find those grades."

I tried to return the key. "Um, I, uh, don't really think that's such a good idea."

"And I really don't care what you think." After executing a perfect 180 on her four-inch spike heels, she returned to her desk. "I've far too much to do to be running over there. So you're it."

She gracefully lowered herself into her black leather executive chair, removed her purse from the desktop, and placed it into the bottom right-hand drawer. "Why are you still here?"

"I'm just not comfortable with breaking and entering. Somehow that seems a bit outside my job description."

She leaned her elbows on her desk, folded her hands, and gave me a stare that was designed to wilt me into submission. "You have the key to his home, a key he entrusted to me to use at my discretion, which I have entrusted to you. Therefore, there is no crime."

"But maybe there has been. After all he's missing—"

"Which is why we need to go to his house in the first place. If he were here, it wouldn't be necessary." She pushed away from her desk. "I've about had it with your insubordination, Glory Harper. If you value your position in this department, you will obey my directive. Now."

I recognized a threat when I heard one. Shaken and more than a little indignant, I left her office.

I was glad to see David was no longer there. It gave me the opportunity to let off a little steam in private.

Yanking open the desk drawer that held the college directory, I grabbed it from beneath a pile of Lila's candy bars and empty wrappers and tossed it on the desk, all the while grumbling to myself. While I was writing down Wallace's address, Lila Samson came in.

"Hi, Glory. Sure is quiet in here." She nearly skipped to the filing cabinet where she deposited her purse.

I shoved the directory back into the drawer, retrieved my fanny pack from another drawer and headed for the door.

"Where ya going?"

"Ask your sister."

Just as I was going out the door, I added, "There's a lot of work to do today, Lila, and no one you can delegate it to. Have fun."

Chapter 9

It always amazes me when I arrive at a destination and realize I can't remember exactly how I got there. It's probably not something I should admit, but I sincerely doubt I'm the only one to experience the phenomenon.

Sitting in front of the brick-fronted bungalow Zeke Wallace called home these last two years, I couldn't help but wonder about the dichotomy of the man's personality. His casual and often unkempt appearance was in complete contrast to the meticulous manner in which he kept his office at the college and in the organization of his class materials. I would have expected his contempt for the community to show in the way he cared for his home. But here again I was surprised.

Despite his being missing for the last two weeks, the grass has been kept trimmed, the plants watered, and papers stacked neatly on the porch. He'd obviously hired someone to keep up the grounds—but even that spoke of someone who cared for appearances, at least to some degree.

The morning sun beat down on the car, heating up the inside of my Corolla to the point that even running the air-conditioner on high wasn't cutting it. Picking up the ring that held the key to Wallace's domain, I ran my fingers over the raised gold letters on the plastic fluorescent orange tag as if they were prayer beads.

That's what I needed right now: a lot of prayer.

Putting the car in gear, I slowly drove past the bungalow, scoping out the yard and doors for any sign of crime scene tape. The dark mesh on the front screen door surely couldn't hide the bright yellow tape. Right?

Once more around the block and back again. The place looked the same—quiet and unoccupied.

I thought about calling Blue Eyes to ask what he thought I should do but threw out the idea almost as quickly as it popped into my mind. I already knew what he'd say. The same thing I said to Hannah when she ordered me to come here.

Still, there was something intriguing about going into Wallace's home and checking out how he lived, what might be in his files . . .

Okay, I admit it. I've got a nosy streak a mile wide. But nosy isn't exactly the right terminology. Um, investigative. Inquisitive.

I liked those terms far better.

Turning the corner, I drove two blocks down and parked. Good investigators wouldn't simply park in front of the place they were going to check out. They would want to approach with a bit of caution, stealth. On the sly.

Besides, if Wallace had neighbors like me around, I didn't want them to know I was here.

By the time I made my way back to the bungalow, I was dripping with sweat. In spite of my mother's adage that "horses sweat, men perspire, and women glow," I was, indeed, sweating.

I came around the side of the house by way of the backyard, cautiously checked out the front, then practically ran up the porch steps to the door. I slipped on a pair of winter gloves I'd found in my glove compartment, then tugged open the screen door.

Manipulating the key into the lock was a challenge with the bulky gloves and my hands growing increasingly wetter by the second, but I finally succeeded. I slipped inside and quietly closed the door behind me, reengaging the lock before I moved forward.

The house was cool. The muffled sound of the air-conditioner and the slight sway of a nearby curtain added to the eerie, empty feeling.

Approaching the house from the outside, I'd noticed that all the blinds were closed, so it took a moment for my eyes to adjust to the dimness of the hallway. Weak sunlight filtered through the house in ghostly shafts filled with dancing dust motes. To the left of the entryway, there seemed to be a bit more light, so I followed the glow to search out its source.

In the living room, a single lamp burned next to a recliner. On the end table beneath the lamp sat a mug containing the dregs of what appeared to have been coffee. A newspaper lay over one arm of the chair. Closer inspection revealed it was the sports page of *The Kansas City Star*, cheering on the Royals and their recent win. The date was a little over two weeks ago.

The neatness of everything else in the room spoke of an occupant who had intended to return. That thought alone caused butterflies to churn in my stomach as dozens of spiders trailed up and down my spine. I tugged the strap of my fanny pack up over my shoulder, pocketed the house key, and after swallowing to stiffen my resolve, moved back into the hall.

The small room to the right of the front door looked like it had once been a walk-in closet. It had a tiny window, blinds tightly closed, and barely room enough for the coats and shoes stored there. The room next to it, directly across from the living room, appeared to have been designed as a formal dining room. The built-in china hutch held rows of books instead of dishes, however. Heavy wooden bookcases crammed full of books, magazines, and newspapers, all neatly arranged alphabetically, lined the remaining walls.

I continued down the hallway, past a bathroom, the kitchen, and a large bedroom. Other than a somewhat rancid odor coming from the kitchen, everything seemed tidy, though covered with a generous layer of dust.

In the doorway of the bedroom, I took in the matching king-size bed and large chest of drawers. The musky scent of aftershave or cologne hung in the air, making me feel an added sense of guilt for intruding upon Wallace's domain. I didn't linger, just followed the hallway down to where it spilled into the final room of the house.

A large, highly polished mahogany desk sat in the middle of the room, surrounded by more bookshelves and several file cabinets. Bi-fold doors on one wall hid what I assumed was a large closet. A nice-sized window to one side of the desk, blinds closed as in the other rooms, lit the room with narrow shafts of sunlight.

There was a constant drone in the room, which I finally realized came from a desktop computer that was angled away from the window. A touch of the mouse slowly brought the screen to life, revealing an Excel file. Closer inspection proved it was what I was sent here to find: Wallace's grades. His grade book remained open on the desk, an acrylic ruler marking his place.

Once again, I shuddered. Visions of the decomposing severed hand with its distinctive signet ring filled my brain.

Something—or *someone*—had called Wallace away from his home . . . and into eternity.

I shoved at the thoughts as though they were physical items I could push out of sight. With my generous imagination, I didn't think it wise to linger on the subject of murder. Not when I was alone in the victim's home, without permission, on a questionable assignment.

Before closing out the Excel file, I noted its name and location on the hard drive, then began pulling out drawers in search of a CD to copy the file. I figured Hannah couldn't gripe with both the grade book and a CD. And if Dr. Hannah Finley was happy, she might stay off my back.

While I searched the drawers, I became aware of another, subtler sound. I ceased inspection of the final drawer and stood perfectly still, barely breathing.

There it was again, soft, nondescript.

I turned my head from side to side, holding my breath and listening. Nothing.

"Just my nerves." The sound of my own voice startled me, but not as much as whatever—or whoever was inside the closet.

Someone was hiding in there.

Thinking things through isn't always a strong point with me. But I do have a little experience in dealing with murderers.

I scanned the desktop for something to use as a weapon, settling on the receiver of an old fashioned, corded office phone. I hastily disconnected it from the cord with as little sound as possible.

The dash to the closet took less time than tugging open the bi-fold doors with one hand—the other poised in readiness to crown whoever lurked inside.

With my heart still thundering, I took in the small female crouched atop a huge safe, her head down and arms crossed protectively in front of her. The red-orange hair and distinctive rose-water perfume instantly told me who she was.

"Elsie?"

Elsie Wilkes lowered her arms. "You!"

Her eyes narrowing, she slid off the safe, straightened her clothing, and strode out of the closet, her head held high. "What are you doing here?"

Vintage Elsie: supercilious tone, classic sneer.

"I was wondering the same thing about you." I lowered my weapon, surprised my voice was so calm.

"I own this property," Was the haughty retort. "I've every legal right to be here . . . unlike you."

She had me there.

As Elsie eyed the bulky winter gloves covering my hands, I figured trying to explain Hannah's directive wouldn't hold water with her. Not when it was obvious I'd frightened her as much as she'd frightened me. Still . . .

"If you're so *legal*, what were you doing in the closet?"

That got her.

Elsie drew herself up to her full height of about 5'3"— the same as mine—straightened her pearl gray silk blouse, and raised an admonishing finger.

That was as far as she got when we heard the front door whoosh open.

Without a word, we both headed for the closet.

Chapter 10

D espite the appearance from the outside, the closet interior was pretty tight with two grown women and an enormous safe occupying the area. Fresh air was at a minimum—the cloying odor of rose-water perfume clung to every inch of the small space. It attacked my sinuses, making it difficult to breathe, let alone keep from sneezing. All I could hope was the intruder would leave quickly.

Intruder. I couldn't very well call him—or her—that, now could I? Not when I was the one hiding in a closet.

The bi-fold doors had stuck as we tried to pull them closed, making me wonder how Elsie managed to shut them without my hearing anything. Of course, *we'd* been in the middle of a *discussion* when we were interrupted. With our nerves on edge, it was a wonder we hadn't tripped over each other and fallen flat on our faces long before we'd made it inside.

I peered through the narrow crack in the doors and tried to take in a breath of air not saturated with Elsie's perfume. The dust we'd churned up on our mad dash for the closet slammed into me now, tickling my nose and throat.

I covered my nose and held my breath, trying to hold back the inevitable. It didn't work.

An explosive sneeze of monumental proportions rocked my body.

"Who—who's that?"

The tentative question was barely audible through the closet doors. Elsie elbowed me in the side before reaching over to cover my mouth. My attempt to swat her hand away when she covered my nose as well caused us both to lose our balance. We stumbled back against the closet wall with a loud thud.

"Who's back there?" A little nearer this time but no less frightened.

And definitely a voice I recognized.

Elsie and I tumbled out of the closet and onto our hands and knees at the feet of a startled Marla Hobbs. But this was a Marla I'd never seen before.

Black jeans covered still shapely legs that were usually showcased by knee-length skirts and nylons. She wore a dark tank top with a daring scoop neck and matching blouse. Her platinum hair was hidden by a black wig, the hair cut to gently curve beneath her chin. Even her make-up was different, more youthful, and a lot more daring.

Exit Stepford wife, enter . . . biker babe? Not quite, of course. But all she needed to complete the ensemble was spike heels and a leather jacket.

I knew she was younger than me by at least five years, but seeing her now had me wondering if I'd been mistaken by at least an additional five years.

"Marla Hobbs, what are you done up for?" Elsie used my head to help her stand, practically shoving my face into the musty-smelling carpet.

Ordinarily, these two would be equally matched, all haughty superiority in a glare for glare stare. Not so today. Elsie wilted this *Extreme Makeover* Marla with a single glance. Her stricken look and quickly lowered eyes said Marla would rather face a murderer than Elsie and me.

Marla shook so hard she would have fallen to the floor had I not gotten up at that precise moment to support her.

I led her over to a chair in front of the desk and eased her into it.

That's when I noticed the key ring in her hand.

"Th-thank you," Marla squeaked out. Her gaze slowly traveled to where my hands rested on her arms, then up to my face. "N-nice gloves."

"Yeah, well, thanks." Tucking my hands behind my back, I moved to the other side of the desk where I could take in both women without being too near either of them.

"You come here in that get up, with a key, no less," Elsie said, still on the attack. "It begs an explanation, don't you think?"

"What about *you*? I can't imagine you picking the lock, Elsie Wilkes." Marla threw her head back with defiance. "Glory's different," she continued, tossing a look in my direction and giving me a little thrill of hope that someone would see my being here as innocent. "I can see her doing just that."

"Now wait just a minute—"

My protest fell on deaf ears. It might have something to do with the gloves.

While the two of them sniped at each other over having keys and parried questions and accusations, I went back to work on the reason I was here, while still paying close attention to what was being said. Which, for all their mutual jabbing, wasn't much.

Examination of the drawer I'd been interrupted in exploring revealed a small stack of CDs and accompanying jewel cases. I extracted one of each and set to the task of copying the Excel file. By the time I removed the CD from the computer, the two women were nose to nose, glaring at each other—and no further along in the discovery process.

"You didn't answer my question." Elsie's posture— hands on hips, shoulders squared in determination, and legs slightly apart—might have been threatening if Marla didn't tower over her by a good four inches. "What are you all done up for?"

Marla's hands went to her short locks, following the cut as it gently curved beneath her chin, a sly smile on her face. "It's not something you could get away with, huh?"

The condescending remark must have shocked Elsie as much as it did me. She backed up a pace or two, her arms falling to her sides. For two people who'd always been such close friends, they didn't look very friendly now.

I scooted out around the desk, trying to decide if I should offer a shoulder to Elsie. But the stricken look was only transient. There was a storm coming, and I didn't want to be caught in the middle of it.

"Hannah Finley sent me here to look for the professor's grades," I said, offering a distraction for the glowering women. "The grade book was right there on his desk, and the program was open on the computer."

Neither woman appeared to hear me.

"Okey dokey." I tucked the CD into the grade book. "See you later."

As much as I'd like to stick around and hear explanations from both of them, I'd already been gone from work long enough. Dealing with Hannah wouldn't be as interesting as what was happening here in Wallace's bungalow, but I didn't want to lose my job.

Marla and Elsie were so occupied with staring each other down, nothing else seemed to matter.

Almost.

The telltale whoosh of the front door broke the awkward silence. I backed away from the entrance to the room, practically tripping over the two women where they now huddled just to the left of the doorway. I saw Elsie glance toward the closet and shook my head. There was no way the three of us would fit in there, and I wasn't about to even try.

"Pro-fess-or, your Mary Ann is here." Came the singsongy voice. "What's with the blinds? It's dark as a cave in here. A light on in the middle of a bright, sunny day? And the *Royals*? Are you sick or something?

"Did you miss me? I have to be honest and tell you I didn't miss you one little bit." She giggled. "I was waaaay too preoccupied." Another giggle. "My goodness, from the looks of this place you didn't get someone over to clean while I was gone. That's gonna end up costing you more in time and money, you know."

There's only one person I know who can transition from one subject to another all in a single breath—aside from most children, that is.

I turned to my companions and mouthed "Ashley Tanner."

Marla looked confused. Elsie simply nodded. With the words and music to *Gilligan's Island* filling my mind, it was difficult to keep from laughing at Ashley's professor and Mary Ann comment, but I did my best.

"Poohie! Smells like you forgot to take out the trash in the kitchen. That's not a bit like you."

The soft footsteps on the carpet were getting nearer by the second. Marla's eyes grew large and frightened. She wedged herself between a bookcase and filing cabinet, though how she managed it, I can't even begin to imagine. I was surprised she didn't attempt to pull Elsie and me in front of her.

"I can hear you back in the office, Zeke," Ashley said. "You can't be all that busy you can't come on out of there and say hi before I get to work. Zeke?"

"Work?" Elsie whispered.

I shrugged. The only thing I knew Ashley did for work was the job she has waiting tables at her parents' restaurant just outside of town.

While the other two looked as though they wished to melt into the floor, I was tired of all this hiding. I started for the office doorway, swatting away hands that tried to hold me back.

Ashley took my sudden appearance in stride—not even missing a beat in her soliloquy.

"Hey, Mrs. Harper. Are you and the professor in a meeting? I'm really sorry if I was interrupting and all. I'm just back from vacation, you know. It was soooo much fun. Ever been to Disney World? My first time. Two weeks that were totally rad." A high-pitched giggle and one of her signature snorts punctuated a dramatic roll of her eyes. "Figured my first stop should be cleaning this place."

"Ashley?" I put a hand on her shoulder, forgetting about the gloves until the startled girl caught sight of them.

"You catch that carpel thingy of the wrists, Mrs. Harper? I know some girls who've gotten it, and it's murder."

Carpel thingy? Ah, carpel tunnel. Best not comment on that.

"I'm fine, Ashley. How about you take a moment and breathe?"

Her quizzical expression proved she had no idea she was the queen of run-on sentences and discordant thought. She waited for me to move aside—which I did most reluctantly—then strode into the room, obviously still searching for Zeke Wallace. Seeing the other two women didn't faze her at all.

"Hi, Elsie. Love your new look, Mrs. Hobbs. Is it a wig or your real hair? I think it's way more attractive. Don't you?" She gazed from Elsie to me for corroboration.

Elsie's eyes widened before she looked away. I figured it was safe to ignore the question. Ashley was certain to move on to another subject in seconds anyway. She didn't disappoint me.

"So where's the professor?"

The million dollar question.

The moment of silence that ensued was only that. Once again the whoosh of the front door caught everyone's attention. The only one who turned toward the hall in expectation was Ashley; the rest of us regarded one another with dread. The room was nearly filled to capacity, and I was more than ready to end this little adventure.

Until I heard the voices echoing down the hallway.

"There have been people skulking around this place all morning long, and I just thought you should look into it."

"I appreciate that, Ms. Naner, but you really should wait outside."

I winced at the sound of his voice. But not as much as Marla did.

"Perhaps I should, but . . . "

"It's too hot outside for that." Ashley Tanner skipped into the hall. "Come on back, guys. I think we're having a party." A moment later she came strolling into the office, arm in arm with my former fifth-grade teacher, Ms. Gracie Naner.

Blue Eyes followed closely on their heels.

Chapter 11

Tarryton Public Safety is a unique combination of police and fire departments. As I understand it, this system is one of a handful of its kind. Not just in Missouri, but in the entire country.

Designed to save smaller communities from the cost of maintaining two separate departments, a Public Safety organization works from a shared budget, within the same facility. The police officers—Public Safety Officers—are cross-trained for fire fighting, though the few full-time firemen are not cross-trained for police duty. There is a heavy reliance on the community for volunteer firefighters, which has never been a problem for Tarryton. Andi's husband, my son-in-law Jared, has been a volunteer for years. And would still be one if his army reserve unit hadn't been called up for active duty in the Middle East.

Now, within Public Safety's inner sanctum, in an uncomfortable chair opposite a stern-faced officer I didn't recognize, I scanned the rows and rows of group photos depicting the members of the department and volunteers over the last fifteen years. If I'd been able to get up and examine them, I would find both Ike and Jared in several photos.

I closed my eyes and leaned back against the hard, slightly dingy wall. It was the best way I could think of to avoid the cold, intense stare of the officer watching me.

I'm not sure if I could pinpoint the exact moment everything left the reality plane and morphed into some kind of weird and distorted dream. Not a nightmare, since it was barely noon, but an otherworldly daymare that threatened to overwhelm my fragile hold on reality as I once knew it.

Jane's oversleeping should have given me a hint that something out of the ordinary was happening, but I'd ignored the sign and gone on my way.

If I skip over the anomaly regarding my sister, then I have to accept that Hannah Finley started the mad trek when she handed me the dreaded key to Zeke Wallace's domain. But even that had grounding in the real world. As did finding Elsie Wilkes cowering inside Wallace's office closet. To some degree, anyway. I mean, you had to know Elsie to fully understand.

The appearance of *Extreme Makeover* Marla Hobbs definitely initiated the warp in the time-space continuum. Motor mouth Ashley Tanner tipped the scales—especially when she invited Gracie Naner and Blue Eyes to join us. But what really convinced me this was no longer the world I'd formerly lived in was what happened as we followed Rick out of the bungalow.

Elsie had grabbed Marla's and my hands and whispered, "Let me do the talking. Just agree you were there helping me with the house. I'll take care of everything."

She'd let go of our hands, tapped Marla on the shoulder and said, "You owe me."

Detective Spencer didn't seem in the least overwhelmed by his catch. Though he did seem to frown at me a bit more than I felt necessary. He called ahead to inform the station he was bringing us in for questioning, then proceeded to tell us he didn't want any more talking—from *any* of us—until we were interviewed downtown.

At that point, I remembered thinking it was a good thing he'd left Ashley behind. I suppose the fact she'd been away on vacation these last two weeks, along with proof she was Wallace's regular housekeeper, helped eliminate her as a suspect. Or whatever the rest of us were considered.

Detective Spencer—not Blue Eyes, and definitely not Rick—had immediately confiscated the grade book and CD, along with the keys both Marla and I had in our possession. Elsie's claim of ownership was likely what allowed her to keep the one she had.

All in all, Elsie was the only one of the three of us Rick treated with any deference. I was curious about that, but in this strange new world, was a little reluctant to let it show. Especially after Elsie kept her word and took care of everything.

Sort of.

They released her and Marla shortly after our arrival at the station. Gus Bradley, Mr. "Just the facts ma-am" himself, had been designated as chauffeur back to their cars—*and he'd actually seemed happy about that.*

What furthered my impression this wasn't quite real was the smile and greeting Gus had for Elsie and her corresponding blush and nervous batting of eyelashes. Never mind that this was the second smile I'd ever seen on the man's face—two in less than twenty-four hours, no less—but it was the only time I'd seen Elsie Wilkes display an interest in any man other than Dr. Steven Acklin, Jane's fiancé, or Elsie's on again off again beau, Rex Stout. This had to be proof that we'd been somehow transported into the *Twilight Zone.* I expected Rod Serling to appear any moment.

Either that, or this mess was some kind of convoluted dream. Right?

Maybe reading science fiction and fantasy weren't the right genres for me.

The familiar sound of Blue Eyes clearing his throat prompted me to open one eye just enough to barely see him and try to determine what kind of mood he was in—and who I'd be dealing with. If it was no-nonsense Detective Spencer, well, I wasn't quite ready to cope with that part of his persona.

Not while I was still drifting in this strange world where Elsie Wilkes actually solved problems instead of being part of them.

"You might as well open your eyes all the way, Glory. I'm not going away."

There was a shuffle of feet and the retreating sound of footfalls. I peered between my lashes to find Blue Eyes perched on the desk in front of me and the other officer nowhere in sight.

There was no quizzical tilt to his eyebrows, no hint of humor or indulgence as he regarded me. The ominous look in his dark blue eyes caused a shiver of apprehension to run up my spine.

"Why didn't you call me when Dr. Finley gave you the key?" He tapped my winter gloves against what I now recognized as Wallace's grade book.

It's too bad Elsie waited so long to tell us she'd get us out of the mess we were in. I'd managed to spill my guts shortly after Blue Eyes's arrival at the house. All it had taken was one disapproving gaze at my gloved hands, and he knew my reason for being there.

"I knew what you'd say," I told him, keeping my eyes locked on his. "And it would have infuriated Hannah if I'd brought you into it."

"So you followed her orders, knowing it was wrong."

Was he just busting my chops, or did he intend to charge me? I prayed it was the former.

"She had a key and what sounded like a good explanation for its use." I hoped my voice wasn't as shaky as it sounded to me. "I didn't touch anything without the gloves, nor did I rifle through the man's belongings. Like I told you before, the grade book was open on his desk, the computer was still on in sleep mode—or whatever you call it—and when I moved the mouse, the Excel file was right there. I looked through the desk for a CD, which you have. That's it."

He barely moved as he continued staring down at me. It made me nervous but also a little indignant.

Unlike my sister, patience doesn't come easily for me. My curiosity makes me more spontaneous and impetuous than is sometimes good for anyone, but it's all part of that insatiable desire to know and understand what's going on. It's given me my fiery resolve, feisty attitude, and overall zest for life. And sitting here like I'd done something wrong was making me more than a little resentful.

Okay, following Hannah's orders may not have been the smartest decision I've ever made. I'd give him that. But in the scheme of things, I hadn't really done anything illegal.

Not in my mind, anyway.

I was just getting up the nerve to stand up to him when he surprised me yet again.

"These are exactly what you said they were." He held out both the CD and the grade book. "I don't approve of how you obtained them, but I understand the bind the school's in."

He didn't move from the edge of the desk. I can't say it didn't bother me, but it wasn't going to keep me in this chair either.

"Thanks."

I stood and snatched up the items in one fell swoop. Before he could change his mind, I headed for the exit.

"You dropped this."

I turned to find him at my elbow, a small piece of paper in his hand. A glance at my fanny pack showed all the zippers tightly closed.

"I don't think it's mine."

"It has Jane's name on it."

"Oh . . . well . . . "

I held my hand out for the paper just as he started to unfold it. I had no idea what it might be, but if Jane's name was on it, there was a good chance it belonged to me.

He tucked the paper into my outstretched hand. "Have you forgotten you need a ride back to your car?"

I had forgotten, of course. As much as I usually enjoyed Blue Eyes's company, being alone with him for the ten or fifteen minutes it would take to drive across town didn't sound all that appealing right now.

"I'll be happy to give you a lift."

Gripping the small scrap of paper so tightly it made my hand hurt, I gave him a wan smile.

"That won't be necessary, detective."

I turned to find a beaming Elsie Wilkes coming toward us.

"I'm sure you have more pressing things to do," she continued. "I'll be more than happy to drop Glory off. Besides, we have some unfinished business. Right, Glory?"

The pointed glance she gave me was barely disguised by the smile she bestowed on Blue Eyes. I had no idea what "unfinished business" she thought we had, but if it saved me from a lecture, I was all for taking her up on the offer.

"Great, Elsie. Thanks."

I looked back at Blue Eyes, trying to gauge his reaction. He'd donned one of those inscrutable policeman expressions he was famous for.

"I'll see the two of you out," he said, gently taking hold of my elbow and guiding me around the front counter.

When we got to the door, Elsie went on ahead after a quick peek over her shoulder. Once she was out of earshot, Blue Eyes stopped and swiveled me toward him.

"You understand that I had to call Dr. Finley to corroborate your story. I'm sorry." He lightly caressed my cheek. "It's not that I didn't believe you—"

"I know." I gave his hand a reassuring squeeze.

If you go out with a cop and you do something legally questionable, then I guess you have to expect him to still *be* a cop.

"Was she . . . upset?"

"She wasn't happy."

I winced. Maybe sticking around the station was the better alternative. Even owing Elsie the completion of that unfinished business didn't sound as bad has having to face my boss.

Blue Eyes placed a finger beneath my chin and raised my head until our eyes met.

It was enough to make me forget about everything but him.

Chapter 12

E lsie barely waited for me to get in the car. "Things are about to get a little freaky around here," she said, pulling out onto the street. "And, well, I want, need someone to confide in I can trust."

Whoa! *Twilight Zone, Part Two* appeared to be just around the corner.

"I don't know how Hannah Finley got that key, but I can guarantee Zeke didn't give it to her."

Zeke? Since when was Tarryton's biggest proponent on a first name basis with its archenemy? I mean, I worked with the guy for two years and would never even consider calling him anything beyond Dr. Wallace or Professor Wallace . . . or jerk, but that was behind his back. Until today, I didn't realize Elsie even knew the guy beyond his reputation.

I suppose renting him a house made all the difference.

"She wasn't his type," Elsie continued. "Not even as one of his flavors of the month."

Flavor . . . oh, I liked that. I quickly tucked it away in my memory banks before I missed anything. This was one time I didn't want to miss a word.

"I also can't imagine his giving her a key for emergencies. Zeke never thought along those lines."

"I hate to interrupt, but maybe a little explanation might be a good thing." I twisted in my seat so I could get a better look at my chauffeur. "You might start by how you know so much about Dr. Wallace. And I'm dying to know what Marla's story was."

Though Elsie stared straight ahead watching the traffic, there was a wicked gleam in her eyes at the mention of Marla's name. "She refused to talk about it . . . for now."

At a stop sign, she turned to me with a confident smirk. "We both saw that get-up and know she had a key. And while it pains me to think about it, Marla's exactly the type of woman Zeke would go after."

As she pulled back into traffic, I wondered what Elsie would think about Wallace's failed advances to me.

I wondered, but not enough to tell her.

"And you know so much about Dr. Wallace because . . . " I prompted.

Elsie's mouth tightened into a thin, straight line. The tautness was reflected in the sudden rigidity of her neck and death grip she had on the steering wheel.

Elsie Wilkes has always fascinated me. Over the years, I've studied her varying expressions and how quickly they can change. Where Ashley Tanner has cornered the market on covering the most unrelated topics all in a single breath, with Elsie one look is truly worth a thousand words.

We drove in silence for several blocks. I knew enough not to force the issue; Elsie would get around to telling me. Especially if she was serious about this trusted confidant thing.

She thawed out sooner than I expected. "Zeke was my brother."

The bombshell brought on a fit of coughing that caused Elsie to pull over to the curb and pound me on the back.

"My half brother, actually," she said as I gulped in so much air I began to hiccup on top of the coughing. Not many people know that when I was a child my father left us for a couple years. Mother always kept it quiet, didn't want people to know he'd taken up with another woman." She patted me on the back once more. "You okay now?"

I nodded, too dumbfounded to even try to find my voice.

"Anyway, Zeke was the result. That ring you recognized on his hand belonged to my father. It's the Wilkes family crest, or some such nonsense. I always thought it was a little garish, which is probably why it was left to Zeke instead of me."

We were just two blocks from where I'd left my car, and I still didn't trust my voice enough to say a word.

And there were a lot of words I wanted to say.

"Never heard you so quiet before, Glory." Elsie stole a sidelong glance. "I guess I've stunned you into silence."

"You can say that again," I croaked.

She laughed. "As I said, freaky."

She parked behind my Corolla but left her car running. "I'd forgotten Gracie Naner lived so near Zeke. We'll have to ask her about what she remembers from a couple weeks ago."

"We?"

Elsie nodded. "I need someone to help me, Glory, and knowing your . . . shall we say, *inquisitive* nature, you're the perfect choice. Besides, I figure you sort of owe me." She tapped the shoulder where she'd been shot.

"*That* wasn't my fault."

"Maybe not. But it does prove you're a capable investigator. In a roundabout way."

It suddenly dawned on me that I'd failed to recognize the bigger picture.

"*You ID'd the professor!*"

Elsie gently inclined her head.

"Which means Public Safety knows your relationship."

"They do now, of course. Thank the Lord Rick Spencer found the card in Zeke's wallet. I'm not so sure the others would've handled it with as much discretion."

I recalled the friendly glances she and Officer Bradley exchanged earlier. It was obvious she had at least one other fan in the department.

"I know your weakness when it comes to mysteries," she was saying. "I remember our old book club and how much you got into trying to figure out the clues and find the culprit before the end of the story. Then, of course, there's your real-life mystery from this spring. If not for your tenacity—"

I raised my hands in surrender. She had me pegged. Besides, I'd fully intended to investigate the severed-hand mystery all along.

But as much as I hated the thought, I had something else to attend to at the moment.

"If I don't get back to the college with these ASAP, Dr. Finley will be sending out a search party."

"Scalping party, if I know Hannah. The way she pulls poor Joe's strings . . . but that's another story."

I gathered up my things, noticing I still held the small square of paper Blue Eyes had found on the floor back at the station. The only word showing on the outside was my sister's name.

"What's that?"

"I'm really not sure." As I told her about the incident with Rick, Elsie leaned over to take a look.

"That's Zeke's handwriting," she said. "Where did you say you got it?"

"Rick thought I dropped it. You don't think . . . " I fanned the pages of the grade book. "Maybe it fell out of this."

"Well it doesn't look like there's anything in there now. May I?"

With more than a little reluctance, I gave her the scrap of paper in a show of that trust she'd spoken about. It didn't mean I wouldn't watch her like a hawk as she carefully unfolded it.

Elsie's muddy green eyes grew large as she read the contents of the note.

"Oh . . . my."

Her usually pale face was even paler than usual as she handed the note back to me.

"Elsie?"

She shook her head and pointed at the scrap of paper. The message contained few words, but the meaning was obvious.

It was a list of instructions to set Jane's house on fire.

Chapter 13

There wasn't actually a tug of war over the piece of paper—we're much too sophisticated for something so childish and unladylike. It was more of an active, physical dispute for possession and the responsibility—and accountability—such ownership would require.

I was ready to trot it right back to Blue Eyes, no ifs, ands, or buts. The sooner it was safely ensconced in his strong, capable hands, the better I'd feel.

Yes, I was expected back at work. But solving Jane's arson was far more important; Hannah would just have to wait a little longer for Wallace's grades.

Elsie, on the other hand, thought there was something hinky about the note. While the handwriting appeared to belong to her half brother at first glance, she felt it looked too contrived, too perfect to actually be his.

"I think it's been forged," she said, taking control of the tiny missive and holding it up to the windshield for the sun to shine through. "Look at the way the letters are formed. It's like they were traced onto this paper from something else. Perhaps from several other items."

I followed her finger as she traced the different letters and the varying lines and curves comprising each one. I'm no handwriting expert, but I had to admit there did appear to be some hesitation marks and the spacing seemed a bit odd.

"It's still evidence." I told her, carefully retrieving the note and quickly tucking it into my fanny pack. "Everything's there, just as the insurance investigator described."

"I'm not saying we shouldn't turn it over to the authorities. I just think we should wait a bit."

"For what? I know you don't want the scandal—"

"That's bound to come no matter what. The moment my relationship to him leaks out . . . " She shuddered, rubbing her arms like she was cold. "But that's not the issue here. Honestly. I mean, Zeke's been blackmailing me—"

"Blackmailing?"

She winced. "In a way it was mutual. I didn't want anyone to know about us; he knew that, and he held it over my head."

"Nice guy."

"Not particularly."

"But he was still your family."

"Half brother by birth but not really family."

It was a distinction I could understand, considering the circumstances.

Elsie shook her head, turned away for a moment, and brushed an index finger across her eyes. She might not consider him family, but it was obvious some part of her still cared.

"Bottom line, he's been scandalizing this town since he showed up two years ago. If he's guilty," she said, turning back to me, "so be it. But what if he isn't? What if this is the one thing he didn't do? *What if he's being framed by whoever killed him?*"

"So he was murdered!"

"Oh . . . well, they haven't done the autopsy yet. And the preliminary report was inconclusive according to Gus, er, Officer Bradley." She blushed. "Nothing's been released. He just told me as a courtesy."

I didn't have to think about my answer. "I'm sorry, but I can't keep this from Rick—or Jane. She's been sick over the fire."

Knowing how Jane and Elsie felt about each other, this might not have been the best thing to say. But Jane *is* family, and I wasn't going to keep her in the dark just because Elsie had a feeling the note was a fake.

The same went for Blue Eyes.

Elsie's cell phone rang. She tugged it from a pocket on the side of her purse, checked the ID, and rolled her eyes.

"Look, I'm late for an appointment to show a property, and this client really doesn't like to be kept waiting." She made a tentative reach for my hand, pulling back at the last second. "Glory, I know Zeke built a reputation around town for being one of the most despicable human beings to ever live here. But no matter what everyone thinks of him, he deserves justice. So before you give the note to Detective Spencer, do me a favor and make a copy. Give me the chance to prove I'm right about the handwriting."

This new, gentler Elsie Wilkes was a little scary in some ways but refreshing too. I didn't see any harm in her request, so I agreed to copy the note.

"I'll call you later," she said as I climbed out of her car. "We've got to get right on our investigation. It's already cold after two weeks."

I still wasn't certain about forming this alliance, knew my sister wouldn't be too happy about it, but also knew that Elsie had information I was unlikely to get anywhere else. If I wanted to have a crack at solving the mystery, a partnership with Elsie Wilkes looked the best bet.

I watched her leave and realized that whether I wanted to or not, it was time for me to face the music. And knowing Hannah, it wouldn't have a great beat or be something you could dance to.

By the time the interior of the Corolla was tolerable enough for me to touch the steering wheel, I'd managed to find my cell phone, buried at the bottom of my fanny pack. With a single touch of a button, I had Blue Eyes's voice mail. I asked him to meet me at the college as soon as he could, then signed off.

The sun was in my eyes as I headed for Tarryton Valley College. From its position in the sky, I knew it was close to noon. I'd been gone for nearly three hours. Hannah wasn't going to be happy about that. But maybe, just maybe, I could appease her with Wallace's grades.

Once I arrived at the college, I had to drive around the various faculty-staff parking lots for several minutes before finding an empty space. Unfortunately, it was the equivalent of three blocks from the science building, and in the heat and humidity, I wasn't moving very fast.

There wasn't a dry place on me by the time I stumbled through the main doors. As disgusted and embarrassed as I was by my condition, I bypassed the restrooms and headed directly to my office.

The chatter of familiar voices spilled through the open doorway. The easy, light-hearted bantering was unexpected, considering that just two weeks ago Lila Samson and David Quinn had been jumping down each other's throats. Entering the office, I found David leaning over the desk—over Lila—whispering something in her ear that caused her to blush and giggle.

I cleared my throat, and David leapt back. He had the grace to blush and croak out, "Hi, Mrs. H. Didn't know you were back."

Lila smirked, clearly pleased the situation made him uncomfortable. Either that, or she was hoping it would make me feel embarrassed or ill at ease. It didn't. After what I'd been through so far today, this was just another in a long list of oddities.

"Your sister in?"

Lila nodded as she studied me, her nose turned up, obviously offended by my appearance. I didn't let that bother me either. In my opinion, Lila Samson is always offensive.

"Hannah's been waiting for you. *For hours.*"

As she reached for the phone to announce me, I marched past her and into the inner sanctum. Hannah wasn't alone. Meg Camden, head of the HR department, was seated across the desk from her.

"See what I mean, Meg? She just struts in here like she owns the place rather than clearing it through Lila first."

Meg and I have been friends since grade school, and in all those years, I don't think I've ever seen such a flush on her beautiful café au lait complexion. She turned to me with an apologetic look in her warm, brown eyes, and I immediately knew my goose was cooked.

"Lila said you were expecting me." I strode to the desk and deposited Wallace's grade book and the CD on it. "If you want your key back, you'll have to discuss it with Detective Spencer. But I guess you already know that."

Hannah doesn't blush, but she does turn a peculiar shade of red when she gets angry. It reminds me of a cartoon bull about to charge.

"Insubordination and a total lack of respect." She turned to Meg. "A simple request turns into a total fiasco involving the police, ultimately placing the entire college in an awkward position. You're a witness, Meg. This department, this college cannot afford to continue an association with Glory Harper. She's not just an embarrassment, but also a blemish."

Meg rose at that. She cast a quick glance in my direction, a warning for me to hold my tongue.

"As chair of the department, you have the right to request Glory's resignation—"

"I want her fired and banned from this school!"

"Dr. Finley, I understand you're upset—"

"She called in the police because she didn't trust me."

"While I didn't trust your word about the key and searching Dr. Wallace's house, I didn't call the police."

"Of all the unmitigated gall—"

Frowning, Meg raised a hand. "We're finished here. I'll have Glory processed out of the department immediately."

Meg indicated for me to follow her. I was happy to comply. Thankfully, the outer office was empty, nor was there anyone lingering in the hallway outside.

"Collect your things, Glory, then come over to HR. I'm really sorry about this, all the more because we don't have another position open right now."

I started to speak, but she stopped me. "Leave it for your exit interview, okay? Not here." She whispered the last two words. "And do yourself a favor and don't dawdle." She left after a gentle pat on my back.

I glanced around the office that had been my home away from home for almost ten years. I'd covered the walls with photos of faculty and student workers alongside those of my family. There was one of former chair, Dr. Lawrence Jensen holding week-old Seth with doting Grandpa Ike looking on. Another photo showed a Christmas party the semester before Dr. Jensen retired and Hannah took his place.

None of them warned of the interdepartmental conflicts that would arise within a year of her appointment. But then, none of us—including Hannah—could have guessed what bringing Zeke Wallace on board would do to the department, the college, and the town.

I emptied the remaining reams of paper from a large box and began loading it with the photos and plants I'd accumulated over the years. The desk drawers had been virtually emptied of my personal items while I'd been out this spring with my broken leg. Lila had limited me to a small corner at the back of a bottom drawer. Even so, I checked through the others in search of items she may have pilfered, finally deciding it wasn't worth the effort.

I'd just sat down at one of the computers to log into my school e-mail account when Lila returned to the office. Her soft, round face was flushed, her eyes a bit glassy. It was not the look of a woman who'd been working—unless it was getting down and dirty with a co-worker in some back closet. The idea made me want to hurl.

And her sister claimed I had no respect for the job.

"Your account's already been deactivated, so you can't access it or any other school account." Lila informed me with another of her self-satisfied smirks, fluffing her bleached hair.

"Was that before or after you checked my messages?"

Lila's eyes went wide. Her attempt at looking innocent gave me my answer.

I flung my fanny pack into the box, picked it up, and headed for the door.

"Just a minute there." Lila sauntered over and peeked into the box. "Hannah said I was supposed to check what you were taking."

Though I'd have liked to whack her on the back of the head, I knew it wouldn't be enough to knock any sense into her. I held my tongue and set the box on the counter. That's when I noticed the large philodendron the school had given me when Ike died. While Lila pawed through my things, nearly upsetting a small prayer plant and an English ivy, I grabbed the phili.

"*That* stays here." She indicated the philodendron. "You can take the rest."

"It's mine, Lila, and I can get a half dozen faculty members to prove it if I have to."

She started to grab for the plant but relented when she realized she'd be in for a fight. Shrugging, she waved me on.

"I'm sure we can count on your cooperation whenever we've got questions," she said, her tone making it an order and not a request.

That was it. The final straw.

"Actually, I've been banned from this department. Looks like you're on your own."

My grand exit was foiled when I ran headlong into David Quinn. He grabbed hold of the box, giving me a grim smile as he relieved me of my burden.

"I take it you've been given your marching orders."

I nodded, unwilling to meet David's gaze. I'd always been comfortable with this kid. But that was before witnessing the little scene between him and Lila.

He asked where I was parked, then followed along like an obedient puppy. We made small talk, the kind you exchange when you're nervous around someone you barely know. After working together for three years, this shouldn't have been an issue, but it's not every day that your boss loses her job.

"I was surprised to see you in the office," I told him as he loaded the box into the backseat of my car.

"It's kind of embarrassing, Mrs. H." He raised a hand to shield his eyes from the sun as he looked at me. "They asked if I'd like your job."

"Really?"

Lila might not use the brain God gave her, but her sister's no fool. David had been my right arm and knew the job better than Lila ever could. Hiring him as a regular employee was the smartest move Hannah made in a long time.

"Congratulations."

David lowered his eyes. "I figured it was a good way to keep your job available."

"Excuse me?"

"You know, if something should happen and you can come back. I'd be glad to give it up, where someone else might not be."

I appreciated the sentiment and told him so. Though it was an unlikely scenario, it was a thoughtful thing for him to do.

But as I headed to HR, I flashed again on Lila and David with their heads together, whispering and giggling. Two weeks ago the tension between the two was so bad, David had decided it was best for him to quit. I'd thought they were fighting, that he was tired of Lila's irresponsibility, and being forced to complete jobs that should be hers. It looked like I was wrong.

Maybe I didn't know David Quinn as well as I thought I did.

Chapter 14

The stress of the morning slammed into me like an eighteen wheeler out of control. I could feel the tread marks where each tire rolled over me as it came back for a second shot—perhaps even a third try at mashing me into the ground.

I was hot, certain my brain had turned to mush, and more than an hour and a half past when I should have eaten lunch. Hunger gnawed at my stomach much as the frustration over being fired ate at my soul. Meg Camden's support and the knowledge that the HR department was on my side helped. Without giving me any details, she'd let me know the college would look into things, and this wouldn't be a permanent banishment.

The single comfort was knowing that even without my job, I would be all right financially—not great, but all right. At least for a while.

From the time we first married, Ike had been very big on life insurance and making certain his family was provided for if he wasn't around. He'd purchased several small, whole life policies that were paid up long before cancer took his life. Between those and what he got through his job, there'd been enough to settle his medical expenses, pay off the house, and give me a little nest egg. I thanked God every day for this blessing and Ike's forethought.

Still, with the way prices continued to rise, having a job and bringing in a little extra income was important. Besides, I enjoyed my work.

Or did before Dr. Finley took over the department.

I was ready to take a cool shower, put on shorts and a T-shirt, and eat anything I could lay my hands on. Especially chocolate. After I was sated, I would take a crack at sorting out everything I knew about Zeke Wallace and the morning's adventure in the *Twilight Zone*. If I didn't pass out from sheer exhaustion first.

Coming up the hill to my house, I noted Dr. Dreamboat's car parked on the street in front, which meant he and Jane were having a much-needed reunion. Since I wasn't expected home until four, I considered turning around and heading to Micky D's rather than interrupting them. Then I noticed Andi's SUV in the driveway.

I drove carefully around my daughter's car and into the garage. The chairs I thought she might be there to collect were still stacked where I'd left them the night before. Maybe they were having lunch together.

My stomach growled, protesting its lack of nourishment. There might be something to Jane's insistence on eating breakfast after all.

I lugged the box and philodendron into the kitchen, disappointed not to find a table laden with delicacies. The house was deathly quiet, the stillness only broken by the faint sound of children's voices and Misty's occasional yips filtering in from the backyard. I hadn't expected Jane and Steven to be making a lot of noise, of course, but it was still a little eerie.

I peered into the dining room, and though I saw no one, there was a murmur of voices coming from the living room. Not wanting to disturb the lovebirds, I decided to forego the shower and change of clothes for the time being. Instead, I kicked off my dress flats, tugged down my knee highs—shredding them in the process—and allowed my feet to breathe for a moment before slipping into a pair of flip-flops left by the door. After grabbing an apple from the fridge and rinsing it, I stole out into the backyard.

Andi was on the patio in the shade, sipping an iced tea, with the remains of a salad in front of her. Two small drinks and a sack from Micky D's sat nearby.

"You're home early." She removed her feet from an extra chair, and I plopped down next to her.

"That happens when you've been fired."

I gave her a rundown of the morning's escapades, starting at the end and working backward. By the time I got to Ashley Tanner's arrival at Wallace's bungalow, Andi was laughing so hard tea flew out her nose.

"I'm surprised Rick didn't toss all of you in jail and throw away the key," she hiccuped. "I'm glad he didn't let you go without a reprimand."

"Yeah, well, that wasn't fun, but Hannah Finley saved the best for last." I took a bite out of my apple, savoring the sweet juicy taste.

We got sidetracked talking about Hannah and Lila, so I never got around to telling her about the new and improved Elsie Wilkes and her relationship to Wallace, or the note.

The note! I'd left Blue Eyes a message to meet me at the college.

I glanced at the back door, thought about calling him, then decided it could wait. This was the most relaxed I'd been all day, and I didn't feel like moving. I took another bite from my apple and settled back in the lawn chair.

Misty gave a sharp bark and barreled toward me with her tongue lolling out the side of her mouth, making it look like she was smiling. After a sloppy greeting of licks and doggy sighs, with me trying to keep her from jumping into my lap, the puppy got a quick drink, then bounded back to the jungle gym. Only then did I notice that Kelly's had come by to erect the small tent on the upper platform. It now had two pairs of legs dangling over the side.

"Looks like Seth and Nathan are having fun," I said, assuming the other set of legs belonged to my grandson's best friend.

"It's not Nathan." Andi leaned toward me, keeping her eyes on the tent. "We've had an interesting morning here too, Mama."

"And here I thought I was having all the fun!"

My facetiousness didn't elicit the expected response. Instead, she leaned in closer, her expression serious.

Had I been so wrapped up in myself I'd missed something important?

My thoughts flew to my son-in-law fighting in the Middle East. I grabbed Andi's hand, searching her face.

"It's not Jared," she said, seeming to read my mind. "Aunt Jane called me after she spoke with the fire chief, around nine or so. When I got here, she handed me a camera and said I was to photograph everything in your house."

"She's become even more cautious than usual since the fire. And after getting that letter from the insurance company yesterday, it doesn't surprise me."

"This is beyond paranoia. She said the new evidence makes it obvious someone was after her. Which means they could strike here next. She doesn't want you to suffer the same loss."

To a degree this sounded like Jane, yet there was a distinct difference—my sister is an optimist, never a pessimist. Cautious, yes, paranoid, no.

Seth's dulcet tones were accompanied by those of the female persuasion. Chloe Henderson, maybe? She's been Seth's girlfriend since pre-school, but they didn't often have play dates. I looked to Andi for an explanation, but that's not where she was headed.

"Did you hear me, Mama? Aunt Jane's packed all the photo albums and most of the pictures you had on the walls. She went around the house gathering papers and folders from your office, dug your lock box out from the back of your closet, then gave it all to me. She made me promise to keep everything safe until whoever set her fire is caught. When Steven got here, she had him put everything in my car."

Trying to wrap my mind around what I was hearing made my head ache worse than it already did. Andi was right; this didn't sound like Jane. Had that fissure I'd detected in her resolve become a crevasse?

Surely that wasn't possible. Not for my big sister.

Seth poked his head out of the tent, spotted me, and headed for the ladder.

"Hey, Bouncy, Bouncy!"

As he ran toward me, Misty galloping by his side, his female companion peered around the tent flap. She stared at us for several seconds before seeming to come to a decision. The flap fell into place as she darted back inside.

Seth wrapped his sweat-slicked arms around my neck and gave me a peck on the cheek. "Mommy said you were at work."

I hugged him back. "And I was. But I decided I'd rather be here with you guys than stuck inside all day."

Misty tried to nose her way between us, her fluffy golden tail wagging so hard I thought she'd topple over. Seth separated from me and plopped onto the patio. He patted his leg and the puppy tumbled onto his lap. She gazed up at him in pure contentment.

"You wanna—"

"Don't say it or even think it," Andi said, meeting my gaze. " 'Cause it ain't gonna happen."

" 'Ain't'? Why Andrea Jane Wheeler, you're a school teacher and should know better than that."

My feigned shock had Seth laughing himself silly. "What about you, buddy boy?" I poked him in the ribs. "Who's your little friend?"

He gave an expressive shrug. "Her name's Becca. Uncle Steven brought her."

Andi put a hand on my arm and nodded toward the jungle gym. The girl was slowly climbing down the ladder.

"Steven?" I glanced at my daughter in question, then turned my attention to the child about to join us.

She wasn't any taller than Seth, with the skinny legs and scraped knees that most kids possessed by summer's end. She had short, chestnut hair touched red and gold by constant exposure to the sun. It lay at odd angles across her head, either from a bad hair day or cut, I couldn't tell which. Her dark eyes were large and wary, reminding me of a deer caught in the headlights of an oncoming car.

"May I have a drink, please?" Her soft voice sounded a little rough around the edges like it would if she'd been screaming a lot . . . or crying. From the dark circles beneath her eyes, I'd guess it was the latter.

Andi handed her one of the drink cups. "I'm not certain it's cold any more."

Becca checked the cup over as though looking for something, nodded, then took a sip from the straw. " 'Sokay." She took another sip, peering over the cup at me while she drank. "I'm Becca. You must be Seth's grandmother."

Seth giggled like he always does when someone calls me his grandmother. I'm not sure why it makes him laugh; I just go with it.

"Good guess." I smiled, wondering about this little girl who was so formal and grown-up one moment and so completely the child she really was the next.

"Not really. I already met the other lady, so that left you."

It wasn't said in a snotty way, more matter-of-fact. While Becca studied me intently, I reciprocated.

She had a tiny oval face with a sprinkling of freckles across her cheeks and the bridge of her nose. Long, dark lashes accentuated the unusual color of her large eyes, which were an interesting shade of brown with generous flecks of green—or perhaps it was the other way around. Her cute, pixy quality was a foreshadowing of the beautiful woman she'd one day become.

"You don't look like *her*," Becca said, pulling me out of my reverie.

While I was trying to figure out who she was talking about, the door opened and Steven joined us.

"Good. I see you're getting acquainted with everyone."

The girl gave Dr. Dreamboat a suspicious look, set her cup back on the table, and folded her arms across her chest. "We going now?"

Steven's eyebrows shot up in surprise at the obvious annoyance in Becca's tone. He didn't admonish her, though it looked like he wanted to. Instead, he held out his hand and smiled.

"I need to check in at my office and thought you might like to come along to see where your mom used to work."

Becca stared at his hand for several moments before stepping forward and slipping her own into his.

"Thank you for lunch, Mrs. Wheeler," she said without prompting. "I enjoyed playing with you and your puppy, Seth."

Misty stumbled out of Seth's lap over to the girl. She licked Becca's free hand, then whimpered softly.

"Looks like you've made a friend." I smiled at Becca while looking beyond Steven's shoulder. Jane was nowhere in sight. I threw a questioning glance in Andi's direction and received a shake of her head in answer.

Misty decided to lie down on my feet at the same time I chose to stand. I fell forward, nearly knocking Becca over, and crashing us both into Steven. Andi and Seth came to our aid, with the puppy leaping up and down as we all broke into laughter.

Giggling, the two kids took off around the corner of the house—and I was praying the new fence and gate would hold.

"Are you okay, Glory? You didn't hurt your leg again, did you?" The orthopedist in Steven had him prepared to examine me. In my hurry to keep that from happening, I jerked back and would have fallen over the chair I'd just vacated if Andi hadn't been there to steady me.

"I'm fine," I insisted, bending down to examine my broken sandal. "I swear that puppy's out to get me."

The skeptical look I received from Dr. Dreamboat and my daughter was a little embarrassing.

"Now I'll have to get new thongs."

"Flip-flops, Mama," Andi corrected, turning a nice shade of pink.

Steven snickered but held his tongue. At least the tone of the encounter had changed for the better.

But I still couldn't figure out what was keeping Jane.

We caught up to the kids at the front gate and said our goodbyes. As Steven and Becca walked hand-in-hand across the driveway, I noticed a similarity in their stride. A cloud blocked the sun and a shiver ran the length of my spine as I recalled Jane's words of the night before.

"Whatever's happening with Steven right now," she'd said, "will change our lives forever."

Chapter 15

I barely recognized my own house. Where portraits of various family members once hung, the sun-bleached walls were now interspersed with darker squares and rectangles, a stark reminder pictures were missing—and that it had been a long time since I'd last painted.

In the dining room, more than half the photos that had been on display behind the glass doors of the china hutch were now gone. The few that remained looked pitiful and out of balance on the shelves.

I wandered from room to room, marveling at Jane's efficiency in selecting items to be locked away for safe-keeping. Notes—tags really—clung to different knick-knacks and furniture, things that had been passed down to us from our parents and grandparents. Some we'd saved from Jane's fire and painstakingly restored, while others were mine, which I would one day pass on to Andi.

My daughter followed along, pointing out things I'd missed, both of us wondering where Jane had gone—not just in the house, but in her mind as well. We got Seth safely ensconced before a favorite game on the computer, Misty lying at his feet, then went in search of my sister. We finally found her in my tiny attic, engrossed in one of the trunks our parents had left with me before they headed out on a seniors cross-country tour several months ago.

"We need to rent a storage unit for the rest of the stuff," Jane said without acknowledging our presence. "There's just so much. So much."

She glanced up at us, then quickly returned her attention to the trunk in front of her. It was enough for me to see that her blue eyes were ringed by heavy, dark circles.

"Have you looked in these?" She held up a small knitted blanket, off-white in color and edged with yellow crocheted scallops.

"I think that's your baby blanket." I stepped carefully along the narrow pathway of plywood that served as a floor. Though the attic had insulated sheetrock walls and ceiling, the flooring was only partially completed. Ike had been in the process of finishing the space when he got sick.

Jane shook her head. "I don't remember seeing it before. That first trunk has our baby blankets and christening outfits. Things like that. This looks older."

Andi came up next to her and gently fingered the blanket. "I'll bet it was grandma's or grandpa's. It's gorgeous and so soft."

Jane handed the blanket to Andi, then continued her search. She came up with a package of letters tied with a faded blue ribbon.

"Love letters?"

"Whatever they are," she said, taking back the blanket and tucking everything inside the trunk, "we can't let them get ruined." She shoved at the trunk, but it barely budged. *"We need to get these down."*

There was frustration in my sister's voice. Worse, there was an anguish I'd never seen before.

"Janie." I reached across the chest, trying to grab her hands. She shook me off and pushed at the container once more. This time it moved slightly.

"Aunt Jane, why don't we go downstairs, so I can show you and Mama the ultrasound of the baby?"

"That's a great idea. Besides, Janie, it took Pop, Jared, and one of his friends to get these old trunks up here. There's no way we can do this alone."

"We can't leave them, Glory. If the arsonist comes looking for me here . . . "

Her face was beet red and dripping with sweat from her exertion. Before she had the chance to shove at the chest again, I was able to capture her hands.

"I'll get Steven and Rick to help, okay? We'll rent a storage unit and put these and anything else you want into it. I promise."

She nodded. Though she was looking right at me, it was clear her mind was elsewhere.

"I thought about checking into one of the motels, but that would just put more people at risk."

"You're not going anywhere, Jane Marie Calvin. Except out of this attic. It's hotter 'n blue blazes up here."

I motioned for Andi to go back downstairs. Once she was out of sight, I placed a hand on either side of my sister's face and waited until I was sure she was focused on me.

"You've been through rougher times than these, Janie. Your faith got you through then, and it'll get you through now. All you have to do is give Him a chance."

A dim spark lit her sad, tired eyes. She bowed her head as tears dribbled down her cheeks. I held her while she cried and prayed silently.

Jane had always been the one I could turn to for help and advice, my big sister with all the answers. She kept me grounded—though sometimes I wished she'd allow me to fly—and knew when enough was really enough. When I called her my Rock of Gibraltar, she'd been quick to remind me that the one true Rock was how she'd weathered every storm—how God had lifted her up when life had beaten her down.

Leaning my head next to hers, I prayed.

She needs me, Lord. I don't know what's going on, but I don't want to fail her. Please grant me the strength and the wisdom I need to get her through this crisis.

Chapter **16**

Jane was starting to look and sound more like herself when the doorbell rang. When Andi got up to answer the door, Misty came running down the hall, Seth close behind.

"Walk," she admonished her son.

Seth and the puppy had gotten settled on the floor by the time Andi showed Blue Eyes into the living room. Misty ran to greet him, but Seth pulled her back before she was able to leave clumps of hair on the uniform he was wearing today.

"Hi, Mr. Spencer."

Detective Spencer—clearly the correct persona—acknowledged Seth's greeting with a smile as his eyes swept the room. That's all it took for those incredible peepers of his to assess the situation and know something was wrong. A single raised eyebrow punctuated his quizzical expression. But he didn't ask.

Of course, I didn't give him much of an opportunity to question me; I darted out to the kitchen to retrieve the note. His curiosity must have gotten the better of him because as I passed back through on the way to the den, he followed me without a word.

"Mind if I ask what's going on?"

I switched on my printer and flipped open the top of the flatbed scanner.

"Glory?"

I held up a finger for him to wait a moment as I tried to decide where best to place the note on the glass.

"You called me, remember?"

Was I detecting some irritation? You couldn't really blame him, though, when it came right down to it. Not with a wasted trip out to the college in the middle of a busy day. Especially when he had a murder to solve.

If it really was a murder.

And I'd lay odds it was.

"I really don't have time for this today." Rick turned me around to face him. His brows were drawn together in a frown that etched deep furrows across his face.

I hated seeing him like this, tired and frustrated. And being the cause of it made me feel even worse.

"I am *so* sorry, Rick. I should have called you back, and was going to, but things kinda got away from me."

Reaching behind me, I punched a button on the machine without looking. The printer began to grind and whine like it was in excruciating pain.

My smile of apology became a grimace that almost matched Blue Eyes's expression. I turned back to the printer, pressed the copy button again, and crossed my fingers.

"First, Hannah fired me. Then when I got home Jane needed me and, well—" I handed him the small scrap of paper the moment the copy began to print. "Here you go." When I tried to direct him out of the room, however, he didn't budge.

"What's this?"

"You found it on the floor at the station, remember? Turns out it wasn't mine after all."

His reaction to the note was the same as Elsie's and mine. He read it once, looked to me as if for confirmation, then read it again.

"Where did you—"

"I didn't find it. You did. It must've fallen out of the grade book." I shrugged. "At least that's the best I can figure."

"You know what this is?" His voice was grave. "Of course you know." He lowered himself onto the corner of my desk. "And you copied it because . . . ?"

"Elsie asked me to. Before you say another word, yes, you're right, I probably shouldn't have. But Wallace is—was her brother."

"That doesn't make it all right. It's evidence."

"What if it's not real?"

There was the raised eyebrow again. How so much can be said by a single action, I'll never know.

"Elsie thinks it's a forgery. If you hold it up to the light—" I reached for the missive, but he blocked my attempt.

"I think we've had enough people handling it, don't you?" He pulled a small plastic bag from out of thin air—or so it seemed—and deposited the note inside. "And real or not, it's still evidence."

"You always carry those on you?"

I wasn't trying to get out of answering his questions. I was just curious.

I also hoped he'd forget about the copy.

He didn't.

"Why does Elsie think it's a forgery?" He took the copy from the printer's tray, folded it, and tucked it into his shirt pocket.

"Because it looks too perfect. I dunno." I sighed, tired and more than a little aggravated. There went this new, friendlier relationship with Elsie. "You'll have to ask her."

"Count on it. Now," he took a deep breath, "I really have to go, so in . . . say . . . fifty words or less, what's going on?" An index finger went beneath my chin to gently raise my head.

That was all it took for the tears to start flowing. I tried to hold them back, tried to be tough, resilient. But it didn't work.

Rick took me into his arms, and I crumpled. At least that's what it felt like.

"I—I got fired," I murmured against his shirt.

The starchy scent of the cotton mixed with the spicy tang of his aftershave enveloped my senses. A scene from *Romancing the Stone* flew into my head. Jack Colton had just told Joan Wilder the yellow-tailed crocodile that swallowed El Corazon had died in his arms. Joan stared deeply into Jack's eyes and said, "If I were to die, there's nowhere on earth I'd rather be."

It was a great line for the movie—a riotous romantic adventure. So why had it suddenly popped into my head?

I tried to push the thought away. But it wasn't easy. This was dangerous ground I was treading.

Perhaps more dangerous than looking for a murderer.

"When I got home," I sputtered, "Jane was—oh, I don't know. She's not at all herself. She's packed away photos and albums and wants to put a bunch of stuff into storage for safe-keeping. I'm afraid for her."

"I noticed the blank spaces on the wall."

Swiping at the tears with the back of my hand, I came out of his arms with more reluctance than I'd like to admit. "And though she didn't say it, I think she and Steven had an argument."

"You've had a busy day." His soft voice, coupled with the tenderness in his eyes, made it difficult to keep the waterworks at bay.

"Y-you going to tell her about the note?"

"Why don't we give this to Lieutenant Holmes and go from there. He's already reopened the investigation. There's no reason to upset Jane any further."

I agreed; this was one secret Jane was better off not being privy to. But keeping my mouth shut wasn't going to be easy.

"Glory?"

"You're right. I'll try."

He gave me a long, hard look, but eventually nodded.

I followed him out of the den and back to the living room, where he said goodbye to everyone. I didn't accompany him out the door, didn't trust myself to get close to him again. If he noticed the omission, he didn't say so. With a brief wave, he was on his way.

And I was ready to discover what had sent Jane over the edge.

Chapter 17

By the time I finally joined them on the couch, Andi was already showing Jane the baby's ultrasound photo. Seth hovered over us, excitedly pointing out different parts of his brother or sister. He punctuated every other sentence with a grin and a gentle pat to his mommy's growing tummy.

"The doctor knows if it's a boy or a girl, but Mommy says we want it to be a surprise like I was." There was a note of pride in my grandson's voice. "*I* think it's a girl, though, 'cause it's so tiny."

Andi poked him in the ribs, and Seth fell dramatically to the floor, giggling. Misty pounced on him, eliciting even more laughter from our pint-sized comedian.

Jane took the picture from Andi and studied it. Despite her smile, tears glistened in her eyes, a single one escaping to roll down her face. Her left hand stole to her abdomen, a familiar sign she was thinking of the twins she'd lost in her second trimester so many years ago.

My sister had always wanted to be a mother. From the way she'd watched over our friends and me when we were kids, it was like her entire life had been geared to the time when she could share her love with a child of her own. When it wasn't in the cards God dealt, Jane threw herself into teaching and into volunteer work with children in whose lives she could make a difference.

Kids adored her as much as Andi and Seth loved her. But sharing in the lives of my daughter and grandson and those hundreds of students she'd taught through the years just wasn't the same as having a child of her own. And though she normally seemed to accept and embrace the role God had chosen for her to play in the scheme of things, I had a feeling that right now it was bothering her more than usual.

"Can I go finish my game, Mommy?"

It's like Seth read my mind. With him out of the room, maybe we'd get down to what threw Jane onto the edge.

I already knew the fire inspector had been by. I guessed it was something Lieutenant Holmes told her that pulled the switch. We needed to find a way to reassure her that everything was going to be fine.

No, better than fine. This incident, which was intended to steal her contentment and unsettle her mind, would be turned into something new and wonderful. I didn't know how. But it's what I chose to believe.

With his mother's approval, Seth darted from the room, Misty trotting along at his side. He wasn't gone more than a couple seconds when he hollered from the den.

"Gramma, you gotta come see this."

He met me in the hallway.

"There's something weird on the computer. It's got Aunt Jane's name and address and a bunch of stuff like—"

I put my finger to my lips to quiet him. If there was a chance Jane hadn't heard his announcement, I'd like to keep it that way.

We hustled into the den where Seth pointed to the monitor.

"See? I think you musta scanned something, Gramma, and not finished it."

Leave it to my seven-year-old grandson to come to a brilliant—and correct—deduction. I peered at the screen, and suddenly the strange whining and grinding the printer had undergone a while ago made sense. Somehow, I'd hit the scan button—an easy thing to do at any time, even easier when you were punching buttons behind your back.

What was lost was now found, sitting on my computer and awaiting a decision to accept or delete the scan. I just needed to make certain to get a printout before the copy was gone for good.

Ordinarily the original would still be on the glass, waiting for that final pass over to finish the scanning process. I had no idea what would happen if I pressed to accept the image without the original available. Would it simply finalize the image already captured or would it delete it altogether? I didn't want to take any chances.

After pressing the "print screen" button to no avail, I searched the tool bar on the scan page for "print." Nothing.

I was about to accept the scan but, at the last moment, changed my mind. Instead, I highlighted the note, pressed control "C" to copy it, opened a Word document, then pasted it there. Once the printer spit out the copy, I accepted the scan and waited. Thirty seconds later I knew I'd made the correct decision.

With my printer and software, all you got without the original still on the glass was a blank page.

I tucked the copy away in a safe place, then got Seth set up with his game. Back in the living room, Jane and Andi were chatting about baby names.

With Jared in a hot spot on the other side of the world, things haven't been easy for my daughter. But she's held it together, keeping Seth and herself occupied as much as possible and praying even more. Andi's always been more like Jane than me: solid, down to earth, and always optimistic.

And as frustrating as she could sometimes be, I wanted *that* Jane back.

"Hey, you two. What did I miss?"

"Not a thing." Jane winked at my daughter, then turned to me. "Something wrong with one of Seth's games?"

I shook my head. "I left a document open, and he didn't want to risk losing it."

The truth is always the best route to take.

"Andi told me about your day, that you've lost your job." Jane wrapped an arm about my shoulders. "I don't understand how the college could let something like that happen after the department gave Hannah a vote of no confidence."

I'd thought the school intended to keep that info under wraps. Even so, things had a way of getting around in a tightly knit community. It's no wonder Dr. Finley had been more stressed than usual.

And typical of her to take it out on me.

"If I know Meg Camden," Jane went on, "you'll be back at work in no time."

"As long as it doesn't mean working under Lila, I'm all for it. Besides, jobs will open up once school starts." I patted my sister's knee. "I—*we'll* be fine."

I wasn't in the mood to discuss my job options or lack thereof. Nor did I want Jane to add this to her worries. Turning her away from this discussion and onto her visit with the fire chief was harder than it should have been. Though it seemed like she wanted to talk about the meeting, there was something else, something more than the arson on her mind.

"I really don't know what to tell you." Jane got up from the couch and walked across the room to examine the few photos she'd left on the wall. "Lieutenant Holmes listened to what I had to say, checked back through his notes, then agreed with me. He said if it had been anyone but me, he would have called in the district fire marshal."

"So even Holmes was suspicious?"

Jane turned back to us. "He said it reminded him of the arsonist they'd investigated in the area about ten years ago. I guess this firebug chose homes and buildings that weren't occupied and—'lit them up,' was how the lieutenant put it."

She moved to an overstuffed chair near the couch and settled into it. "He said the arsonist used things like pennies in fuse boxes, old paint cans and rags, and anything else he could find in the homes. It wasn't until we were talking that he realized how closely my fire resembled the last one in the spree."

"They never caught the guy?" I asked, recalling the incidents but not the end result.

Jane shook her head. "After six fires and running the department ragged, they stopped."

"That's when Jared and I were looking into buying a house. It was a scary time for the firefighters. Jared said the arsonist always chose a point of origin that would do the most structural damage. The fires burned hot and fast." Andi shivered. "As frightening as that was, I'd rather he was here fighting fires than in the Middle East fighting terrorists."

That was something we could all agree on.

"The bottom line is if you hadn't lost Misty that night—"

"I didn't *lose* her, Janie. She slipped her collar."

"A collar I'd already warned you wasn't the right size."

"True, but—"

"And that chain you were using," Jane shook her head. "It's a wonder she hadn't gotten loose before."

"You were still living here before that," I muttered.

"And when you discovered she was missing, you ran out of the house in bare feet and your pajamas!"

"Bare feet, yes, but it was a T-shirt and shorts."

I spied Andi from the corner of my eye, trying to keep from laughing. To be honest, I felt the same way. But Jane was on a roll, and I wanted to keep her going.

"Whatever." She waved her hand as though dismissing the information. "Did she tell you how she conducted her search that night?"

I was certain Andi had heard this before, but she shook her head anyway.

"Your mother was using her cell phone as a flashlight!"

"It worked, didn't it? Besides I was holding the phone when I realized Misty was gone. I didn't want to take the time to find a flashlight that actually worked."

"You were running around the neighborhood half dressed in the middle of the night. It's a wonder you weren't picked up by the cops—"

"Actually, I was," I said with a grin.

"By Rick."

"Yep. He got here before you did."

"Which brings me back to the beginning of this conversation. Because of you, my dear sister, I was out of the house when the water heater blew. If you hadn't—if Misty—"

I went to my sister and enfolded her in my arms. "You're welcome, Janie."

Chapter 18

"It's incredible the way God works," Andi said, tears in her eyes. "Just when we think we have things figured out on our own, we realize He was in the mix all along."

"That's exactly what I need to keep in mind right now." Jane sniffled. "I know you two think I've gone off the deep end, packing things away and all. Maybe I have to a degree. It's not every day you realize someone's deliberately set out to harm you. It changes things."

"I've already promised to get the storage unit, Janie. We'll do it tomorrow if we can get the help. In the meantime, we'll take precautions, okay?"

"I appreciate that—and both of you. Today's one of those days you're just not prepared for." She flashed us a weak smile. "I should have known something strange was about to happen when I slept in so late this morning."

Uh oh.

"I thought I was ready for Lieutenant Holmes and dealing with the idea someone hated me enough—"

"Not true," Andi and I said in unison.

"Let's be honest, okay? I've got an enemy. He, she, whatever, set my house on fire. Sure, it could have been random—I hope it was. But either way, I have to deal with it. And right now, that means keeping you safe, Glory, and making sure we don't lose all our photos—our memories—to this freak."

I liked the determination in her tone; it meant Jane was pulling back from that dangerous precipice she'd been on. I just wished her eyes weren't still so haunted.

"Which brings me to the next piece in the puzzle." Jane inhaled deeply. "Andi, sweetheart, I want to thank you for taking care of Becca so Steven and I could talk. It's another sure sign God was looking out for me today."

"Not a problem. She's a very polite little thing. She and Seth got along great."

Andi's sidelong glance held a question I couldn't answer. I didn't know where this was headed, but the icy tentacles that wrapped around my spinal column didn't bode well.

"I'm glad." Jane laced her fingers, separated them, then finally settled her hands in her lap. She drew in another deep breath. "I know you both remember Rachel Eberling."

My stomach felt as if it had been turned inside out. Andi reached for my hand and grabbed on tight.

A movie reel from ten years ago flickered through my mind—Steven at church functions, suddenly accompanied by the young nurse who worked in his office. When he'd introduced us to Rachel, her bright green eyes barely strayed from the object of her affection. Ike and I had joked about it, wondering if our old friend had any idea the girl was in love with him.

"When she and Steven got engaged, it took you two weeks before you told me. Don and I had a big laugh about it." A secret smile flitted across my sister's lips as she recalled the time—and her late husband. "After all those years alone, Steven had finally found someone to share his life with. I was so happy for him."

Andi and I clung to each other as a faraway expression settled over Jane's features. I didn't know if Andi sensed what was coming, but I did.

"We've talked about her, about Rachel." Jane continued. "Steven knows how I feel about honesty—I know he would never deliberately break my trust again."

Again? That would imply Dr. Dreamboat and Jane had trust issues in the past. I couldn't remember anything that raised a red flag, but then Jane isn't quite as transparent as I am.

"He had no idea Rachel was pregnant when she broke off their engagement. She left him a note saying that she just couldn't compete with my ghost any longer. Then she was gone." Jane sat up straight, her back suddenly ramrod stiff. "She has his eyes, don't you think? Becca has Steven's eyes."

I could see a burden the size of Manhattan had been lifted from Jane's shoulders. But while she seemed relieved to have shared the information about Becca, Andi and I were waiting for the rest of the story.

That's when things unraveled even more.

A phone call from Steven had Jane sequestered in the kitchen around the same time Seth came running out of the den in a panic. We'd been so preoccupied with Jane's confessions, time had gotten away from us. Seth had less than fifteen minutes to get home and change for soccer practice. His last game of the season was tomorrow, and he didn't want to miss an opportunity to brush up on his skills. Before they left, Andi reassured me that she'd have someone help her carry the boxes Steven had loaded into her SUV.

They'd just gotten into the car when Elsie pulled up. She didn't waste any time. She was marching across the yard and up the porch steps within moments of parking.

"I would've called but thought coming to get you would be faster," she said when she reached the porch. Her red-orange hair glistened in the sunlight, every strand lacquered in place. She didn't appear tired or frazzled after the long day. She looked fresh, energetic, and raring to go.

And I felt like that eighteen wheeler had run over me a few more times.

"I'm not sure this is the right time—"

She slipped past me before I could stop her.

There'd been more on Jane's mind today than cleaning up after last night's meeting, so the house wasn't very presentable—especially for company like Elsie Wilkes. But instead of turning up her nose and making a snide comment, she got right down to business.

"It's the perfect time. Gordon won't be back from his business trip until tomorrow morning, and I doubt Marla's in the mood to go out. If I know her—"

"After this morning, I wonder if *any* of us know her."

"True," Elsie conceded. "But I still have a feeling she's holed up in her house. I've tried calling several times, but she just lets the machine pick up."

"Then how do you know she's actually there?" I was a little confused by Elsie's line of thought.

"I drove by and peeked in her garage."

It took a lot of brass to do that. And people think I'm nosy!

"Then why didn't you just stay and talk with her?"

"More power in numbers."

"I thought that was safety." I tried to herd her back to the front door, but she was having none of that.

"Same thing." She stood in the middle of the living room and glanced around her. "Are you getting ready to paint?"

The room had a polka dot effect from the missing pictures—light space here, darker squares there. I wasn't about to tell her what was really going on, so I agreed with her assessment.

"Probably a good idea. You'll have more time now you're not working."

How did she know that?

Silly question. This is Elsie Wilkes, after all.

"Get your shoes on," she said, heading for the door. "We need to get to this."

"I don't know—"

"Get to what?" Jane entered from the dining room.

I'd hoped talking to Dr. Dreamboat would make her feel better. From the way she looked, I'm not sure it did.

"Glory and I are going down to my office to discuss the terms of her employment."

"Huh?" My eyes flew to Elsie, who bowled me over by actually giving my sister a real smile.

"That's good." Had Jane heard what Elsie just said?

"I agree. The moment I found out Hannah Finley let her go, I decided to snap her up," Elsie continued as I tried hard to unlock my jaw from the open position. "I've been needing someone I can depend on, and Glory fits the bill to a tee."

Elsie's self-satisfied smile was almost as unnerving as my sister's absent gaze. But who was I to argue when Jane offered her encouragement? That alone confirmed the suspicions I'd had all day.

This *had* to be an alternate universe.

Chapter 19

As Jane shoved my fanny pack into my arms and hustled us out the door, she whispered in my ear that Steven would be back at the house any moment. That explained her wanting to get rid of Elsie, but what about me? What if things didn't go any better between her and Dr. Dreamboat than they had earlier? And what about the little girl, Becca? Was she coming along?

I turned back to Jane before starting down the porch steps. She had one hand on Misty's collar; the other was shooing me on. Her expression was set and determined, even if her face was a little haggard. At least she didn't look as lost as she had earlier.

Elsie was on her cell phone by the time we got into the car. In spite of the heat, she didn't put the key in the ignition until she'd hung up the phone.

"She's still not answering." Elsie pulled onto the street. "But I know she's there."

"And if she isn't?"

"We've other people to talk to. Besides," she glanced over at me and winked, "I meant that bit about the job. I really could use someone at my office."

"Me?" I was still marveling at the wink. *Who was this woman?* It certainly wasn't the Elsie Wilkes I've known my entire life.

"Don't act so surprised, Glory. If you can't manage to wrap your head around the fact that I know you'd be an asset to my business, then accept it as the Christian thing to do."

I was too stunned by her statement to do anything more than offer a humble, "Thank you."

I knew she'd become the exclusive agent for the most prolific builder in Tarryton. Between the development south of town and the condos near the college, Elsie kept busy. People said she knew what they wanted even before they knew themselves.

In the same way she always seemed to know what was going on in the lives of everyone in the city.

I eyed my chauffeur and potential future employer. However she managed to do it, it's what made Elsie Wilkes Tarryton's premier real estate agent and information broker extraordinaire.

"I noticed the paper on your porch, so I doubt you know that Hazel and her irritating son have broken the news about my relationship to Zeke. By now it's all over town."

"I'm sorry—"

"It was bound to happen, of course. I'd just hoped for a little more time." Elsie cleared her throat before continuing. "I'm sure my business will suffer for a while, but I've faith people won't blame me for Zeke's actions once they've a chance to stop and think. I was born here, never lived anywhere else, and have been a member of the Chamber of Commerce for years. They'll remember my support of community projects and volunteer work."

"I'm sure they will." I was also certain they'd remember all the stories and gossip she'd passed along, which wouldn't be helpful at a time like this.

Maybe this wasn't the best time to become part of Elsie's team.

"I know what you're thinking, Glory." She pulled up to a four-way stop and took the opportunity to glance over at me. "You're stiff as a board, wondering if you shouldn't make a break for it before people start pointing fingers at you too."

"How'd you—"

"Know what you were thinking? You, my dear, are an open book."

The tinkle of her laughter surprised me. It wasn't at all derogatory or nasty. It had a light, merry ring to it that I never would have expected.

"It's not so much listening to what people say as it is hearing what's not said, Glory. A look, a nod, even a sigh is just as revealing as the spoken word." Elsie paused as she turned right in the direction of the Hobbs's home. "You study a person's body language. Can they meet you eye to eye or do they look away when they speak to you. It's a skill, you know, not at all the common misconception that I'm a nosy old gossip." She laughed again— though this time it was a little harsher. "Still, that misconception has often worked to my advantage."

We pulled into the Hobbs's driveway. But instead of jumping out of the car right away to confront Marla, Elsie kept the engine running and turned toward me.

"I wasn't always this astute, you know. I used to be as dumb as a post, totally blind to everything that wasn't spelled out for me. And I got worse before I got better." She removed her hands from the steering wheel and rubbed them together.

"It was the last half of my senior year when my father decided to come clean about his second family," she continued. "My mother turned to the church to help her get through. Not me. One look at the photo of my twelve-year-old half brother and I lost faith in everyone and everything. I looked at my friends and suddenly doubted their sincerity. I figured they were out to betray me just as my father had."

"I think I can understand that." I patted her arm. I didn't know quite what to make of her confession, but it certainly seemed to be the day for them.

"I was going steady with Rex Stout, had a beautiful promise ring, and thought my future was all set. I'd just found out about my dad when Rex dumped me. Just like that. He decided he could do better."

I was really feeling uncomfortable now.

Elsie gazed over at me, her eyes soft, her expression one of regret. "Jane's never told you, has she?"

Here I was on the brink of discovering what had happened between Jane and Elsie, and she had to ask a question that was bound to put a stop to the great reveal.

But I couldn't lie.

"No," I admitted with reluctance.

Elsie nodded. "Well, when she tells you, you'll have the background, which is something I never gave your sister. I was too proud to show my weakness and too ashamed to disclose what my father had done to us. That's when I decided it was time to sit up and take notice, to become aware of anything and everything that might eventually affect me. If I kept my eyes and ears open, no one would ever be able to hurt me like that again."

"Elsie, I—"

"I know you've thought of me as stuck up," she interrupted. "But I'm really not that way inside. It's a combination of shielding myself against betrayal and the professionalism I've sought to achieve. I'm a real marshmallow inside."

I took in the arrogant tilt of her head, the confidence of her voice, and everything I'd ever known about Elsie Wilkes before today. Somehow she didn't strike me as a marshmallow.

Unless they'd drastically altered the recipe.

Yes, I was seeing sides to Elsie I never knew existed— and God help me, I wasn't sure if this new and improved version was the real McCoy, but I hoped it was. I could see us becoming true friends.

Before I had the chance to comment, Elsie shut off the ignition and opened the car door in a single motion. She slid out of the seat and stood with the fluidity of a dancer. Peering in at me, she flashed another of those mysterious winks.

"Now let's go grill Marla."

Chapter 20

"**W**hy can't you just leave me alone?"

Marla Hobbs's muffled voice barely made it to us through the thick oak door. She was clearly exasperated, and who could blame her? Elsie had been calling all afternoon. Now here we were on her porch, demanding entry.

Elsie was, anyway. I'd been inching away from the door since Marla's first plea to be left alone.

"You need us, dear," Elsie answered calmly.

"Like I need a hole in the head. Go away!"

I tapped Elsie's shoulder to get her attention. Maybe there was a way to persuade her this wasn't a good idea after all.

"Perhaps we should—"

She jerked away from me and, with an adamant shake of her head, rang the doorbell yet again. "Come on, Marla, be reasonable. Let us in."

"I'll call the cops."

Elsie gave me one of her cat-that-ate-the-canary looks. "Before you make a hasty decision, Marla, you need to think about this very carefully. Do you really want to deal with Public Safety for a second time today?"

Moments later the distinct sound of locks being disengaged filtered through the solid oak before it opened a crack. A red-rimmed eye peeked out at us.

"I'll let you in on one condition: You have to promise to leave the moment I tell you to. No argument."

"You've our solemn promise."

Elsie didn't wait for Marla to change her mind. She pushed the door open wide enough to admit her, motioning for me to quickly follow as Marla had backed away from the entrance.

I closed the door behind me, eliminating the only light in the vast entryway. Every blind in the house seemed to be closed, with the curtains tightly shut. It was an eerie reminder of how I'd started the day by breaking into Zeke Wallace's home.

Okay, technically it wasn't breaking and entering— though I'd done both. That's still what it boiled down to even though I'd had a key. Especially in Blue Eyes's way of thinking.

I knew the large entryway spilled out into an enormous living room/dining room area just up ahead and to the right. Or was that left? Maybe it would be best to stand here until my eyes adjusted from the bright sunlight to this weird fog-like interior.

"Come along, Glory," Elsie said, grasping my arm. "She's not going to let us stay long."

She tugged me forward, making all the correct twists and turns. Which made sense, of course; Marla and Elsie have been friends for years.

"Why have you shut yourself up like this?" Elsie deposited me on a loveseat, then turned on a nearby lamp.

"I felt like it."

Marla's petulant tone didn't go with the sweep of her black satin robe over her head. While the tone spoke of a wayward child, the action was reminiscent of Count Dracula.

Gone was the wig and the biker babe togs. Wisps of platinum hair peeked out from beneath the robe, and fuzzy pink slippers completed her ensemble. Marla continued to sit with her head covered, statue still. Perhaps she felt if she remained this way long enough, we'd leave.

I was fairly certain that wasn't on Elsie's agenda.

Before my team member took a seat, she handed me a pad of paper and a pen. Looked like I was relegated to the steno pool. Guess this wasn't the time to tell her I didn't know shorthand.

"If it makes you feel better to hide like that, you go right ahead and do it, dear." Elsie's words dripped saccharine in bucket loads. "We understand you're upset and embarrassed. We're just here to help you get through this rough patch."

"In a pig's eye!"

The exclamation would have held far more punch if it hadn't been issued from behind a swath of material.

"Now dear, let's remember who your friends are. Because of my generosity, you were exempt from explaining your presence and ridiculous outfit to the police. Why, I even gave them a logical explanation regarding the key you had to Wallace's home."

I shrank down in my chair about the same time Marla seemed to curl up into a little ball in hers.

I couldn't picture myself interrogating anyone—not like this. Asking questions someone might not want to answer . . . yes. But trying to force anyone into submission was beyond my ability. I'd feel too guilty.

Casting a glance at Elsie, I didn't think she had that problem. Scruples were something I never associated with the old Elsie Wilkes, but this new one . . . I was still trying to figure this one out.

But even this new incarnation appeared to thrive on ferreting out secrets from unsuspecting individuals. She could give one of her wide, plastered-on smiles, offer a shoulder or sympathetic ear, and BAM! The person spilled their guts, never knowing what hit them. Hadn't she just worked her magic on me?

Maybe Elsie should give up the real estate business and get into undercover work as a spy. I had a feeling she'd excel in such a career.

With all this in mind, teaming up with Elsie to solve Wallace's murder was actually a pretty good idea. Maybe she could even get a bead on the arsonist.

Even if it wasn't her half brother.

By the time I returned from my reverie, Marla had begun to unwind her long limbs from the near fetal position she'd curled herself into. One eye peered out from behind the robe, and even in the light from the single lamp, I could see how red and swollen it was.

I couldn't help feeling sorry for her and whatever she was trying to hide. While I understood that she might possess an important clue to the mystery surrounding Zeke Wallace, I felt compassion for her misery and guilt for intruding where I didn't belong.

"He's really dead then?" Marla's plaintive voice caught on each syllable.

"Yes," Elsie answered without elaboration.

Confirmation of Wallace's demise appeared to assuage at least part of what tortured Marla. She slowly unwrapped from her cocoon until her feet touched the floor and her head was completely uncovered.

"That's it, dear," Elsie cooed. "Why don't I go make us some tea while you pull yourself together?" She took off in the direction of the kitchen, leaving Marla and me alone.

"I—I'm sorry, Marla. We won't stay long."

With a derisive laugh, Marla flapped the wide sleeve of her robe. "If that's what you think, then you don't know Elsie Wilkes. I shouldn't have let you in." She rose and shuffled out of the room, her fuzzy pink slippers slapping against the oak flooring.

I felt small and insignificant among Marla's expensive furniture and doodads. Chairs and sofas were oversized and plush in appearance, though a might scratchy to the touch. Not well-versed in upholstery materials, I'd no idea what the pieces were covered in, only that I'd have gotten something you wouldn't be afraid to sit on in a pair of shorts.

Even in the filtered light, I could tell the house was spotless. Everything sparkled and shone, polished to the nth degree. There were no dust motes floating in the tiny shafts of sunlight in this place—they wouldn't dare.

"Good, she's freshening up." Elsie's sudden appearance startled me. "Help me with these windows."

In a matter of seconds, the rooms were flooded with afternoon sunlight. I switched off the lamp, then sought out a more comfortable chair—far away from the elegant figurines that seemed to decorate every flat surface. I didn't know what they were but knew they had to be worth a small fortune.

"Aren't they beautiful?" Elsie lifted one graceful lady from a nearby end table. "They're Lladró porcelains. The colors are exquisite, don't you think."

"I'll thank you to put that down, Elsie Wilkes. *A Flower's Whisper* cost me five hundred bucks."

Marla floated into the room on a cloud of midnight blue satin—another robe of some sort that whispered against the shining oak floor as she passed. Her platinum hair lay across her shoulders with a sheen that could only have come from a bottle but still looked beautiful against the deep blue of her robe. She gave the impression of an old-time movie star granting an audience with fans who were far beneath her station in life.

Elsie returned the piece to its spot on the table, her mouth twitching into a sly smile. "A little something you gifted yourself or . . . "

"Unless you want to leave right now, you'd better stop right there."

The whistle of the teapot broke their glaring contest. Without a word, Elsie left the room. Once she'd gone, Marla seated herself in an overstuffed chair situated at the apex of the conversation area, an obvious power play. She didn't say a thing, didn't even look in my direction.

"You have some lovely things," I offered with a smile. "I don't remember seeing them when I was here before."

She inclined her head in my direction but didn't meet my eyes. "It would be far too dangerous to have them out and risk all those women from Bible study pawing over them. Gordon and I always secure everything inside the curio cabinets when I'm hosting." An index finger indicated the polished oak and glass cabinets nestled in the corners of the giant room.

Elsie came in carrying a silver tray set with a pretty milk glass tea service adorned with hand painted roses. She set the tray on the beveled glass top of the large wrought-iron coffee table situated between us.

The formality and efficiency with which Elsie prepared each cup of tea fascinated me, bringing to mind English novels I used to read. Personally, I've never understood drinking something hot when the temperature outside was close to boiling. And as attractive as Elsie made everything with the delicate cup and saucer, sparkling silver spoon, and lemon wedges, I still declined the beverage.

Instead, I sat back and watched the women prepare their tea with a precision that amazed me. When they finally lifted those delicate cups to their lips to take a sip, their little fingers crooked just so, I had to wonder if I'd been transported to England during high tea.

Captivating as this was, it didn't reveal a thing about why Marla had shown up at Zeke Wallace's house today disguised in her sleek black wig and tight clothing. I didn't mind helping her through a rough patch, as Elsie called it, but I'd had a hard day too. A hot shower or a long soak in the tub still beckoned me.

And then there was Jane. I said a quick prayer for my sister, Dr. Dreamboat, and whatever was going on between them.

"I hate to break up this idyllic little soirée, but exactly what were you doing at the professor's house this morning?"

Marla gulped in a sip of the hot tea, then fanned her mouth with one hand while steadying the cup and saucer with the other.

Elsie's jaw dropped open momentarily, but her recovery time was faster than Marla's. "You have to forgive Glory for being so tactless, dear. She was fired today."

"I'm surprised she lasted this long." Ever graceful, Marla leaned forward and placed her cup and saucer on the tea tray. "No offense intended, Glory," she added hastily. "The moment Lila convinced Hannah to give her a job, it was only a matter of time before you were squeezed out. I don't expect it to last, however."

"In the meantime, Glory's going to be working for me."

"Oh, that *is* good news! You've been needing someone at your office—"

"Ladies—"

"Glory, these constant interruptions are simply not polite."

Leave it to Miss Manners to try to correct my short-comings. Now that Marla had snapped out of her earlier funk, she'd slipped back into her *Stepford Wives* persona.

"You were in disguise," I said, refusing to take the bait and determined to get this over with so I could go home.

"She's right, dear." Elsie set her cup on the tray, her eyes trained on Marla. "It wasn't a very good one, but it was a disguise."

"Why, I—I—" Marla glared at us. "The two of you were in the closet!"

I didn't have an answer for that. But from Elsie's expression, I knew she did.

"Glory was admiring your beautiful figurines, weren't you, dear? I'll bet you're wondering how she can afford them on Gordon's modest salary."

I wasn't wondering, but I was curious where this was heading. And from the way Marla stiffened, I imagine she wondered as well.

"Marla frequents garage sales and estate auctions, always looking for items she can resell over the Internet. Isn't that right?"

"Yes, eBay and places like that. They're gold mines if you have the right things. One man's trash, and all that, you know." There was a sense of pride in Marla's voice and smile.

"And you're very resourceful." Elsie rose from the love seat and walked about the room. "I've checked out your auctions from time to time, and you do very well. But it hasn't kept me from questioning . . . " She stopped before one of the curio cabinets and attempted to open the glass door. "Um, locked. Probably a good thing."

She turned and smiled. "Before we leave, Glory, you really need to take a moment and look inside all the cabinets. It'll take your breath away."

Marla mumbled something I couldn't quite catch.

"What's that, dear?" When Marla didn't respond, Elsie moved to a curio on the other side of the room. "This one contains one of my favorites," she said, indicating something inside. "I believe it's called *Bridge of Dreams*. It's worth over five thousand—"

"*You're just like him!*" Marla screeched, rising out of her chair. "Oh, I know all about you and your brother. I always have."

"*Always?*" Elsie jumped on the last word and crossed the room in a flash.

Realizing she'd said too much, Marla blanched. While the two of them glared at each other toe to toe, I added it all together and came up with the only logical conclusion.

"You were having an affair with Wallace!"

Chapter 21

"I—we were not!" Marla's face was as red and swollen as a ripe tomato. "Not since college."

Her hand flew to her mouth, and I thought for a moment she might faint.

Leave it to me to come to the wrong conclusion. But not by much.

Marla shrank away from Elsie and returned to her chair. She practically fell into it. Elsie remained where she was, clearly stunned by these startling revelations. I'm not sure I've ever seen either woman at a loss for words or so totally exposed.

"So . . . you knew him—Wallace—in college?" Yet another example of my brilliant conversational skills.

"Zeke." Marla glared at me. "His name is—was Zeke."

In the time it took for me to check on Elsie, who hadn't moved an iota, Marla began spilling her guts.

"It was my freshman year of college. Even though he was a senior, he didn't have a problem mingling with underclassmen. We kept running into each other at parties. One thing led to another . . ."

Her voice had a dreamy quality to it that I found particularly apropos, considering how I'd felt all day. She tossed her head and her sleek, white-blonde hair slid in concert across her robe.

"You said you knew—"

"About you being his sister, yes. I've often wondered if it was my link to Tarryton—to you—that first drew him to me. Later, of course, there was no question it was just co-incidence." Marla's lips curled into a sly smile that she quickly tried to hide behind her hand.

"Zeke wanted to know everything about you and your mother," she continued. "He asked a lot of questions I couldn't answer. You're almost eight years older than I am, so aside from going to the same church, we didn't have anything in common. But he wanted info, so I got it for him."

I'd just convinced Elsie to sit back down on the loveseat, and now Marla's bomb had her perched on the edge in what appeared to be attack mode.

"You fed him information about my mother and me?"

"It was nearly thirty years ago, Elsie, and not a big deal in the scheme of things. Actually, we have Zeke to thank for our friendship."

Elsie didn't look thankful. She did look furious, how-ever.

"Thank him?"

By the time Elsie pushed herself out of the loveseat I was by her side, urging her to sit back down. I expected her to shove me out of the way and go for Marla's throat and was pleasantly surprised by her acquiescence.

My mother used to say that no matter how well you thought you knew someone you'd be shocked by what they kept hidden. Appearances were deceiving—as were works and actions. Who would've guessed that Marla Hobbs, a Betty Crocker wannabe/Stepford wife clone, had such a steamy past?

Badly as I wanted to go home, I was so caught up in the unfolding story a bulldozer couldn't have moved me.

"So you kept in touch?"

Marla turned to me, rolling her eyes. "Hardly. Monogamy wasn't Zeke's thing, and I got tired of sharing."

She shrugged. "I hadn't seen him since I left UMKC after my third semester. And I wish it'd stayed that way."

"He was blackmailing you—"

"Don't you dare look at me like that, Elsie Wilkes!"

I placed a hand on Elsie's shoulder, but this time she threw it off. I had no desire to break up a brawl—and from what I could see, one looked imminent.

"So if it wasn't for sex, why was he blackmailing you?"

Once again I managed to catch my companions off guard. Elsie's jaw dropped open, and Marla's complexion became tomato-colored once again. The tough questions had to be asked, after all. And if Elsie was sidetracked . . .

"I—he—it—" Marla's mouth slapped shut as she glared at me.

"Money." Elsie croaked her first words in several seconds. "It's all about the money. About all of this." She waved her hand about the large double room, her eyes narrowing as they returned to Marla. "Gambling."

"I—he made me keep doing it. He threatened to turn me in if I didn't get him his cut."

Marla sank into the depths of the overstuffed chair. I was surprised she didn't pull her robe over her head as she had earlier.

"I suspected as much. But I hoped you'd kept your vow."

Elsie knew Marla gambled?

"I did keep it—till Zeke showed up two years ago and said he'd tell Gordon about us, about Vegas and Atlantic City."

"You never told your husband? Wasn't that one of the steps?"

Marla cringed. "You've no idea what it was like—the pressure Zeke put on me. And once I folded, he had even more to use against me."

"But the lies . . . "

I wasn't following this conversation at all. I mean, I was still stuck back on the comment about Wallace threatening to turn Marla in—but to whom and for what exactly?

"Ladies, I'm a little lost here. If you wouldn't mind explaining the part about Wallace turning you in, I'd be grateful."

From their startled expressions you'd have thought I hadn't been in the room with them all along.

"To Gordon, of course."

Ah, there was the haughty tone of the Elsie Wilkes I've known and tolerated for years.

"Actually, he was threatening me with the casinos and the gaming commission." Marla wrapped the midnight blue satin robe more closely around her. "You see, I count cards."

Chapter 22

Zeke Wallace's torrid affair with Marla was only rivaled by the one they shared with the game of Blackjack. The moment Wallace recognized Marla's talent for the game at a casino night fundraiser held at the school, he'd set in motion an addiction that would last a lifetime.

Trips to Vegas and Atlantic City were fun, profitable, and dangerous. Marla was so enthralled with these new experiences that she failed to attend classes just so she could practice her newly discovered skill. God only knows what might have happened to her if she hadn't been separated from Wallace when she flunked out of college.

By the time we left Marla Hobbs, she seemed more at peace and ready to accept the responsibility of confessing to her husband the dual life she'd been leading since Zeke Wallace arrived in Tarryton. I wondered if that included telling him about the biker babe alter ego she'd created to travel to different casinos in the tri-state area. It wasn't a conversation I'd want to have.

"She has a motive," I told Elsie as she backed out of the driveway. "I really feel sorry for what Wallace put her through, don't get me wrong. But with him dead . . . "

"Much as I hate to admit it, you're right." Elsie pulled onto the street, but instead of turning in the direction that would take me home, she headed the opposite way.

"I know you're tired and it's been a long day, but it's dinnertime and I'm really not in the mood to eat alone. I thought we'd run out to Tanner's for their Friday night special."

Tanner's Truck Stop sits at the north edge of town at a major intersection of two busy highways. Ashley's parents ran it now, but there's been a member of her family operating the restaurant and gas station for as long as I can remember. Their old-fashioned recipes and down-home atmosphere has made it a popular place to eat for locals and truckers as well. And if I remembered correctly, their Friday night special was the best chicken fried steak I'd ever tasted. As picky as my sister is about her food, even Jane agreed no one could outdo Tanner's when it came to their chicken fried steak, mashed potatoes, creamy white gravy . . .

Jane!

"I admit you've got me salivating over here, Elsie, but I've got to get home. Jane's—"

"Likely still with Steven." She glanced at me, then returned her attention to the road. "You knew Rachel Eberling died, didn't you? A car accident."

How does she learn these things?

"She was taking her mother in for chemo when a drunk driver blew threw a stop light. It killed Mrs. Eberling instantly. Poor Rachel hung on for several days. Thank the Lord Becca wasn't in the car with them."

Was Elsie fishing for information or just making conversation?

I got the strangest feeling that neither assumption was correct.

"I don't have a crystal ball, Glory. I kept in touch with Rachel. When she had the baby so soon after leaving Tarryton, it wasn't hard to guess who the father was."

"*You knew?*"

"Rachel never said anything, if that's what you're wondering. Her mother sent out announcements when Becca was born. Probably sent them to everyone in Rachel's address book. Rachel was horrified I knew and swore me to secrecy. I honored her request."

Elsie took a deep breath before continuing. "Suzanne Acklin was in St. Louis visiting her sister when she saw the accident on the news. She went to the hospital and was able to convince them to let her see Rachel."

It didn't surprise me that Dr. Dreamboat's mother was able to pull strings and get what she wanted—seeing her son's former fiancée included. Suzanne is one of the movers and shakers of our community. She's been superintendent of the school district, sat on the Board of Education, and is one of the biggest supporters of Tarryton Valley College. Even at seventy-nine, she is the woman every little girl in town wants to be when she grows up.

"Mrs. Acklin told you?"

"No. My source was a worried babysitter who'd been left my number and a message to pass along in case of an emergency."

"And the message?"

"Tell Steven." Elsie entered the parking lot of Tanner's, pulled into an available slot, and shut off the car. "By the time I got the call, Steven and his father had already taken off to join Suzanne in St. Louis."

"Dear Father in heaven." No wonder Jane was on overload. "I really think I need to get home. Jane will expect me for dinner, and she's been through so much—"

"And she needs the time alone with Steven to sort things out." Elsie patted my hand. "I know you don't trust me on this, so why don't you give her a call. I'll wait for you inside. If I'm wrong, come get me, and I'll take you right home."

I opened my door at the same time she did, then waited until she was well out of earshot before making the call. Jane answered after the fourth ring—just before the answering machine picked up.

"How are you?" we said at the same time.

Jane's laugh warmed my heart. "Elsie putting you through your paces and making you change your mind about working for her?"

"Actually, she's been really nice."

"That's when you have to be the most careful, sister dear. Elsie's not as Christian and ethical as she'd like people to believe. If she's asked you to help her, there's something in it for her. Just keep your eyes open, okay?"

I agreed, wondering what Jane would think of the Elsie I'd been introduced to today.

"How are things going between you and Dr. Dreamboat?"

"I was just about to leave you a note. We're heading over to his parents' for dinner. I'll tell you about it tonight. Will you be all right?"

"Yep, fine. As a matter of fact, Elsie invited me to Tanner's."

"Well, make her pay." Jane laughed again. It wasn't her usual laugh—free, open, and catching. It was a bit more subdued, tentative, but at least she felt well enough to laugh, which gave me hope she was feeling better.

"By the way," she said, breaking in on my thoughts, "Rick called a while ago and asked if you'd call him back when you've got the chance."

"Did he say why?" It would be nice to have a heads up in case I was in trouble for breaking another law.

"Just for you to call him. Look, we've got to go. Say a prayer for us." With that she was gone.

I accompanied a group of people headed into the restaurant, marveling at Elsie's prediction of what was happening with Jane and Dr. Dreamboat. She claimed not to have a crystal ball, but it did appear she had a sixth sense the rest of us didn't.

The restaurant was bustling as it always was at this time in the evening. Ashley caught my eye and motioned for me to follow her. I squeezed through the throng of people to join her. Now in full waitress mode, she led me to where Elsie was already seated, grinned, and said she'd be back in a moment to take our orders.

"Everything all right?" Elsie closed her menu and set it at the edge of the table.

"Just as you said."

She nodded. "Don't look so worried, Glory. Your sister is on the cusp of getting everything she's always wanted."

Her smile made me believe she was genuinely happy for Jane. At any other time, on any other day, that alone would have made me suspicious. Today, it made me curious.

What was it Jane always wanted? And how would Elsie have that answer?

I studied the menu even though I already knew what I would order. It gave me a moment to ponder again this new Elsie Wilkes without her perceptive eyes studying me.

But the moment was only that.

Elsie tugged at my menu, giving me a sly grin.

"I've got an idea . . . "

Chapter 23

"Ashley's scheduled to take her dinner break in a few minutes. I think we should ask her to join us."

"I like Ashley, but more than once in a day . . . " I didn't know if I could take her enthusiasm and nonstop, run-on sentences—especially when I was trying to eat.

"She worked for Zeke," Elsie said. "She might know something to help with our investigation."

"Hey, ladies. How cool is this, huh, seeing one another again today? Why, there are days, even weeks, I don't see you, and now here we are again. Not that we were here earlier, you know. I just mean," Ashley gave one of her signature snorts of laughter, "it's such a hoot."

Seeing us again or her laugh? Her laugh was certainly a hoot—to me, anyway.

"I think we've both settled on the special, dear." Elsie smiled, handing Ashley our menus. "Am I right, Glory?"

I agreed and asked for an iced tea to drink. Ashley wrote everything down, then read it back to confirm our orders. She might be a motor mouth and seem like a ditz, but she was an excellent waitress. Within seconds of taking our order, she was back with our drinks, place settings, and extra napkins, all delivered with a smile and her natural enthusiasm.

"You look tired, Ashley. When do you go on break?"

I didn't know what made me ask after my earlier reluctance. It seemed to make Elsie happy though.

"Actually, I was supposed to go a few minutes ago." Ashley blew her bangs off her forehead. "I sent another girl, instead, so I could wait on you guys."

"I—we thought that rather than sitting in the hot kitchen you might like to join us."

Ashley regarded Elsie with surprise, then grinned from ear to ear. "I'd love to as long as my mom doesn't need me in the back. Thanks, Ms. Wilkes, Mrs. Harper. Thanks a lot." She scooted around a fellow waitress and moved on to another table.

"What made you change your mind?"

"Like you said, she might have information."

And I figured Elsie would win whether I agreed or not. Better to make it look like it was my idea. Besides, Ashley's known me since she and Andi started kindergarten. She'd trust me.

The tinny sound of Elsie's phone could barely be heard above the din in the restaurant. She grabbed it, looked at the caller ID, asked the caller to hold for a moment, then slipped off to find someplace not quite as loud. When she returned to the table several minutes later, she was flushed to the tips of her ears.

I recognized that look; I'd seen it in my own mirror a lot recently. And if I was right, it had nothing to do with the heat.

But maybe everything to do with the sudden change in Elsie Wilkes.

Ashley arrived with our meals, expertly balancing a large serving tray containing three steaming platters of chicken fried steak, mashed potatoes covered in thick, creamy gravy, green beans seasoned with bacon and onions, with sides of homemade applesauce. The tantalizing aroma was enough to make me forget about interrogating Ashley—at least for now.

"My first day back, and the place is hoppin'." Ashley set the last of the dishes on the table and handed the tray to a passing waitress. "Didn't think Mom would be so understanding, but I'm sure glad she was. After walking all over the Disney parks, you'd think I'd be fine comin' back to work, but my feet are killin' me." She plopped down in a vacant chair and picked up her fork.

I put a hand on Ashley's arm, nodded toward Elsie's bowed head, and followed suit. Elsie's blessing was short and sweet and over none too soon for Ashley. She dug into her food like she hadn't eaten in a month.

"So you enjoyed your vacation?"

"Loved it," she answered around a bite of steak. "The weather, the parks, the people. Do you know that every other person down there speaks another language? It was incredible, all these people talking and not being able to understand a word. Hey, Mrs. Harper, your hands are better."

"My hands?" Remembering the gloves I'd been wearing when she saw me this morning, I quickly answered, "Yes, much."

"That's great 'cause that tunnel thingy is a bear. A couple of the girls who work here had it and were out of commission for ages. So you really need to be careful."

"Thanks for your concern, Ashley. I appreciate it."

"No problem, Mrs. Harper. At your age it could be, well, like fatal or something."

"I think you're getting it mixed up with breaking a hip." I could have taken what she said as a slam but knew Ashley wouldn't have meant it that way—even if she'd known what she was talking about.

"Dear," Elsie said, trying to get her attention, "I was wondering if you'd mind us asking you a few questions about Professor Wallace."

"He's dead, you know. Like, I couldn't believe it when that gorgeous cop told me. Isn't he just the most good-looking older guy ever? He reminds me of someone, some movie star or other. I can't pin it down, you know? It's, like, on the tip of my tongue."

"Harrison Ford," I offered quietly.

"Huh?" Ashley downed about half her glass of tea. "It's that guy—oh, what's his name? He was in those action flicks back in the eighties. Real cute, for an older guy and all."

"Harrison Ford," I reiterated, louder this time.

So loud, in fact, the people at the next table stopped eating and gaped at me. I apologized to them, then turned to find my dinner companions staring at me as well.

"I'm not sure if that's who I was thinking of, Mrs. Harper. It's the dude that was in those Indy-something movies. I'm horrible with names, but I really liked those when I was a kid. But, hey, come to think of it, you might be right."

"Yes, well, now we've got that settled perhaps you can help me out." Elsie touched Ashley's hand, tapping it until the girl turned to her.

I guess Elsie knew Ashley well enough to realize that if she wasn't looking at you, you didn't have her attention. Even then you had to wonder.

"Did you notice anything out of place or unusual at the house today?"

"The blinds were shut. He never shuts them." Ashley took another bite of her dinner. "I'm really sorry, but I don't have a long break, and I'm starved."

"I remember you saying something about the newspaper, the sports page," I prompted.

Ashley nodded. "Far as I know, he doesn't like baseball. Football and basketball, yes. That was a little strange, the paper being open to a story on the Royals, but maybe he took the rest of the paper with him when he went out. Right?" She looked at her watch and shook her head. "I've gotta get back to the grind, ladies. Thanks for the company."

"If you think of anything else, will you give one of us a call?"

"Sure thing, Mrs. Harper. You guys enjoy your supper." She picked up her half-empty dishes and stood. "You know, I just clean the place, I don't really look at it. He could've changed a lot of things while I was gone. I mean, it's been two whole weeks since I saw him last."

"What day?"

That was such a good question I was tempted to give Elsie a thumbs up. I wondered if anyone had established a timeline for when Wallace was last seen.

"Friday, July 31. I stopped by to pick up my check before I left for KCI." Ashley pushed in her chair. "You should talk to Lizzie Cawley. She was really into the professor."

I'd known Lizzie was interested in Wallace, but I'd thought it was more about trying to save his soul than anything else. Was it possible they'd become romantically involved?

"Eat up, Glory," Elsie said, sliding the small dish of applesauce toward me. "We've got another stop to make."

Chapter 24

I'd made a decision and was determined to stick to it. It had been a long, eventful day, and I was ready to go home. This latest encounter with Ashley Tanner sapped the little strength I had left.

Elsie wasn't pleased with my decision, especially when I told her I would be unavailable until after Seth's soccer game the next morning. She grumbled and groused for a moment or two, then acquiesced with a grace that surprised me. Though it shouldn't have, not after all the other changes in her personality I'd seen that day.

I was reminded of Hayley Mills's character in the movie *The Trouble With Angels*. She constantly had these "scathingly brilliant" ideas, which consequently got her and her cohort into hot water. Elsie hadn't gotten us into trouble yet—as far as I knew—but the ideas had certainly been plentiful. And exhausting. No matter how brilliant her suggestion might be, I'd had as much excitement in one day as I could handle.

So Lizzie Cawley was granted a reprieve—at least until tomorrow.

I hated to think of Lizzie having any part in the demise of Zeke Wallace. The thought of anyone I knew being involved wasn't pleasant. I was more inclined to believe he'd been offed by his CCR buddy Renée Brent or some other stranger, rather than one of my friends or neighbors.

By the time Elsie dropped me off, we'd ironed out a few details regarding my new job. She offered me a far more generous salary than I'd imagined possible, plus a bonus for assisting her in going through Wallace's belongings. As the man's only living relative, disposition of his household possessions had been left to her. And she wanted to get started immediately.

"In case there are clues to what happened to him," she explained.

I didn't bother to remind her about the plethora of keys that seemed to be floating around. Blue Eyes had confiscated three today. Who knew how many more might be out there?

Misty yipped the moment I opened the door. As I neared the kitchen, I could hear her nails clicking against the metal door of her kennel. She wiggled all over when she spied me, her thick, pink tongue lolling out the side of her mouth in a goofy doggy smile.

"Were you lonely, girl?"

I opened the kennel, and the puppy fell out at my feet. She rolled over, offering me her tummy for loving. I rubbed her stomach and spoke to her like she could verbally answer all my questions. She *did* answer in a way that only a dog is capable of doing. Each contented sigh and whimper conveyed that she listened and understood. Her chocolate eyes regarded me with unconditional love and acceptance, something I really needed after the day I'd had.

After making certain she had plenty of water and a few puppy treats, I left Misty out in the backyard, then finally took the shower I'd longed for. It was still over ninety degrees outside, but the cool seventy inside the house said there wasn't a need to skimp on the hot water. Steam quickly filled the bathroom as I luxuriated beneath the pulsating shower head.

A sudden—and deafening—racket startled me out my peaceful interlude. I screamed and the bar of Ivory flew out of my hand, bouncing, and then sliding around the bottom of the tub.

Grabbing for something to steady myself, I caught hold of the shower curtain with one hand, bringing the rings that held it around full circle. It detached from the rod and threw me even more off balance.

Blinded by the streaming hot water, I windmilled, fighting to stay upright. That's when I stepped on the fallen soap.

I managed to keep my face from hitting the edge of the tub when I fell, but twisted my right wrist and slammed both knees against it in the process.

The smoke alarm in the hallway continued to blare, a reminder that I'd failed to heed the hard and fast rule of closing the bathroom door before turning on the water.

I staggered out of the tub, almost losing my footing again on the puddled floor, and pulled what was left of the curtain closed against the still-running water before fumbling for a towel. Once in the hall, I fanned the area repeatedly with the towel until blessed silence finally reigned.

That's when I heard the doorbell and pounding on my front door. I recognized the muffled voice calling my name at the same time I realized I was standing there buck naked—and the tiny hand towel I was holding wasn't going to cut it.

At the sound of Rick's shoulder hitting the door, I screeched out a warning not to come in. I flew into the bathroom still dripping, tugged on my clothes, and hurried to open the front door.

"Are you all right? I heard screaming." Rick rushed past me, his eyes scanning the area for danger.

"It's—I—everything's fine. I was taking a shower and the smoke detector went off."

My hero turned to give me one of his heart-stopping, lopsided grins, and pointed to his head. At first, I didn't have any idea what he was getting at, then I felt the drips down my back and the side of my face.

"Oh, good heavens!"

My hair was still matted with a deep conditioner I'd decided to try. Talk about being mortified.

I was about to run back to the bathroom when Rick took hold of my hand and led me to the kitchen.

"Relax. This won't hurt a bit."

Fascinated, I watched as he adjusted the water temperature.

"You're not gonna—" I tried to pull away, but he maintained his grip on my hand.

"Your dish towels?"

I pointed to the drawer, more than a little uncertain, yet unable to do anything other than follow his directions to lean over the sink.

The first spray of water was a little chilly, but it quickly changed to the most perfect, soothing temperature—or maybe it seemed that way because of how incredible his hands felt on my scalp. My embarrassment changed to a self-conscious awareness of his close proximity, then changed again to total peace. I was putty in his hands.

I'd just closed my eyes to enjoy the decadent pampering when it was over. Blue Eyes shut off the water and gently squeezed the excess from my hair. As he placed an oversized dish towel on my head, he kissed the nape of my neck, sending a cascade of shivers down my spine.

A girl could get used to this.

"You having trouble with your water pressure?"

It took me a moment to process what he'd said.

"Oh!" I lit out of the room and ran all the way to my bathroom. After shutting off the shower, I exchanged the kitchen towel for a fluffy bath sheet, and rubbed my hair.

"Glory?"

"Be right there," I said, drawing a comb through curls so tangled it would take a pitchfork to get through them. I threw up my hands in despair, tossed the comb on the counter, then rejoined Blue Eyes in the living room.

"Better?"

"Um. Thanks."

He'd no idea how difficult it was to keep from messing with the riot of damp curls or how conscious I was of the way his eyes kept straying to them. The gleam in his dark blue eyes said he was either amused at my dilemma or admired my hair. With my luck, it had to be the former.

"I wanted to check on you," Rick was saying, a hint of a smile dancing across his mouth. "Make sure you were all right."

"I'm tired, a little freaked by the way my shower was interrupted, but fine. Elsie offered me a job." I motioned for him to have a seat, but when he remained standing, so did I.

"Wilkes?"

I nodded. "It might be an interesting change of pace."

"With Elsie? I didn't think you were—"

"Friends?" I shrugged. "She's changed. I hung out with her most of the afternoon, and it was a real eye-opening experience."

I wouldn't mention we were investigating her half brother's murder.

"You and Elsie? Well . . . that's great then. While we're on the subject, I talked with her about the note you found."

"You found."

"Right. Anyway, she's going to bring by some of Wallace's papers for comparison. I'll take the lot to a handwriting expert I know down in Kansas City."

"Did you mention any of this to Jane?"

He shook his head. "I talked to Jack Holmes, and he agreed that it's best to keep her out of the loop for now. He said she was really upset by the time he left here this morning. And after what you told me earlier . . . "

It was funny how awkward things seemed now, him on one side of the room, me on the other. I mean, it hadn't been fifteen minutes since my sensory receptors had been on overload while he rinsed my hair. I know he'd felt it too. Hadn't he?

I noticed he was studying me and felt heat radiate throughout my body—and it didn't have anything to do with how hot it was outside.

"So," we said at the same time.

We both laughed, and then drew in deep breaths. He indicated I should go first.

"I was just wondering if there's any news on how Zeke Wallace died."

That was one way to chill things down. From my boyfriend Rick to the inscrutable Detective Spencer in less than five seconds flat.

"If you're looking for proof the man was murdered, I can't give it to you." He grimaced. "Wouldn't, even if I had the information."

"He had a lot of enemies."

"You'd do better to count his friends."

"Meaning?"

"It would take less time. Look, I know you like your mysteries—"

"Isn't that why you're a cop?"

"—but you're going to have to sit this one out."

"Because the body's so decomposed you can't readily tell what happened. Right?" I'd seen enough episodes of *NCIS*, *Bones*, and *CSI* to figure that much out.

Blue Eyes raised his hand like a traffic cop stopping an oncoming car. "Don't even go there, girl."

"Don't—do you guys have a timeline established? Do you know the last time anyone saw him—admitted to it, anyway?"

"Glory?"

"Something's not right. I can feel it. More important, Elsie feels it."

"I'd tell you to stay out of it, but I know it'd be a waste of breath." He shook his head. "I am warning you, however, that if you bother people with your questions and they complain—"

"You'll throw me in the slammer."

"And maybe lose the key."

Rick crossed the room in a few long strides. He ran an index finger along the side of my face, and just when the fire started anew, chucked me under the chin, then walked away.

"I'll see you at eight tomorrow night, little miss detective. See if you can find something other than murder and mayhem for conversation."

He was out the door before I even had a chance to move.

Chapter 25

When Jane came home, I was on the patio, stretched out on a lounge chair, watching Misty chase butterflies and the first fireflies of the evening.

Misty ran to greet her, tumbling over her big feet in her excitement. She waited long enough for a cursory pat, then was back to jumping after the lightning bugs.

Jane looked more like herself, if still a bit haggard, though that was to be expected after the long, hard day she'd had.

"How was the chicken fried steak?" She pulled up another lounger and eased herself onto it.

"Wonderful. I meant to bring you what I couldn't eat but left it in Elsie's car. Sorry."

"Let's hope she finds it before it sours on her. In this heat, that wouldn't take long." Jane lay back on the lounge chair. "And the job?"

"I think it might be fun. It's definitely different from anything I've done before." I told her about the salary offer and the bonus for helping with Wallace's belongings. That's when it occurred to me Jane might not have heard about Elsie's relationship to the dead man.

"Her generosity has me puzzled. Not that she can't afford it because she can. Just don't let your guard down."

I thought about sharing the remarkable change in Elsie—and my guess as to what prompted this sudden conversion—but didn't think now was the right time. What I wanted more than anything was to know how things had gone at the Acklins' tonight. Usually, I would pry it out of her. But there was nothing usual about the present situation.

The sky deepened in shades of the richest blues, crimsons, and purples as twilight fell. The heat of the day had gradually cooled with a gentle breeze blowing in from the north, bringing a welcome relief from the persistent high temperatures of the last several days.

Misty darted to and fro after anything that caught her attention. Now and then she would stop what she was doing and stand still, sniffing the air. Once or twice I thought I could hear a low growl, but it was gone before I could be sure.

Jane and I sat in silence. I wanted to question her but was too afraid of bringing up something that might cause the pain to return to her eyes.

I stole a look at my sister. Her face was perfectly composed as she stared up at the darkening sky. She seemed to have regained the peace and serenity she'd always exuded—the stable, no-nonsense attitude that had endured through the hardest of times.

Until the fire.

"How was dinner?" I finally asked, hoping it wouldn't intrude, only spark a conversation.

"Pleasant. Suzanne made spaghetti in honor of Becca joining the family. She has impeccable manners—Becca, of course."

"I noticed that earlier."

"Um. She was very taken with Seth. They're only six months apart in age, which Becca thought was great."

"So they'll be in the same class. That'll make it easier on her in a new school."

"Actually, Suzanne intends on picking up where her other grandmother left off home schooling. They'd already started lessons at the beginning of the month." Jane sighed. "I looked through the books and was very impressed with the curriculum and Becca's progress. She's very bright and eager to please. That should help this period of adjustment."

Jane rubbed her eyes. "I can't imagine the turmoil the poor child is going through, losing both her mother and grandmother inside of a week. Suzanne thought perhaps I'd like to take over teaching Becca, but with school starting in another week, it's just not possible. There's no way they could get a replacement on such short notice."

The haphazard delivery wasn't typical of Jane, but it got the information across.

"So there's no doubt?"

"That Steven's her father? None. I'm surprised Elsie didn't tell you. She knew all about it. According to Suzanne, Elsie was Rachel's failsafe in case of an emergency. Ironic, isn't it?" Jane readjusted the chair into a more upright position. "It's probably the only time Elsie kept anything to herself. Though I imagine that's how her brother found out."

"You know, then, about—"

"Zeke Wallace being Elsie's half brother?" She nodded. "It was one of many topics of conversation tonight. At least it explains how the lowlife knew there was something shocking in Steven's past. The woman should be ashamed of herself."

It hadn't occurred to me that Elsie might have fed Wallace the information he tried to use against people. But who better than Tarryton's information broker?

"He was blackmailing Elsie. Guess we know what he had on her."

"Yeah, all the gossip she was able to glean about everyone else. It makes me regret encouraging you to take her job offer. Had I known in advance—"

"Maybe it's her way of apologizing," I said.

"Or of trying to get the skinny on what's going on. Who knows? Elsie will have to answer for it in the end."

While that was true of us all, somehow I didn't think Elsie looked at it that way. After our time together, I got the feeling she had turned a new leaf. Though I didn't think my sister was ready to hear that at the moment.

"There's nothing we can do about what's past. The best we can do is to make sure she isn't privy to any more secrets."

I hunkered down in my chair and stared straight ahead. How would Jane feel when she discovered Elsie knew about the note we'd found implicating Wallace in her fire?

"Glory?"

Change the subject before she suspects anything. Good thought, but from the look on Jane's face, it was already too late.

"So Steven is really Becca's father?"

"Rachel listed him on Becca's birth certificate, even named the child after both grandmothers." There was resignation in my sister's voice. "Rachel's dying confession to Suzanne, the papers her lawyer had already drawn up . . . and, of course, the paternity tests all prove Becca's his. I've no idea if they're running a full-panel DNA, nor does it matter."

Even in the dimming light, I could see Jane narrowing her eyes in one of those looks that always made me feel she was capable of seeing right into my brain. She flipped around on the lounger and placed both feet firmly on the concrete between us.

"I know when you're hiding something, Glory Harper. After everything I've been through, I haven't the patience to deal with more secrets. Spill it."

"It's not really a secret—" *And if I tell, there are a lot of people who are going to be very angry with me.*

"One."

This wasn't a good sign.

"Rick doesn't believe you should know—"

"Two."

"Janie, please."

"Three." Jane rose and started for the back door.

"I—we . . . there was a note, a list really, stuck inside the grade book."

Jane stopped but didn't turn around.

"It had your name and address on it." I gulped, not wanting to continue.

"And?" Jane came to hover over me.

"It looked like directions to—to start a house fire."

Chapter 26

By Saturday morning the rumor mill was in full swing. The *Tarryton Tribune* had broken the story of Elsie's kinship to the deceased town bully, which was a coup in itself; the latest information gleaned from an unknown informant sent it over the top.

Somehow word had leaked about the note implicating Wallace in Jane's fire. Innuendo and speculation followed, creating an avalanche of finger pointing and whispers at the soccer match. Spectators seemed more intent on spreading gossip than on watching the final match of the season. Though the kids played their hearts out, they'd lost a good deal of their cheering section.

I felt vindicated about spilling the beans to Jane about the note the night before. There was no mention of Elsie or me in the exposé, thank heaven, leaving me to wonder where the leak came from. In the end, sharing the information with Jane not only put a plus mark in my column, but also kept her from being blindsided. While she took this article in stride, the same couldn't be said of the blurb in the "People" section of the newspaper.

Suzanne Acklin's visit to family in St. Louis was enhanced by the news she'd returned home with a newly discovered granddaughter. Dr. Dreamboat's name wasn't spelled out, but as Suzanne's only child, it was a foregone conclusion. If Hazel Garrett's propensity for truth and facts had been skewed more toward gossip, Jane and Steven would have been dragged through the mud—as would Rachel Eberling and little Becca. Thankfully, the snippet stopped short of this. It was, however, enough to set the rumor mill on its collective ear, giving it more to chew on.

As a result, Jane was a little more subdued than usual. She wandered off during Seth's biggest play, which left Andi and me cheering him on from the sidelines. All the yelling had Misty jumping up and down in excitement, trying to run after the kids each time they crossed the field in front of us.

"You think Aunt Jane's ready to become the mother of an eight-year-old?" Andi tore her eyes from the players to glance over to where I stood with the puppy.

"I think she's too stunned to have thought that far ahead."

Elsie's comment that Jane was about to get everything she'd always wanted flashed through my mind.

Jane had always wanted to be a mother . . .

"Even stunned, Aunt Jane would be looking at every angle, every possibility," Andi said. "She's the original multi-tasker."

A true statement. But in her present state of mind, I wasn't sure.

Looking across the field, I saw my sister huddled with Pastor Connor Grant and his wife Madison. Madison had an arm about Jane's shoulders. Connor's earnest expression as he spoke, and the nod of my sister's head, said the discussion was serious. It didn't take a genius to figure what it was about.

"You're right, sweetie. Jane's the strongest, most focused person I've ever known." I smiled at my daughter. "Her faith is unshakable—till now, anyway. I'm praying it still is."

"That little girl couldn't ask for a better stepmother."

We both clammed up when we noticed Randi Gregar and Kelly Greene coming toward us. The girls had all been in school together and, though Randi and Kelly were at least a year or two older than Andi, had been friends all their lives.

Misty gave an excited yip, pulling tighter on her leash the closer the girls came.

"I heard what happened to you at the college yesterday, Glory," Kelly said, reaching down to give the puppy a pat on the head. "If you're interested, I usually need an extra hand at the nursery in the fall."

Lila Samson had been wagging her tongue again. It had to be her. I'm sure her sister wouldn't have risked the criticism that firing me, and then bragging about it, might bring—especially after her recent no-confidence vote by the department faculty.

"Thanks so much, dear, I appreciate the thought. But I've already accepted a job with Elsie Wilkes."

The surprise on both girls' faces had me wondering if I should have blurted it out like that. But with the way news spread in this town, it was only a matter of time before everyone knew. I figured that by Monday evening the wildfire of gossip would exceed the boundaries of Tarryton. All I'd done was start the process a couple days early.

"Are you sure that's wise? After the way Elsie's behaved . . . " Randi placed a hand on my arm, which caused Misty to jump up at her. She pushed the puppy away at the same time I reined Misty back.

"Would you have told anyone that the person they all hate happens to be your half brother?" My daughter interjected. "I don't think I would. Zeke Wallace waltzed into town with a chip on his shoulder. He dared everyone to try to knock it off—and he did it without provocation. Jared helped him set up his bank accounts, tried to befriend the man, and he treated him like garbage."

"There's a story like that from most everyone in town," Kelly agreed. "He wasn't looking for friends here; he was out to get anyone he could."

Elsie had admitted Wallace was blackmailing her—even though she'd tried to downplay it by saying she was doing the same to him. We'd discovered that Marla Hobbs was also one of his victims. He'd gone after Jane with Steven's secret, and he'd attempted to convince me he could find something in my past that would make me come over to his side. It wasn't difficult to believe he was pulling the strings of several individuals—or, at the very least, attempting to do so.

Elsie's stock in trade had always been the information she could discover about people. How much of that information found its way into Zeke Wallace's hands?

And, more important, did Elsie know what he was doing?

"Did he try pulling anything like that on either of you?"

The girls laughed.

"After he accused me of trying to poison him with one of the candies he bought—which was totally bogus since it states right up front it contained peanuts—he said he would let it go if I voted for his referendum to the city council. When that didn't work, he threatened to tell some deep, dark secret I was keeping." Randi shook her head. "I told him to go right ahead."

"What secret?"

I couldn't imagine Randi having anything in her past that Wallace could use against her. She'd always been such a sweet girl—just like the goodies she baked for Randi's Dandies.

But then, who would've dreamed Marla Hobbs wasn't the perfect Stepford wife she portrayed?

Randi touched the bridge of her nose and sighed. "The idiot thought he could blackmail me with the nose job I'd had. Guess his informants failed to tell him it was to correct the damage from a car accident when I was a kid."

"That's my cue to go, ladies." Andi waved and headed over to help the soccer mom of the week dole out snacks.

I turned back to the field in time to see Seth pass the ball to a fellow teammate, who then kicked in the final goal. The winning team went crazy, jumping on each other and their coach, exchanging high fives, and just being kids. The coaches finally got control of the field and lined everyone up for the traditional high fives between the opposing teams.

Seth and his fellow teammates descended on the soccer mom, whooping and hollering in celebration of their victory.

"Oh dear, now we missed the last of the game. I've got to run help with snacks and soothe the losing team." Randi took off across the field.

"If you change your mind about the job, just let me know." Kelly patted my arm. "Things will be tough for Elsie for a while. You too, if you're working for her. But I'm sure it'll pass."

"Did Wallace try to blackmail you?" I asked before Kelly left to join her friend.

She laughed. "He hit on me every time I saw him. Didn't matter that I'm engaged, he said he wouldn't tell. All he wanted was a little—'afternoon delight' is how he put it. I thought about slugging him, but I'm too much of a lady for that." She rolled her eyes. "I know he tried to pull the same thing with Ashley Tanner. But you know Ashley; she didn't get it. I've no idea how she worked for the sleaze."

I'd wondered the same thing.

Kelly said goodbye and headed across the field. A moment later, she returned.

"If you're trying to figure out who knocked him off, you'll have your work cut out for you. I don't know a soul who liked the man—except that CCR woman." She reached down to pat Misty. "You might want to check out Olav Cawley. He and Wallace had quite a fight at the nursery a couple weeks ago. I finally had to ask them both to leave."

That didn't sound like Ollie.

"Do you have any idea what it was about?"

Kelly shook her head. "I know Mr. Cawley didn't like Lizzie associating with the man, but I don't think the fight was about Lizzie. Wallace showed up while Miss Gracie was at the nursery picking out her fall flowers with Mr. Cawley. She was so flustered, she put everything on the counter and went out to the car. Next thing I know, I'm breaking up a fight."

I thanked Kelly for the information, then watched as she made her way across the field. I'd known Ollie all my life; he and his wife were good friends of my parents. He had a crusty side, but he'd never struck me as having a mean bone in his entire body.

But as I walked over to join Seth's team, I remembered Ollie's reaction to something Blue Eyes said the day we found the hand. His harsh tone had surprised both Jane and me—even though his comments hadn't. I wondered if it had been an accurate assumption.

While many in the town might be celebrating Wallace's demise, I had a feeling tears were indeed being shed.

And I had a sneaking suspicion who was shedding them.

Chapter 27

With the help of Pastor Connor, Steven, and a few other men they'd managed to round up, transporting our keepsakes from the house to the storage unit took a little over two hours. Jane and Andi were in their element, overseeing the placement of items in the trucks, wrapping everything securely with heavy moving pads, and generally directing every phase from start to finish. I stayed out of their way the best I could and kept an eye on Seth, Becca, and a very excited Misty.

While the kids played on the jungle gym, Misty divided her time between the two ends of the house. She would peer in through the patio door, making you believe she had her own special way of handling traffic inside the house. She seemed to have a second sense as to which way the men were going with their burdens—on the garage end was Andi's father-in-law's big Ford truck, which was parked in the driveway. If she darted to the other end, items were being loaded in the Dodge Ram pickup Dr. Dreamboat borrowed from his dad.

I tried not to worry or even wonder how much would be left when they were finished. Since most of the good furniture had belonged to our grandparents, it was a sure bet Jane would include the majority of it. I just hoped she'd stop when it came to the beds. I didn't relish the idea of sleeping on the floor until they caught the firebug.

Elsie called several times, wanting to know when I would be available. She didn't seem to understand the concept of my babysitting. By the third call, she got pretty huffy when I refused to meet her right away. But after a few minutes, she calmed down, saying she had some work she wanted to have ready for me when I came into the office Monday morning. With that settled, I eased back in the chaise, enjoying the cooler weather while keeping an eye on Seth and Becca.

Today, Becca's chestnut hair showed its true beauty; the red and gold highlights kissed by the sun almost glistened, and the ends were no longer ragged or unkempt. Her laughter was spontaneous and honest, exchanged with a camaraderie that belied the amount of time she and Seth had known each other.

It was obvious they'd become fast friends. Little Becca Eberling-Acklin would be needing as much support as she could get.

"Hey, Bouncy, Bouncy!" My grandson called from the trapeze bar where he hung upside down. "I can't touch the ground."

I assumed that was a good sign. After all, the new set wouldn't be any fun if he was already too tall to use it, right? Still, I sauntered out to where he hung, his shirt practically covering his entire head. I pulled it back, so I could see his face.

"So is that a good thing or a bad one?"

"Good, of course," he giggled. He flipped around and landed at my feet. "See, I couldn't of done that if it was too short."

"Couldn't have," I corrected. "But I see your point."

"Why does he call you that?" Becca's voice came from inside the tent on the upper platform.

" 'Cause that's who she is, silly. She's my bouncing gramma. Sheesh." Seth shook his head. "Girls."

There was a rustling sound on the platform and soon Becca's tiny oval face appeared. Her large greenish-brown eyes peered out at us—or rather, at Seth.

"Well, boy, I don't understand. If you expect me to know what you're talkin' about, you're gonna have to explain."

I felt a chuckle coming on as Seth stood below the platform, hands on his waist, his legs slightly apart. He reminded me of a miniature version of Blue Eyes.

"First of all, if you're talkin' to me, you need to call me Seth, not boy. Second of all, she's *my* gramma, and I'll call her anything I want."

I knew he hadn't meant to hurt her, but he had. As he walked away from the jungle gym in search of Misty, I turned toward Becca in hopes of softening the sting of his words.

Tears had formed in the corners of her eyes, and her little mouth was drawn so tightly it looked like a thin line. One freckled fist slammed against the platform floor; the other whisked away the tears.

"He didn't hurt me, if that's what you're thinkin'," she told me, her voice far steadier than she appeared.

"I'm glad. But I am disappointed he was rude to you."

Becca raised her narrow shoulders in an expressive shrug. "I shouldna called him boy." She gazed down at me, a speculative look in her eyes. "He's got two grandmothers, right?"

"That's right. And two great-grandmothers as well."

"Wow. That's a lot of family. There was only just Mommy, G-ma, and me." Her lower lip puckered. "Until now."

I searched for something to say, something to make her feel that everything would be okay. She wasn't crying, but I could see those tears weren't far off.

Please, Father, please help me comfort this child. Help me show her that though she has lost so much, You are still providing for her, loving her.

"Mommy and G-ma are in heaven now," Becca said, her voice barely above a whisper. "I'm angry at that man who ran into them. He was drunk."

"I know."

"I really miss them."

My heart ached for her and what she was going through. I held out my arms and was surprised—and pleased—when she came down from her perch and not only accepted the hug, but returned it.

"You will never forget them, sweetie, or stop loving them. No one expects you to, okay?" She didn't respond, just clung to me even tighter. "Whenever you need someone to talk to, to share your memories, or just to keep you company—"

"You'll be there?" She pulled out of the hug and gazed up at me in expectation.

"I'll try." I was going to say that Jane would be there for her, but staring down into those sad eyes, I was unable to do anything other than agree with her.

"I wish you were the one engaged to my new father," she said, throwing her arms back around my waist. "You're so much nicer than *her*."

Nicer than Jane?

"Becca, honey—"

"Oh, I know what you're gonna say. You have to, 'cause you're her sister."

I hugged her tightly to me, then pulled back slightly so I could kneel in front of her.

"Jane hasn't been herself since she met you, honey. You see, there was a fire at her house about a month ago, and just about everything she had—pictures of her husband, mementoes of their life together, they were destroyed. She's been living here with me since then, trying to put the pieces back together again."

"I still have pictures of Mommy and G-ma. I wouldn't like it if they were burned up." Becca took a deep breath. "But at least your sister didn't have someone die too."

"Not this time, no. But four years ago she lost her husband."

"What about her kids?"

"Maybe someday she'll tell you everything you want to know about her. But right now, she's just like you, trying to get used to the idea of having someone new in her life."

Becca backed up until she felt one of the swings behind her. She grabbed hold of the chains and lowered herself onto the plastic seat.

"But I like you."

"It doesn't mean you can't like her too, does it?"

She chewed that over for a moment.

"Granny Suzanne thinks Miss Jane is wonderful. When I asked her about Seth and his mom and you, she said you were all my family. I like that idea."

"So do I, Becca. I've always wanted to be an aunt."

Her greenish brown eyes lit up with pleasure. "You have?"

I nodded. "And you're exactly what the doctor ordered."

"Huh?"

Misty slammed into my back, nearly knocking me over. Seth and Becca ran to my aid, helping me to my feet.

"Hey, Becca, I'm sorry 'bout earlier. Okay?"

"Sure," she answered with a smile. "No big deal."

"Great!" Seth ran to one swing and Becca to the other. "Know why I call Bouncy Bouncy? 'Cause that's what she does. Bounces balls, bounces on my trampoline, stuff like that."

"Oh, okay. What do you call your other grandma?"

Seth screwed up his face and looked around—I assumed he was checking for his mother. With a sly wink at me, he put a hand in front of his mouth.

"Mad Gramma," he whispered.

I backed away as both kids started to swing, laughing so hard I thought they'd tumble to the ground.

🔍 🔍 🔍

It was close to noon when Steven came out onto the patio to let me know that Jane and Pastor Connor were taking the last load of furniture to the storage unit.

"Is there anything left?"

Steven laughed. "Not much. When they get back we're all going out to eat. My treat. Marcello's sound good to you?" He stretched before lowering himself into one of the straight-backed chairs around the patio table.

His hair was mussed, revealing more gray than brown strands, and his color was heightened by all the activity. Even so, Steven was one fine male specimen. I just hoped my sister realized how lucky she was.

"Sounds great, but I'll have to bow out."

"I'm sorry to hear that. Becca will be as well."

"While I hate to disappoint her, it can't be helped. Besides, Seth and Andi will be there, right?"

"Yes. And Connor is having Madison and his daughter meet us at the restaurant."

"Good. I think Becca and Kelsey will take to each other immediately."

Kelsey Grant would be in third grade, just a bit older, but she was a real sweetheart. I was sure she and Becca would be the best of friends in no time at all.

"She likes you, Glory." Steven watched Seth and Becca as they vied for who could swing the highest.

"She'll like Jane too. You can count on it."

Dr. Dreamboat shifted around in his chair, splaying his hands on the table in front of him. "Do you think Jane will come around? Do you think she'll forgive my—sin."

I gazed from him to his beautiful daughter and back again. Sitting, I swung my legs over the side of the lounge and stared directly into his dark eyes.

"Whether it's a sin or not is up to God to judge, not man. As for my sister, I doubt she sees anything to forgive. For heaven's sake, Steven, she was married, you were engaged to Rachel."

"But she's just—so . . . distant." His voice broke, and he looked away. "I love her so very much, Glory. I always have. I don't want to lose her."

I leaned forward and touched his hand. "Then don't let go."

Steven, Jane's very own Dr. Dreamboat, raised his head, his earnest expression so like Becca's a few minutes earlier. I could feel tears forming at the back of my eyes, but I refused to give in to them. Going over to him, I threw my arms around his shoulders and squeezed.

"Never, ever let her go."

Chapter 28

After everyone but Andi and Seth headed for the restaurant, I forced myself to walk through my nearly empty house.

The dining room looked desolate without the oak table and chairs and matching china hutch that belonged to my grandmother. Andi assured me that everything—including the china her father had given me on our fifth anniversary—had been packed carefully and stored with equal care and attention. Gone was the sewing chair we'd saved from the ashes of Jane's home, as were two massive chests of drawers. Newer furniture from Andi's old bedroom replaced the older pieces and antiques. If I hadn't known better, I'd think I was in the middle of a move.

"At least she left the beds."

Andi gave me a quick hug. "She was ready to put the mattresses on the floor, but Connor talked her out of it. He convinced her that caution was fine, but giving in to fear was just playing into the devil's hands."

"Remind me to thank him."

While Andi went to check on Seth, who was supposed to be getting cleaned up for the restaurant, I made my lunch—a pre-packaged salad, an additional carrot or two, and a tall glass of iced tea. I was seated at the dinette set—circa the nineteen seventies and definitely not a sentimental piece—when they came in to say goodbye.

"You gave up Marcello's for this? Why?"

"I promised to help Elsie today. I'm already later than she wanted."

Andi rolled her eyes. "I just don't know about this, Mama. It seems to me Elsie is relying a bit too heavily on you. Makes me question what's in it for her."

I wasn't about to admit that we were trying to solve the mystery of Zeke Wallace's death. I figured she already knew anyway.

"I intend to stay on my toes," I assured her.

"It hurts to walk that way for very long, Gramma," Seth giggled.

Andi pulled down the bill of Seth's Chiefs cap, then gently shoved him toward the hallway.

"Be careful," she told me, kissing the top of my head.

"I always am."

That received another roll of her eyes before she followed Seth down the hallway. They called out a last good-bye right before I heard the door close.

Outside, Misty yipped, then came barreling to the back door. She peered in at me and whined. It was hard to ignore her, but I did the best I could. Since I'd be leaving soon, I wanted her to have as much free time as possible, and running around in the yard was the best I could offer right now. But when she started jumping up and pawing at the screen door, barking—two things she rarely did—I figured I'd better find out what was going on.

The moment I opened the door, Misty dashed past me, running for all she was worth toward the front of the house. I found her barking and growling at the front door. A moment later the doorbell rang.

I peered out through the frosted window in the upper part of the door, instantly recognizing David Quinn.

Grabbing Misty's collar with one hand, I opened the door with the other. The low rumble in Misty's throat erupted into a full-fledged growl the moment David touched the screen.

"Hey, Mrs. H, doesn't look like your puppy likes me, huh?"

"Don't take offense, it's been a crazy day." Which was true, with so many people coming and going. But I'd never seen Misty act like this before.

"What can I do for you, David?"

"I was going through the files and cabinets at the office and found more of your things." He held up a small wooden crate. "There are some gifts in here from the faculty too. They asked if I'd mind bringing them by."

"That's very thoughtful of you." I stood back from the door, practically dragging Misty with me. "Come on in."

David entered the house, his eyes going immediately to the patchwork walls.

"Looks like you're in the middle of remodeling. Heck of a time to lose your job."

As much as I've always liked David, I didn't feel like telling him what was going on or about my new position at Wilkes Realty. He could get it through the grapevine like the rest of the town.

"Everyone wanted me to pass along how much you'll be missed." He set the crate on an occasional table Jane must have overlooked.

"Please let everyone know how much I appreciate that."

David took a step toward me, and Misty leapt forward, dragging me with her. While I got her back under control, David retreated to the door.

"I'm really sorry. She never acts like this."

"Hey, no problem. She probably smells my cat. Besides, I can't stay." He opened the screen, turning back after he stepped out onto the porch. "I found a set of house keys in the back of one of the desk drawers. None of us recognized them, so I figured they were yours."

"Good guess." There'd been a time while Ike was sick when I'd constantly misplaced everything—especially house and car keys.

"Take care of yourself, Mrs. H. See ya around."

I called out another thank you, then quickly shut the door and let go of the puppy. Misty galloped to the picture window, pawing at the curtain so she could look out. But without the chair that once sat there, she was out of luck. She didn't relax until she heard David's car drive away.

$$\mathcal{Q} \quad \mathcal{Q} \quad \mathcal{Q}$$

"I'm glad I caught you," Elsie's voice sounded a little frantic, making me wonder if she was all right. "There's been a change of plans."

"Not a problem. What's up?"

"Lizzie agreed to see us out at her grandfather's at four. I thought we could go by the uh . . . um . . . rental till then. I've arranged for Joe Finley to come by to look at the safe."

Besides being Tarryton's number one in appliance sales and repair, Joe is also the best locksmith in the area. I wasn't certain those things qualified him to break into a safe, but then what did I know?

"I'm leaving as soon as Misty's in her kennel." Hearing her name, the puppy perked up her ears.

"Why don't you bring her along? We'll be working in the back room, and, well, after all the activity the other day, it might be handy to have a dog around to warn us if someone decides to, er, pop in."

Since she had a valid point, I agreed. Elsie was waiting on the porch when we arrived. I was curious about how she and the puppy would get along. Elsie didn't strike me as a pet lover, but I needn't have worried. Misty nearly dislodged my shoulder trying to get to my new employer, and when she did, Elsie cooed and hugged the puppy like they were long lost friends.

"I didn't know you like dogs."

"There's a lot you don't know about me." She flashed me a mysterious smile as she straightened to unlock the door.

The moment she slipped the key into the lock, I could tell something was wrong. She turned to me, put a finger to her lips, then tried the doorknob.

"It's unlocked," she whispered.

"Maybe we should call—"

Without waiting for me to finish, Elsie cautiously opened the door. She was about to step over the threshold when Misty squirmed around her. One whiff was all it took for Misty to jerk the leash out of my hand. Growling and barking, she flew down the hallway to the back office. In the quiet house, she sounded like a dog twice her size—and I for one was glad not to be on the receiving end of her fury.

By the time Elsie and I entered the office, Misty had the CCR rep, Renée Brent, pinned in the closet. The woman was swearing worse than a sailor on leave—not that I've ever heard a sailor on leave before, but from the language coming out of Brent's mouth, I figured the saying was appropriate.

"Call her off or I swear I'll hurt her!"

"Oh, give me a break, *Miss* Brent," Elsie said, pulling her cell phone from her purse. "She's a puppy, not a set of tires that'll just sit there while you slash them. Besides, Glory won't take too kindly to your threat to hurt her dog."

She was right. I'd already grabbed my friend, that heavy, old fashioned telephone I'd chosen as a weapon the last time I was here.

"Everything under control?" At my nod, Elsie slipped into the hallway to make her call.

I took in the scene before me, amazed. Renée Brent had managed to open the safe. Strewn all over the floor were file folders, manila envelopes of varying sizes, padded and unpadded, even bundles of money that appeared to have been sorted into specific stacks.

A paper shredder stood nearby. From the looks of it, Brent had been making considerable use of it.

"I have every right to be here." The woman glared at me, causing Misty to growl even more fiercely.

"Hold that thought. You'll need it when Public Safety arrives."

I maintained my hold on the receiver, not afraid, but figuring it was always a good idea to remain prepared.

Still holding a stack of files, Brent tossed her long, blue-black hair over her shoulder and leaned against the side of the safe, glaring at me. I took her lead and eased myself onto the corner of the desk.

"I have a key to this house," Brent seethed.

"So does half the community."

Though her eyes went wide, she didn't seem all that impressed with the news. "These are files Zeke and I compiled."

I wasn't impressed with her news either. "When was the last time you saw him?"

"Excuse me?"

"It's not a trick question, Ms. Brent. As a matter of fact, I'm sure it's something Public Safety will want to know as well."

"And why should I tell you anything?" She looked down her rather long, hooked nose, and tossed her head in a manner that said she'd dismissed me.

Then Misty growled again.

"Why don't we just say inquiring minds want to know," I answered with a smile.

She rolled her eyes, staring at me as if she could see straight through me. It didn't faze me a bit.

"The cops are working on a timeline," I continued. "It will help narrow down the suspects, being as there are so many possibilities. You included."

She huffed and puffed at that. "Me? You're as nuts as people say."

If she was trying to get a rise out of me, it didn't work. I've been called nuts by better people than her.

"While you're 'investigating,' Mrs. Harper, you might want to take a good look at your sister."

"Oh really?"

Brent smirked. "You are about as transparent as a window, lady."

"I'm not trying to hide anything."

"Well, maybe you should. Especially with your sister being at the top of my list of people who could've murdered Zeke."

"And just why would Jane want to murder my brother?" Elsie crossed the room to stand right behind my growling puppy, going nose to chin with the woman in the closet.

"Calvin thought Zeke had something to do with her fire. She threatened him."

"Half the people in Tarryton have threatened Zeke Wallace at one time or another. Why should anyone believe her threat was any different?"

Brent drew herself up and stared pointedly at me, a malicious smile on her thin lips. "Because she had a gun."

Chapter 29

I was still lost in the idea of Jane having a gun when Elsie's laughter startled me.

"Jane Calvin wouldn't touch a gun to save her life." Elsie gulped back another hoot of laughter.

"Zeke said she threatened him with one, and I believed him."

"Of course you did, dear. Just like you believed you were the only woman my brother was sleeping with. I can understand how you wouldn't want to accept that the only reason he was interested in you was for the support you and the CCR gave him."

"You've no idea what you're talking about!"

"No, Miss Brent, that would be you."

Their arguing was giving me a headache. It must have had the same effect on Misty because she suddenly started barking again. That's when I realized Brent was trying to inch her way out of the closet.

I pushed Elsie behind me and stood in front of the nearly six-foot-tall CCR representative. "Stay where you are. Misty and I may not look dangerous to you, but you'd be wrong to underestimate either of us." I tapped the receiver against my palm. "Now, I'll ask you once more, when did you last see Professor Wallace?"

"Why should I answer you—"

"Actually, ma'am, that's a question I'd like the answer to as well."

Elsie and I turned to find Gus Bradley standing just inside the office, his hands resting on his fully equipped duty belt. "I'm Officer Gus Bradley, ma'am. I understand you broke into this residence."

"I. Have. A. Key."

"Given to you by Zeke Wallace?" 'Just the facts ma'am' Bradley matched Brent's precision with a dead-on stare I was glad wasn't directed at me.

"Of course, you moro—"

Bradley bristled. "Yes?"

Brent shrank slightly, her eyes burning holes through Elsie and me.

"And are you aware, ma'am, that Dr. Wallace is deceased?"

"Yes, of course. That's why I'm here. To collect our files."

"And shred them too, from the looks of it," I added.

"It would also appear she was intent on walking off with my brother's money."

Misty barked her agreement, wagging her fluffy tail at the officer.

Bradley reached for the radio on his shoulder, but one glance from Elsie stopped him. He raised his eyebrows in question.

"Is there a problem, Miss Wilkes?"

"I was wondering if you could just take her in on the breaking and entering charge, Gus."

"*I have a key!*"

Elsie waved away Brent's explanation and smiled at the Jack Webb wannabe. "She broke into the house—"

"I didn't break in, you idiot! Don't any of you get it—"

"—and Glory and I caught her before she was able to take anything."

Officer Bradley glanced from the angry and frustrated Brent to the smiling woman before him . . . and *smiled.* "If you're certain you don't want to press any other charges."

Elsie nodded. "I'm sure. I would, however, like to have Miss Brent write down the combination to the safe before you take her away."

"And I'd like an answer to my question," I spoke up. "About when she last saw the professor."

"For the love of God—"

"I thought you didn't believe in Him," I said, picking up Misty's leash and tugging her away from the closet door. "Isn't that what you and your organization are all about?"

"The separation of church and state is in the Constitution," Brent stated as she came out of the closet. "You people have carried things too far."

"Technically, the term comes from a letter written by Thomas Jefferson. I don't recall who it was addressed to, but Jefferson was referring to the rights and provisions adopted in the First Amendment." I smiled at the astonished woman. "So you see, it's *you people* who have forgotten that the Bill of Rights guarantees freedom of religion. And that really is part of the Constitution."

That seemed to take the wind out of her sails.

As Brent passed by Misty, the puppy's menacing growl had the woman practically jumping into Officer Bradley's capable hands. Bradley procured a promise from Brent to behave, so he left the handcuffs on his duty belt.

With a triumphant smirk on her face, Elsie held out a pad of paper and a pen to Brent. The woman took the items with reluctance, glanced from Elsie to me, then jotted down the combination to the safe. Rather than giving the pad back to Elsie, she tuned it over to Officer Bradley, who then passed it on to Elsie. When their fingers lingered a moment longer than necessary, Brent rolled her eyes and headed out the door.

"Ma'am—Ms. Brent—aren't you forgetting something?"

Bradley's deep baritone vibrated through the silent house, pulling the woman up short. She turned back around, lingering in the doorway while Elsie made sure the combination was correct. Once Elsie reopened the safe, Brent started her retreat once again.

"Ms. Brent?" Officer Bradley beckoned her back into the room with a wave of his hand. "The last time you saw Dr. Wallace, please."

Her stance—her whole attitude—radiated disgust, but she seemed to realize Bradley wasn't about to relent. "I talked to Zeke on the phone Friday night, July 31," she finally said, her voice tight with barely controlled anger. "We made plans to meet outside Mount Pleasant Church on Sunday. There were some people he needed to—connect with."

"And?" Bradley prompted.

"When he didn't show, I came over here," Brent sighed. "He didn't answer the door, but I could hear someone inside the house. I used my key and came inside." She looked away, blushing. "He . . . he was in bed."

"But not alone," I offered.

"No. He wasn't." She tossed her hair over her shoulder.

Despite her hooked nose, she was really very pretty in an Amazon woman warrior sort of way. Dangerous too, if I didn't miss my guess.

"There was a blonde in his bed," she finally said. "And I'm positive it was that little tramp Lizzie Cawley."

Chapter 30

Neither of us said a thing in response to Renée Brent's bombshell about Lizzie. Even though it was the second time today her name had been brought up in connection with Wallace's, I chose to believe she was innocent. I couldn't imagine Lizzie Cawley going against everything she believed in to have an affair with anyone, let alone a cad like Zeke Wallace. Besides, her grandfather would kill her.

No, not *her* . . . the man who lured her into his bed.

Misty lay just outside the office in the hallway, her rich chocolate eyes drowsy from all her hard work. She'd expended a lot of energy protecting us from Brent, and after hugs of thanks from both Elsie and me, she deserved some down time. I left her to nap, eager to get my hands on some of Wallace's files.

While Elsie busied herself counting the bundled cash, I began an inventory of the items on the floor. Each of the padded envelopes held photographs, and though I was curious as to who or what might be in those pictures, I curbed my natural instinct to investigate further. Instead, I used the numbers on the outside of each envelope as an ID for the list I was making. Then, with great reluctance and more self-control than I thought I possessed, I set them aside.

"Dear God in heaven."

I looked up from the stack of files I'd just set on my lap to find Elsie clutching her chest.

"Elsie?" The folders dumped on the floor as I stood and rushed to her side. "Are you all right? Do you need me to call 911?"

She shook her head, thereddish orange curls flying. "It's . . ." She patted her chest and the stack of money at the same time. "There's nearly two hundred thousand dollars here. What the devil was Zeke doing with all this cash?"

"CCR financing? Brent may have been trying to get it back."

"But why give it to Zeke?"

"You've got a point." I gazed at the files now spread haphazardly across the floor. "I'll bet the answer's in those." I pointed to the folders. "After all, if he was blackmailing Marla, he was probably leaning on others as well."

" 'Leaning on'?" Elsie shook her head. "I think you watch too many crime shows, Glory."

"Or not enough. Otherwise I may have figured out what he was up to a long time ago. You know," I fingered the money as a thought suddenly occurred to me, "we never did find out the last time Marla saw the professor. At least part of this might be from her."

"You think she won this money?"

"It's a possibility. It would also explain why she was here yesterday."

"Trying to take back some of her ill-gotten gains. Makes sense. I'll see what I can find out."

"And I'll put together a timeline."

One glance around the room, taking in the money on the desk, multiple envelopes filled with photos, and stacks of files, told me what we should do. It was practically screaming at me.

"You know, we really need to get Public Safety involved in this." The thought didn't make me happy. The moment they stepped in we'd be forced on the outside, no longer privy to what was going on. And with all the info bound to be in this room, that wasn't at the top of my agenda.

Even if it was the right thing to do.

"I'm not very pleased with the way they're handling Zeke's death." Elsie's voice was frigid. "There's been no definitive cause of death established, which is outrageous. It seems the coroner is mystified by the whole thing."

"Has he established time of death? I mean, they should be able to come to a conclusion based on insect activity." It was out before I could stop myself. "I'm sorry, Elsie. I shouldn't have. I mean . . . "

"More knowledge gleaned from your crime shows?"

"Among other things," I admitted.

"I don't know how you watch those things." She shook her head. "But your information's correct. As a matter of fact, that's been the most surprising information I've gotten—"

Misty sprang to her feet and took off down the hallway, barking and carrying on like crazy. Within seconds, the doorbell rang.

"Is she always like this?"

"She has been today," I answered, still trying to recover from shock as I followed Elsie to the front door. The puppy's sudden flurry of activity wouldn't have bothered me nearly as much if we hadn't been talking about Wallace's demise.

I captured Misty, sinking to my knees and holding her tightly around the middle. It was probably more effective than trying to control her with the leash. But not by much.

Elsie opened the door to Joe Finley, there to help with the safe. True to his usual easy-going personality, Joe didn't make a fuss about the trip being for nothing. Instead, he offered to take a look at the safe to see if he could help Elsie change the combination.

"You don't want any more surprises," he grinned.

Elsie agreed, then suggested they wait in the foyer while I got Misty's leash from the office and tried to get the puppy under control. I liked the suggestion even if Misty didn't. She fought to stay where we were, obviously wanting to keep an eye on this latest intruder.

I finally managed to half drag, half carry her back to the office, but getting her to stay still long enough to latch the leash was another thing. She calmed a bit when she saw Elsie, allowing me the opportunity to fasten the leash to her collar just before she lurched toward Joe. By the grace of God, I maintained control and kept her from reaching him.

No matter what I said, what I did, Misty refused to settle down. Her barking and growling were so intense, Elsie finally suggested I shut her up on the back porch.

"It's screened in, but I don't think she can damage the screens, as high as they are," she assured me. "And the door can be locked and is very strong." She pointed me through the kitchen. "There's an overhead fan to keep it cooler for her."

I tugged the reluctant puppy the short distance down the hallway and in through the kitchen. The room still smelled of rotting garbage. Between that and the over-abundance of flies, I was anxious to get Misty settled on the porch so I could get back to the den.

It didn't stink in there. And I just knew something interesting was about to happen.

I opened the porch windows, made certain the door to the outside was locked, turned on the fan, then scooted out while Misty was busy investigating.

The first thing I noticed coming back into the den was that the bundles of money had been removed from the desktop. Elsie must've been able to hide them while Joe was trying to keep Misty from tasting him.

It still surprised me the puppy had gone after Joe the way she had. Until today, I'd thought she liked everyone. But inside of a couple hours, she'd shown her dislike of David Quinn, Renée Brent, and now Joe Finley. And the only one of the three I felt was justified was the CCR rep.

"Now you see here, Elsie? See where he's got these instructions taped to the underside of the shelf?"

Joe was on his hands and knees in front of the safe, flashlight in hand. He tugged on something—the safe instructions he was referring to?—until a manila envelope came loose.

Elsie held her hand out for the envelope. I wondered if she was as concerned as I was that it might contain something other than the instructions.

Joe didn't appear to notice Elsie. He slit open the envelope with a pocket knife, then removed the contents.

"Yep, this is what we're looking for," he said, scanning through the pages. "Long as you've got the original combination, you can go ahead and reprogram it to anything you want." He turned the items over to Elsie.

"Thank you so much, Joe. I would never have thought to look beneath the shelves like that."

She gave him one of her wide, plastered-on smiles, which surprised me. I'd thought these two were closer friends than that.

"Yes, well, sometimes you've got to get into the client's head, you know. I figured Wallace for the sneaky sort, trying to keep things from being too easily found. I practically had to stand on my head to find that thing."

"We do appreciate it."

I don't know if it was the word *we* or not, but Joe turned around then and gave me a kind of grimace. "I'm real sorry about your trouble at the college yesterday. I know Hannah will be too, when she gets a chance to think about it." He shook his head. "With Wallace gone, things should start running a bit smoother. He was always shaking everyone up and causing trouble."

He cast a sidelong look at Elsie. "I'm sorry to have to say that, his being kin and all, but you know I'm right, Elsie."

I was pleased to see Elsie's reaction was a simple nod. Not that she could deny her half brother was a trouble-maker. But it still had to bother her to have to hear it.

"I pray you're right, Joe. That's a good department with some of the best faculty at the college. They need a leader they can depend on." I hoped this didn't sound too harsh. It was the truth, after all. "As for me, I've moved on. Elsie's offered me a job in her real estate office."

"Oh, well, that's great, isn't it?" He gathered the few tools he'd removed from his toolbox and tucked them back inside.

Elsie came around the desk holding what looked like some kind of invoice. "Before you go, I found this bill on the desk."

Joe gave it a cursory glance. "Yeah, I was out on a service call when this came up. One of my guys said there was a bit of a panic about the refrigerator not working. The person who called asked about one we had in the store, if we still had it. Since it was in stock, they put it on a credit card and asked if it could be brought right over."

"Whose card?" I asked.

"Wallace's, I assume. My bookkeeper ran it through with no problem, or else she would have told me. One of my guys brought the fridge over a couple hours later—top of the line baby. He got it set up and carted off the other one with no problem." Joe narrowed his eyes. "Are you having problems with it, Elsie? It's still under warranty, and I'll be happy to see to it right away."

"I'm sure it's working fine, thank you. I was just wondering if you could tell me who signed for the work. The signature's not very clear."

He peered over Elsie's shoulder, took a look at the invoice, and flushed right down to his fingertips. He moved back nervously, shifting from one foot to the other. Maybe he was trying to figure out if there was some kind of an appliance man's code that forbade him to reveal the name of a client.

"Well, um, that kinda looks like Hannah's signature. She musta been over for a meeting at the time of delivery."

"Your wife, my ex-boss, *Dr. Hannah Finley?*"

My mouth watered in excitement. Had we found another of Wallace's babes in Joyland?

Still looking like an overripe tomato, Joe nodded. "Could I see that again, Elsie?"

She held the invoice out to him, all the while keeping a tight hold on it.

"I can't for the life of me understand it, to be sure." He shook his head. "But that certainly looks like the way Hannah signs her name. It's just a bunch of squiggles, if you ask me, but you know how these academics can be."

I couldn't help feeling sorry for the man. His tomato-red complexion wasn't at all healthy looking, and the usual congenial atmosphere he naturally exuded faded quickly.

He hurried past us down the hall to the front door. He didn't wait for us to catch up to him, didn't turn around at all. He was out the door in a flash, almost running to where his truck sat in the driveway.

Misty barked and carried on so loudly I wondered if she'd gotten off the porch. I trotted back through the smelly kitchen and opened the door, only to be barreled over by the anxious puppy, who was bent on finding Joe. She ran through the house and into the living room, searching for a window she could see out of.

Elsie raised the blind and pulled back the drapes just as Joe's truck sped out of the drive. Misty growled until it was no longer in sight, then she padded over to Elsie, sniffing her and rubbing up against her. When she was finished with Elsie, she repeated the behavior with me.

"I think she's making sure we're all right," Elsie said.

"Are we?" I held my hand out for the invoice. "Besides Hannah's name, what's in there that could make Joe act so strangely?"

"You'll find it." She walked past me down the hall with my puppy following happily at her side.

I took the yellow invoice copy over to the window and studied it. I recognized Hannah's scrawl—after two years, I was an expert at interpreting her handwriting. Her name on an invoice for this place was definitely incriminating. But what else?

Then I saw it: the date. I did a double take, but it didn't change what was written there.

It didn't make sense. I mean, Dr. Finley had been the one to tell everyone that Professor Wallace was missing without turning in his grades. She'd repeated the story over and over again about how he'd come in on July 31, they'd gotten into an argument, then he'd slammed out of her office. I'd called him every few hours until his body was found. So had the dean and practically everyone else at the school.

How could this be possible? How could she have . . . lied? And why?

But the date was clear as day.

Friday, August 7.

Chapter 31

Names and numbers. That's what each file folder contained on the tab identifiers. And it wasn't full names or numbers that made sense; most of the time the letters appeared to have been chosen at random. They were followed by one or more periods, dashes, slashes, or other symbols, which were then followed by two- or three-digit numbers.

Elsie thought they might be related in some way to the Dewey Decimal System; I decided this odd shorthand had been created solely to confuse and addle the brain. It had that effect on me.

We did our best to make sense of the folders, neither one of us anxious to peer inside and see what mysteries awaited discovery. There was something a little freaky about the idea that we could be handling files containing the deep, dark secrets of our friends and neighbors. And as much as Elsie was into collecting information, even she appeared to have a limit on how it came to getting the intel.

Elsie's phone rang, disturbing the relative quiet of shuffling papers and Misty's soft snores. Her even tones and the mention of Marla's name told me not only who she was speaking to, but also that the conversation wasn't going well at all. By the time she hung up, she looked like she needed to sit down—and she already was!

"Marla's on her way over," she told me with a sigh. "I guess I shouldn't have mentioned the safe was open."

"She wants her money back."

"And her file." Elsie stared at the folders we'd already logged into our inventory. "Have you seen anything that might be Marla's?"

"Maybe." I checked my part of the inventory. "Here's an 'mar..79-09@bljk' that might be hers."

"Huh?"

"Oh, well, I think I'm getting the hang of this weird shorthand. I'm guessing, of course, but it could be 'Marla, 1979-2009, blackjack'." I grimaced. "After writing a dozen of these down, it was making my head swim, so I tried to come up with a solution."

Elsie stared at me dumbfounded. "Jane always said your mind worked in ways no one else's did."

I smiled.

"I don't think she meant it as a compliment at the time, Glory. We were about thirteen and tired of you tailing us everywhere we went."

"I kinda remember that." I giggled. "I'd just read some *Hardy Boys* and *Nancy Drew* and was testing my sleuthing skills."

"Well, you drove us crazy." There was a hint of a smile on her lips, and her eyes took on a faraway gleam.

I think Elsie missed my sister more than she'd ever admit.

"You know you can't just give Marla what she wants."

Elsie nodded. "As much as I don't want to do it, I suppose it's time we called Public Safety. How many of these folders do you have left to log?"

"Maybe five or six. I can't believe he had all this stuff in the safe. I hate to think what's in these file cabinets."

"It's astonishing—not to mention disconcerting." She picked up her phone. "Do you think you can finish yours and what's left of mine before the officers arrive?" She handed me another seven or so folders.

"Shouldn't be a problem—unless someone's in the area. Think I should relegate Misty to the back porch?"

"She'll be fine. She liked Gus, er, Officer Bradley, and I'm assuming she gets along with Detective Spencer, right?"

I grinned. "He has a way with her that boggles the mind. What about Marla?"

Elsie shrugged. "I think she could use a little more shaking up. I'm not saying that to be cruel. Marla has a way of compartmentalizing things that's not healthy. From the way she sounded just now, I doubt she's told Gordon about the gambling or that she was being blackmailed. She can't be helped if she doesn't admit she needs it."

Elsie sounded like she knew a thing or two about seeking help—maybe through one of those twelve-step programs.

Stepping over my sleeping puppy, Elsie slipped into the hallway to make her call. I returned my attention to the remaining stack of folders, jotting the tab information onto my log sheet before setting each one aside.

Several of the files were stuffed to the two-inch expandable capacity, which made it look like there were more folders than there actually were. Relief flooded through me to finally see an end, especially when the doorbell rang.

I hustled to record the IDs of the top two, moved on to the next one and felt my heart beat a strange staccato. The identifier on this folder was different than the others, clear and precise.

CALVIN was written on the tab with a jolly roger drawn next to it.

The folder was thin, not expanded at all. I wanted to look inside, but the hum of voices at the front of the house, and Misty's sudden interest in the visitor, changed my mind. I grabbed it up, glanced to where my small fanny pack sat on a nearby chair, then scanned the room.

Voices raised in anger echoed down the hall. Part of my brain recognized the angry tones, but most of my mind was intent on searching for a hiding place for the file in my hands.

I spotted Elsie's zippered portfolio on the corner of the desk. Perfect.

But trying to stand after kneeling for so long wasn't an easy task. My right leg, the one I'd broken earlier in the year, didn't want to cooperate. It tingled and stung so badly that I crashed back onto my knees, dislodging the remaining folders in the dwindling pile.

The click clack of high heels on the tiled entryway and Elsie's protests had me struggling even more to gain my feet. I set my hand atop a folder, bowed my head, and readied myself for a powerful push into action. That's when the file under my hand caught my attention. It was in the largest expandable folder I'd run across yet—and it was stuffed beyond capacity.

5I5.MSTR!!Pln

Misty's excited yips and Elsie's continued protests stopped our visitor's forward progression. I twisted my head around, turned the folder, and looked again at the tab. The writing was draftsman precise, as on all the tabs, but the smudging said it was more frequently used than any of the others.

"Get this dog off me!" Hannah Finley's demand was followed by a high-pitched screech.

Misty yipped again, the kind that said she wanted to play. The incongruity of that, of the puppy *liking* Hannah, might have been what finally turned on the light in my overtaxed brain.

I tucked the enormous file under my arm with the other one, shoved to my feet with all my might, and limped to the desk. I was zipping the portfolio when Hannah burst into the room, flushed down to her press-on nails.

"Get off me!" She pushed at Misty, which only seemed to excite the puppy more.

"You need to go." Glaring at her, Elsie took hold of Misty's collar.

"*You* need to cooperate, Elsie Wilkes," Hannah sneered. She noticed my hand on the portfolio and advanced across the room directly at me. "Where is it?"

"I don't know what you're talking about."

It was an honest answer. If one of these files contained information about her, it hadn't been obvious to me.

Not like the two I'd just hidden. I was sure the one was Jane's, and if I was right, the second file was probably what initiated all the others.

Looking past my enraged former boss, I stared into the muddy green eyes of my new employer.

How would she feel when she saw it? Or did she already suspect?

We exchanged a long glance as I patted her portfolio. The question in her eyes cleared to one of understanding, and I knew I was right.

It wasn't '5I5' it was 'SIS'.

SIS Master Plan.

Chapter 32

"I've tried to be nice about this," Hannah Finley said, her jaw rigid, her hands clenched.

She didn't look nice. Angry, furious even, but not *nice*.

"And *I've* tried to explain that Public Safety will be here any minute." Elsie continued to hold onto Misty's collar.

The silly puppy was salivating all over the place, struggling to reach her newest acquaintance. She didn't understand Hannah's scorn; she just wanted to be friends.

Misty's reaction to the pompous, condescending woman perplexed me. How could she dislike a sweet guy like Joe but fall in love with Hannah?

"If you're planning on using that invoice to blackmail me into giving your job back—"

"Whoa there, sister. I don't want to burst your bubble, but I've no desire to work with you again. Besides, if I'd wanted to blackmail you, Lila would be all the ammunition I'd need."

That seemed to take the wind out of her sails. Maybe she knew about Lila playing hooky for a little nooky in the storage closets.

I clipped Misty's leash to her collar, relieving Elsie of puppy duty. My new employer took the opportunity to cover her smile with her hand.

Hannah huffed and puffed so much I thought she'd hyperventilate. But like everything she does, she managed her embarrassment with such aplomb that she was able to maintain her outraged expression even while she blanched.

"*Please* may I see that invoice?" Her tone was a bit more polite, but only a miniscule amount. Behind her, Elsie shrugged and shook her head, clearly recognizing that it was unlikely Hannah would leave without getting her way.

"Why don't you ask to see Joe's copy?"

Though it seemed a logical solution to me, the look on Hannah's face told me logic wasn't involved in this particular situation. Elsie retrieved the invoice from a desk drawer, studied it for a moment, then gazed up at Hannah.

"You have to promise to leave once you've seen it."

I was pleased to hear the firmness of her tone. And her glare said she'd accept no argument over this stipulation.

Hannah finally nodded, holding her hand out for the paper. But instead of giving it to her, Elsie went over and held it up in front of her.

When Hannah attempted to take the invoice, Elsie jerked it out of her reach. "You can look, but don't touch."

Hannah frowned, released an undignified "harrumph," and removed her hand.

Misty responded with a sympathetic whine that I was certain Hannah didn't hear. All her concentration was focused on the yellow paper in Elsie's hands.

"So, when was the last time you saw Professor Wallace, doctor? The real date this time."

Hannah twitched at my question, but she didn't answer. She slung the strap of her purse over her shoulder, turned, and strode from the room.

Misty lurched on her leash, pulling me off balance in her effort to follow her new friend. I maintained my hold until she suddenly turned a *Dr. Jekyll and Mr. Hyde* on me and began barking her head off. The puppy flew down the hallway, Elsie and I running after her.

We were in time to see Hannah exit the house and Marla enter. Misty had her pinned in seconds.

"What the devil!" Marla screamed.

Elsie beat me to the leash and tugged the growling puppy away from Marla, while tucking the invoice into her pants pocket.

"No, Misty!"

I knelt in front of her and gently took hold of her face. Her big brown eyes sad, she lowered her head onto my knees.

"Is that what you're doing now, scaring people half to death?" Marla straightened up and took a step forward.

Despite my scolding—slight though it was—Misty was bound and determined Marla wasn't coming any farther. She leapt away from me, growling and snapping at the intruder. I captured her collar with one hand, the leash with the other, and pulled her into the nearby living room.

"I'm here for my file." Marla rearranged her blouse and patted her stiff blonde hair with shaking fingers. "Let's just get this over with now, Elsie. You're not putting me off."

Though she didn't bark, Misty's growl grew steadily louder as Marla approached Elsie.

"I told you on the phone that's impossible."

The two women glared at each other so intently I didn't know if either remembered my presence. As I stood there, trying to control my puppy, an idea suddenly popped into my head.

I've never thought of Marla Hobbs as a soft touch, but the last few days had been hard on her. Her secret identity had not only been compromised, but she'd also been caught in one lie after another because of her gambling.

She might seem in full possession of her faculties and back into the Stepford wife persona, but there was a desperation in her eyes that told me the idea just might work.

Marla loomed threateningly over Elsie. "*And I told you—*"

"When was the last time you saw Zeke Wallace?" I piped up.

"A week ago."

Marla's irritation was palpable. So was the realization that she'd revealed information she'd had no intention of sharing.

She slapped a hand over her mouth and wilted before our eyes. Sinking back against the screen door, she reverted to the woman we'd spoken with the day before: weak, broken, helpless.

"Please, Elsie, Glory. You can keep the money. All I want is the file."

"What time?"

"Huh?" Marla turned tear-filled eyes to me.

"What time on Saturday?"

"Not Saturday. Friday." She shook her head. "It was a little after lunch. I rang the doorbell, but he didn't answer. His car was in the lower driveway behind the house, so I knew he was here—most likely in bed with one of his floozies."

"So you used your key?"

"I—didn't, I mean . . . no."

"You didn't have a key, did you, Marla?" Elsie peered closely at her old friend.

"It's . . . he . . . " Marla shook her head again. "He finally came to the door. He was sick or something, stumbling all over the place. He nearly fell about where you're standing now, Elsie. I gave him my, er, payment, then he asked me to help him back to bed. He passed out almost immediately. I thought maybe I should call someone, that he shouldn't be alone when he was that sick, but who could I call? I would've had to explain why I was here, why I was dressed like—like I was." Marla gulped back a sob. "His keys were right there on the dresser. So I—I—"

"Took his house key." Elsie finished for her.

"I thought I could come back later to check on him, maybe find the file I knew he kept on me." Her eyes were wild as her gaze darted between Elsie and me. "I didn't kill him. I swear I didn't."

"That's good to know, Mrs. Hobbs."

Blue Eyes opened the screen door and caught Marla as she tumbled backward, startled. He set her firmly on her feet inside the door, then walked her into the living room where he encouraged her to sit.

Officer Bradley brought up the rear. He made certain the screen door was closed before proceeding further into the house. While Misty whined in ecstasy upon seeing Rick, temporarily distracting him, Bradley and Elsie exchanged a smile that could have melted the polar ice caps.

"Is there someplace you can take the puppy, Glory? She seems a bit agitated."

"She's been trying to attack me," Marla accused in a whimper.

So, once again, I led Misty through the smelly kitchen and onto the back porch. I reopened the windows, switched on the fan, filled a bowl with water, then skedaddled out of there while she was distracted by an outside noise.

By the time I'd rejoined the group, it had grown by two. Officer Roberts was standing next to Renée Brent, and she was not a happy camper.

"Are you telling me I can't have my own property?" She tossed her black hair across her shoulder and went toe to toe with Rick. "Do I have to get a court order, detective? Is that what it'll take to get you morons to release—"

"You like that word, don't you, Ms. Brent? I understand you called Officer Bradley a moron earlier, right before he escorted you down to the station. Now here you are again, another of my officers in tow, trying to throw your weight around." Rick stood his ground, legs slightly spread, elbows bent with his hands on his duty belt. "I don't know who you think you are, but you're in no position to make demands. As a matter of fact, if I were you, I'd see if I could manage a low profile and keep my nose clean while we conduct this investigation."

Brent staggered back a step, her face aflame. "You won't get away with this."

"I was actually thinking the same thing about you. You see, after we processed you earlier, we ran your prints against the ones found on the side of Albert Donovan's car after his tires were slashed. Guess whose they matched?"

"That's not possible," she seethed. But the guilty look in her eyes proved otherwise.

"I'm afraid it is. And it's enough for us to take you in. You want to do the honors, Chris?"

The younger officer came slowly forward. "She convinced me that Mrs. Harper and Miss Wilkes had stolen some files from her, sir. I had no idea—"

"Not a problem. But let's say we do this one by the book. Ms. Brent would you please place your hands behind your back."

Officer Roberts snapped the cuffs on her like an expert. As he turned her toward the front door, I caught a glimpse of the fury on her face. It was unlikely anyone would get information out of her now. She was bound to lawyer up the moment she got to the station.

But there was one more thing I wanted to know, and she was the only one who could tell me.

I followed them out of the living room but didn't get very far. A firm hand on my shoulder stopped me. I turned and gazed into those amazing blue eyes.

"If you won't let me do it, then you have to. Now, before she gets into the squad car."

"What's so all-fired important it can't wait?"

"Once she calls her lawyer, she won't give you a thing. You know I'm right. Please, Rick! It's really important for us to know who she and Wallace were supposed to meet outside Mount Pleasant Church on the second."

He stared down at me, his confused expression making me doubt he'd help get my answer. But once again, he surprised me. Without a word, he walked out of the house and across the yard to where Roberts was assisting Brent into a squad car.

Standing in the doorway, I glanced up to find Marla at my elbow, watching the scene unfolding before us.

"Will that be me?" she asked, her voice small. "Because I took his key?"

I put my arm around her shoulders—not an easy feat since she's at least four inches taller than me. "If you didn't do anything more than that, I'm sure everything will be just fine."

"I didn't kill him, Glory. I swear to God I didn't."

I patted her shoulder, hoping, praying, she was telling the truth.

Blue Eyes loped back across the yard. The curious look on his face quickly changed to one of aggravation when Will Garrett pulled up in front of the house.

"Gus," Rick called as he hustled up the steps. "We've got company."

Bradley shoved past Marla and me and joined Rick on the porch. I watched as *Tarryton Tribune's* most disliked reporter got out of the car, followed by his mother.

Hazel waved at the officers. I could hear Blue Eyes cursing softly, then he turned and strode past us through the door.

"Gus will hold them off until we get reinforcements." He scrutinized each of us in turn, his eyes finally settling on Elsie.

"You've got a story to tell, right?"

Elsie drew in a deep breath and nodded. "It appears my brother was blackmailing quite a few people in town. I don't know who, and I don't want to know. Glory and I have spent the last couple of hours trying to log the folders and cash Zeke had stuffed in his safe." She bent her head and sighed. "I thought maybe I could try to make things right, fix it so no one would get hurt anymore, but it's just too much."

"And against the law. To blackmail someone, I mean. That's why we called Public Safety."

Blue Eyes gave me a half smile, then returned his attention to Elsie.

"And you think one of the people he was blackmailing may have killed him?"

She nodded. "I know the coroner's stymied about the cause of death, but I need you to consider something important. Zeke was allergic to everything from bee stings to penicillin to food. Peanuts and shellfish were deadly to him. Just because he wasn't shot or stabbed doesn't mean someone didn't kill him. And I think the answer's in those files."

"And you're one of his victims," Rick said, turning his attention to Marla.

Her eyes instantly filled with tears, and she looked down, unable to meet his eyes.

"I'll want to talk with you later, Mrs. Hobbs. Keep yourself available. But right now, we need to get you out of here."

The commotion outside on the porch grew louder by the second. Though I was curious about what might be happening, I knew that with the front door open, people on the porch could easily see anyone who walked into the hallway—and vice versa. I wasn't anxious for one of the Garretts to see me. Being hounded by the press wasn't in my day's agenda.

Marla, Elsie, and I held back while Blue Eyes checked out the scene. "I assume there's a back door."

"There is, but I just put Misty on the porch."

"I don't want to go anywhere near that devil dog," Marla screeched.

"I won't let her hurt you—"

"Where are they? Where're Wallace's files?"

Rick moved quickly to intercept Albert Donovan, who nearly knocked him over as he tumbled into the house. Donovan's face was a florid, unhealthy-looking color with white blotches interspersed among the red, and his breathing was ragged and uneven as if he'd been running for blocks.

His wild eyes searched the dimly lit area beyond the swathe of sunlight illuminating the hallway. When Rick caught hold of his arm, Donovan fisted his other hand and swung.

Rick blocked the blow before it connected with his face.

"Mr. Donovan, I think you'd better settle down. I'd hate to have to charge you with assault."

Rick felt behind him for the door, managing to slam it closed just as Hazel Garrett reached to pull open the screen. He threw the deadbolt, then turned with a sigh.

"Well, ladies and gentleman, maybe we'll have a moment or two of sanity before someone else busts in. At least we can hope. Any more keys out there, Elsie?"

"I've no idea," Elsie responded, still taken aback by Donovan's sudden appearance.

"All I want are the photos of my daughter. Give them to me and I'll go."

Donovan's wild eyes glazed over, and he crumpled to the floor.

I dialed 911.

Chapter 33

Before the ambulance arrived, Donovan regained consciousness and spilled his guts. His daughter had been caught on video during spring break, wearing nothing but a smile. Wallace had threatened to send a copy to the mayor—her future father-in-law—if Donovan didn't cooperate.

"The maniac came into the store with one of the photos. He slapped it on the display counter where everyone could see." Donovan clutched his chest.

"Save your strength, Albert," Elsie said, dabbing his face with a cool cloth.

Donovan pushed her ministering hands away and grabbed Rick's arm. "He could ruin her life, her career, and he didn't care." He swallowed hard, and his voice shook, but he maintained his grip on Rick's arm. "He said he was going to the state legislature with a petition to force the schools here in Tarryton to eliminate any mention of God. If I didn't agree to support him—"

I peered through the peephole, watching for the ambulance while keeping my ears open to what was going on behind me. My mind was off and running in a thousand different directions.

"It's all right, Mr. Donovan," Rick told him, releasing himself from the man's grasp. "Wallace can't hurt your daughter now."

"But that witch Brent can!" Donovan attempted to rise from the floor but didn't have the strength. "Wallace said he'd be back in a week with the petition. When he went missing, I thought that'd be the end of it. Then Brent showed up yesterday, making demands. But I stood up to her, told her I didn't believe she had the guts to go it alone."

"I'll bet that's why she was here today."

Blue Eyes pointed me back to my ambulance-watching duty. It wasn't easy to stare through the tiny peephole and keep an eye on what was going on behind me at the same time. But I did my best to do both.

At least while Rick was otherwise engaged.

"But she didn't get any of the files, isn't that right Elsie?" Marla patted Donovan's shoulder. "So everything's going to be all right, Al. Just lie back and take it easy. Detective Spencer will take care of everything."

I felt a glow of pride at that statement. I cast a sidelong glance at the handsome detective, and my heart did a little flip-flop.

Donovan's eyes went wide, and he clutched at the air in front of him. Elsie caught one of his hands, Blue Eyes the other as he began flailing about. Tiny as Elsie is, I expected her to be tossed around like a rag doll, but she stayed firm, trying to soothe Donovan. He seemed to calm when suddenly his entire body gave a hard jerk, then lay perfectly still.

"I can't feel his pulse!" Elsie cried, pressing her fingers against his wrist, then his neck.

As the wail of a siren sounded off in the distance, Rick went to work applying his lifesaving skills. By the time paramedics came through the door, Donovan was breathing again.

And I'd had a front row seat to watch real heroes in action.

Backup for Rick and Officer Bradley arrived about the same time the paramedics were loading Donovan into the ambulance. Roberts had returned from the station with a bruise developing on the side of his face where he'd run into the car door while trying to assist Brent out. The poor guy was already embarrassed about falling for her ruse; now his gallantry had been rewarded with a shiner.

Rick patted the younger officer on the back and assigned him to escort Marla home. To his credit, he didn't say a word, only shook his head as he watched Roberts and Marla leave.

With other officers arriving to cordon off the area—if that's what they were doing, I wasn't sure—and keeping out undesirables like the Garretts, Rick was finally ready to listen to what Elsie had to say. She repeated her insistence that her half brother had been murdered, pointing Rick to the smelly garbage in the kitchen.

"As badly as it stinks, I deliberately left it for Public Safety to search."

"So you believe that whoever killed him was intelligent enough to use something he was allergic to but not smart enough to clean up after himself?"

Rick's solicitous tone could be maddening; I knew that firsthand. It didn't, however, seem to strike Elsie in the same way.

"But you'll consider this a crime scene now, right? And doesn't that mean you'll search everything?"

"We'll do our best, but you have to understand that with as many people who've been in and out of this place in the last few days—and who knows how many before that—it's not going to be an easy task. And we still have no confirmation from the medical examiner as to cause of death."

"But the evidence we do have—all these people he's blackmailed—that's motive."

Blue Eyes nodded. "Of course it is. And I promise you we'll do our best."

"Have you got a timeline?"

Rick turned his baby blues on me, and lifted a single, quizzical eyebrow. I refused to go weak in the knees this time.

"And I would tell you that why?"

"Because if you don't have one, I'll be happy to share mine—once I've gotten it set up."

"In exchange for?"

"The information I asked you to get from Renée Brent." I shrugged. "I'd give it to you anyway, my civic duty and all, but I'd really like to have the answer to my question."

From Rick to Detective Spencer in two seconds flat. He stood, stretched slightly, and gave me a long, hard stare.

"Since this is now a possible murder investigation, all information pertinent to the case will be released to the public only when, and if, the department sees fit."

"So that would be a no?" I rose from my chair and glanced over at Elsie. "I think that's our cue to leave. Besides, aren't we expected someplace in about thirty minutes?"

"That's right. I'd almost forgotten with everything else." She stood, giving the detective a hint of a smile. "Would it be all right for us to go into the office and get our things?"

"Not a problem."

Since Misty was still locked up on the back porch, I didn't wait for Elsie. Nor did I check to see if Mr. Meany Detective was following me. I stomped past him, which wasn't very successful considering the plush carpeting in the living room. Once in the hallway, I scooted along to the kitchen and retrieved my grateful puppy from the porch. I shut the windows, turned off the fan, then headed to the office.

Elsie and Rick were already there, talking so low I couldn't hear a word. Misty gave an excited yip when she saw them, tugging on the leash till I finally let go. She wriggled between them, wagging her fluffy tail and giving wet puppy kisses every chance she had.

Rick knelt in front of her, held up the index finger of one hand, and pointed to the floor with the other. Misty instantly responded by calming down and sitting at his feet. He rewarded her with a gentle pat on the head.

"Are you a dog whisperer?"

Elsie's amazed assessment seemed to embarrass him. The tips of his ears turned a slight shade of pink.

"It's one of his many talents, isn't that right, detective?" I entered the room and went directly to where I'd laid my fanny pack. "Police officer, firefighter, paramedic, hero, and dog whisperer, just to name a few."

I couldn't help but grin at him. It wasn't worth it to be angry or upset when I knew it was all about the job.

"You're making me blush."

"You should do it more often. It looks good on you."

We gazed into each other's eyes, and like always, there was this strange electric current that made me tingle all over. I knew the air conditioning was still on, but it suddenly felt like a hundred degrees in that room.

"Yes, well, um, Glory, we really should be going." Elsie picked up her purse and portfolio from the desk.

"Right." I smiled up at Rick once more, then, as an afterthought, grabbed the inventory I'd made, and handed it to him. "I don't know if this will help, but it lists everything Elsie and I found on the floor in front of the safe. We think that's where it all came from. Of course, Brent shredded some things before we got here. It's a cross-cut, so I doubt you'll be able to piece any of it together."

"This is everything?"

He had to go and ask that question. I glanced up at him, then over at Elsie, knowing I needed to do what was right and not what I wanted.

"Glory?"

His hand on my arm was warm, his rich blue eyes penetrating. Misty wriggled between us, her little chuffs and puppy sighs mirroring my own emotions.

"It's okay," Elsie said, unzipping her portfolio. "I don't need to see it in black and white to know that most—if not all—of the information Zeke used against people came from me."

She handed Blue Eyes the two files I'd hidden. "She only took them to protect Jane and me. Neither of us looked inside the folders, detective. Not these or any of the others."

Rick took the folders and set them on top of a nearby file cabinet.

"I'll wait for you in the car, Glory." She picked up Misty's leash. "Go through the backyard so you can avoid the Garretts. I'll meet you a block over."

I stood there for a long time after she'd gone, my head down, afraid of the disappointment I would see in Rick's eyes. I could hear other Public Safety officers enter the house. It was only a matter of time before they came in here.

"I only wanted to protect them—Jane and Elsie."

"I know."

I raised my head and met his gaze. "Am I in trouble?"

He released a heavy sigh, touched me lightly on the shoulder, and said, "You better get out of here before I have a chance to think about that one."

I took him at his word.

Chapter 34

"You do realize my car's still in front of Wallace's house?"

"Not a problem. I'll drop you by after we talk with Lizzie," Elsie said, pulling onto the main road that led out of town. "The vultures should be gone by then."

"Yeah, but they know my car." And where I live, and my phone number . . .

Misty shoved her nose between the seats and proceeded to give both of us slobbery kisses. A firm "no," and a whimper later, she settled in the back, goobering up a window.

"She's a sweet puppy, Glory. Smart too."

"And a handful. If it wasn't for Seth, she'd be bored out of her mind. Even though Jane and I take her for walks, it's not the same as running around after Seth. Don't get me wrong, she's a sweetie, I'm just not, well, I don't know . . . "

"Owning a dog is a lot harder than people realize. I'm surprised you got her."

"She was a gift from Jane and Dr. Dream—er, Steven. Jane was concerned about me being lonely after she moved back home."

I didn't add that I'd been looking into getting a kitten at the time. Since Misty basically saved Jane's life the night her water heater blew up, I wasn't going to complain about the little inconveniences the puppy caused.

"By the way, that was awesome back there, how you handled Albert." I wanted to switch subjects before she started asking questions about Jane and how she was dealing with the news of Steven being a father.

"Thanks." Elsie brushed a strand of her red-orange hair out of her eyes. "I didn't really do anything. Rick was impressive, though, the way he saved Albert's life. He's a real hero, you know."

We came to a four-way stop not far from where Jane and I grew up. The house was gone now, torn down to make room for a gigantic garden for the people next door. It choked me up just thinking about it.

Even though there wasn't any other traffic, Elsie lingered at the corner. There was something about the little half smile and glow in her eyes that made me nervous.

"You're a lucky woman," she finally said. "Maybe a little of that luck will rub off on me."

"So I was right!" I clapped my hands. "You and Gus 'Just-the-facts-ma'am' Bradley?"

Elsie giggled. "I can see why you call him that." Her blush almost matched the color of her hair. "We started seeing each other after I was shot last spring. He's been so nice, stopping in the office to visit whenever I'm there. I've known Gus more than twenty years, and never once thought anything about him—other than as a police officer, that is. Isn't that horrible?"

"Not at all. If he didn't show any interest, how were you to know?" Of course, she'd been too busy running around after men she couldn't have—Rex Stout and Dr. Dreamboat among them. "I'm really happy for you, Elsie."

She nodded her thanks, finally turning the corner that led to where I used to live.

Corn tassels blew in the breeze approximately where my bedroom had been, judging by the old cottonwood at the back of the lot. It was the last tree I climbed, the summer I was nine. I got stuck up there when my ladder fell, leaving me stranded and screaming my head off for help.

Jane had always told me that if it hadn't been for the strange boy who alerted her to my predicament, I'd still be in that tree. An exaggeration, of course, but it was enough to make me think twice before climbing another tree that required a ladder.

It hadn't been until I'd gotten acquainted with Rick last spring that Jane and I figured out he was the grandson of our next-door neighbors, the Todds—and the boy who had rescued me.

"Haven't they done a nice job on the Todd's old house?"

"Yes, it's beautiful."

And it was, with new white vinyl siding, black shutters and trim around pristine double-paned windows, an oversized attached garage, and a neatly trimmed and landscaped yard. I just wished they could've done it without tearing down my childhood home.

Elsie must have sensed what I was thinking because she reached over to pat my leg as we drove past. "The owners restored all the hardwood floors on the inside. Rick's grandparents would be pleased."

We spotted Olav Cawley at the end of the long drive to his farmhouse. Though his wave seemed friendly enough, the scowl on his face said he was unhappy about something. I hoped it wasn't our visit.

Elsie pulled to a stop and rolled down her window. Ollie ignored the invitation, tramping over to my side of the car. I threw Elsie an apologetic glance, then quickly lowered my window.

"Glory-girl. You're lookin' a mite tired. You been keepin' late hours with that beau of yours?" He chuckled.

"I like that boy. Told your mama and daddy that when they called last week. I think they were headed for the Grand Canyon this time."

"Sounds about right," I grinned. "They're really enjoying this Scenic America Tour, but we'll be glad to have them home. Seth misses them a lot."

"Betcha he does with his daddy away. The rest of you too." He squinted over at Elsie. "Miss Elsie Wilkes. You know the only reason I'm lettin' you in to see Lizzie is 'cause Glory's here?"

"Yes, sir," she answered, lowering her eyes.

"After invitin' that devil into our town—"

"I didn't—"

"—and not havin' the decency to warn people about his character or let us know he was your brother . . . We're mighty ashamed of you right now, missy. Your mama's probably rollin' over in her grave at all these goin' ons."

I covered his grizzled hand where it rested on the edge of the open window. "In Elsie's defense—"

"No, he's right. I should've owned up to my relationship to Zeke. Maybe if I had . . . " Elsie shook her head. "It's my fault, and I accept the responsibility. I just hope you can see your way to forgive me, Ollie."

Eighty-two year old Olav Cawley was was the oldest farmer in the area—and the town's conscience. He pulled back from the car and drew in a deep breath.

The lines on his face were like a road map showing the twists and turns in the journey of a life lived in the sometimes harsh Midwest weather. His eyes crinkled in hard cracks at the corners, and his mouth had its own set of tracks. But the crystal blue of his eyes, the color of a clear winter's day, held the warmth of summer.

Life and love shown out of his weathered face, revealing a compassion that welled up from the core of his being.

He could be a hard man when he needed to be, I was sure of that, but until the other day, all I'd ever seen was the care and consideration he had for his fellow man . . . and woman.

"I accept your apology. And though I'm still a mite peeved, I know you ain't the root of all the trouble. So you're to stop blamin' yourself right now, hear?"

"Yes sir."

"And quit callin' me sir. I've been Ollie to you since you were a young 'un, and that's what it'll be till I meet my maker. Understand?"

"Yes, si—Ollie."

"All righty, then. You go on up to the house. Lizzie and Gracie Kay are waitin' for you. I'll be along directly." He stepped back from the car and waved us on.

We rolled up our windows, and in the silence that ensued, my thoughts crashed against the sides of my brain. While one side yelled that Ollie was a prime murder suspect and I should have questioned him about the fight he'd had with Wallace at Kelly's, the other side countered that he was a good man who would never resort to violence— even if the victim warranted it.

"Ollie's right. You can't blame yourself for what's happened."

"You do," Elsie answered quietly. "Isn't that why you tried to take that folder?"

"I was trying to protect you—and Jane, from whatever that monster put in there." She stiffened when I said 'monster,' so I rushed on to explain. "Look, somewhere along the line, I kinda figured the professor had gotten his information from you. It's not blame, Elsie, just fact. Like the ones you're so adept at collecting. I took those files to keep you from being hurt and embarrassed, not so I could point a finger at you."

"There will be enough of those," she sighed. "And rightfully so."

She pulled up in front of the house and parked alongside cars already in the drive. "I'd write him letters off and on to go with the money my father left him in his will. After mother died, Father kept trying to get Zeke and me together. His mom had passed away years before, and Father thought the three of us could become a family. There was too much anger on both sides for that to happen, of course. But then I was forced to dish out his inheritance over a five year period. It just didn't feel right sending the check by itself, so I tried to open up a line of communication."

"And you told him about what you knew best: the citizens of Tarryton."

She nodded. "I'd no idea he would end up here and use those tidbits against my friends and neighbors. You've got to believe that."

"It might sound crazy, but I believe you. In all honesty, if this had come out a week ago, I'm not sure I could have taken you at your word."

"But you do now?" She seemed amazed.

"Yep. You've become a real person to me now, Elsie, not just someone who has some weird grudge against my sister."

"Or the biggest gossip in town?"

"Well, yeah. You *have* come off that way, you know. Kinda like I come off a little wacky."

"A little?" We both laughed.

In two short days, Elsie Wilkes, Tarryton's information broker extraordinaire, had gone from the character you most dreaded to run into, to one you could count on when you had a run-in. By the time we reached the Cawleys' porch, I knew I was standing next to a friend.

Chapter 35

Lizzie Cawley answered the door. Her gentle eyes were tinged red from crying.

"Come on in, ladies," she said, her hoarse voice reinforcing my first impression. "Miss Gracie's in the kitchen making iced tea."

Lizzie stood back for us to enter. Her frame was so tiny she made a thin line when turned sideways. At no more than ninety pounds, Ollie's pretty, twenty-six-year-old granddaughter was barely five feet tall—if even that. Standing next to her, I felt like a giant at my mere five feet, three inches.

Her long, white-blonde hair caught the afternoon sunlight, sparkling as if sequins or miniature diamonds were entwined with each strand. The highlights formed an incredible cascade down her slender back to the almost nonexistent indentation of her waist. She'd inherited her grandfather's crystal blue eyes, but that's where the resemblance ended. Unlike Ollie's deeply tanned and weathered complexion, Lizzie possessed the beautiful pale skin tones of her Scandinavian heritage, her cheeks touched with subtle pink.

"Is there somewhere I can put my puppy while we visit? I don't want to leave her in the car."

Lizzie looked beyond me to where we'd parked the car. Misty's nose was pushed as far out of the slightly lowered window as it could go, and her pitiful whines broke my heart.

Like the nymph she resembled, Lizzie skipped lightly down the porch steps, her tiny bare feet hardly seeming to touch the ground. Her gauzy white dress floated around her, giving her an entrancing, ethereal quality. The garment reminded me of the peasant dresses popular when I was in high school. And with her long, straight hair, and other-worldly persona, she could easily fit the bill for a sixties flower child. All she needed was flowers in her hair.

"She's adorable, Glory. May I?"

Lizzie had the car door open and the puppy in her arms before I could respond. Misty licked her, crying in ecstasy.

The girl took the puppy's leash and led her to the porch. There was no pulling, tugging, or dragging, as Misty behaved—misbehaved—with me. She walked sedately at Lizzie's side.

"I'll just take her to the mud porch. It will only take a moment. You ladies go inside and make yourselves at home."

Elsie and I followed her into the house. I didn't know about Elsie, but Lizzie's poise and grace made me feel like an oaf by comparison.

The loving touch of a woman's hand was evident everywhere I looked. Furniture that had become shabby in the years since Sarah Cawley's death had been beautifully repaired or recovered. Delicate doilies and crocheted throws I recognized as Gracie Naner's handiwork brightened the room.

The rumors of Miss Gracie's and Ollie's upcoming nuptials was clearly more fact than fiction. It was a joy to see people I cared about discovering such love and happiness this late in life.

Elsie and I sat on a comfortable Early American style sofa decorated with some of Sarah Cawley's signature pillows, which combined quilting, needlepoint, unique style, and imagination. She used to sell dozens of these at church and school fundraisers. I believed every family in Tarryton owned at least one Sarah Cawley original. I certainly did.

Lizzie drifted into the room. "I've been waiting to talk with someone about Zeke," she said, lowering herself into a chair opposite us. "Gramps felt I should stay out of it for now, that it was best not to get in the middle of things. I wasn't certain it was the right thing to do, but . . . " She shook her head. "Have they determined how he d-died?"

"Not that I've been told," Elsie said. "My inside source says the M.E. is rather mystified and has deemed it suspicious circumstances."

"What about, well, when are they saying Zeke passed?"

I leaned forward, gazing from Elsie to Lizzie. This was something I'd like to know as well. Elsie had been about to reveal something when we were so rudely interrupted back at Wallace's house, and we'd never had an opportunity to get back to it.

"That's the curious thing. Based on the 'forensic evidence'—my source's words—the coroner is sure Zeke died sometime late on the ninth or early on the tenth."

"What about the rumor that he's been missing these last two weeks?" I was confused. "I mean, I know we've gotten info contrary to that, but it does beg the question as to who perpetrated the ru—"

"That would be Dr. Finley," Lizzie stated quietly. "I apologize for interrupting, Glory. It just saved time and energy since I already knew the answer."

"Why?" Elsie and I asked in unison.

"They'd fought. She refused to accept his grades, something about supporting documentation." Lizzie shook her head. "She wanted to get him fired because of everything he'd put her through. He'd organized the faculty petition."

"The no-confidence vote?" How had he managed to do that? I didn't know anyone who liked him—or trusted him, for that matter. Maybe they'd figured Hannah was the worst of two evils.

"Yes. He hand delivered it to the dean and made certain Dr. Finley was aware of what he'd done." Lizzie took in a deep breath, straightening her spine as she stretched her arms above her head. She breathed out slowly as she lowered her arms. "And his funeral, have you . . ." A single tear slid down her cheek.

"Monday at three," Elsie answered quietly, her gaze locked on the small figure across from us. "Pastor Connor will conduct a brief service at Winston's Funeral Home."

Lizzie nodded. She laced her long fingers together, closed her eyes, and bowed her head. Though her lips moved, no sound issued forth.

"She's praying again." Miss Gracie set a tray containing a pitcher of iced tea and glasses onto a side table. "If she's not talking to God, she's crying. The prayers are more productive."

"Is she all right?" I whispered, noticing the pallor of the girl's face.

"She will be. Now." Miss Gracie handed me a glass of tea and a coaster. "And you, Elsie Wilkes? Will you be all right?" She pierced my companion with the keen eyes of a teacher detecting a mischief-maker.

In fifth grade, I'd always believed Miss Gracie Naner was capable of seeing into each of her students' brains to determine exactly what they were thinking at any given time. Now, as she stared at Elsie, I was positive she possessed this unique ability—and was glad not to be on the receiving end.

Taking the offered tea with slightly trembling hands, Elsie met Miss Gracie's gaze. "I—I apologize for keeping my relationship to Zeke a secret and for any trouble he may have caused you."

"I accept the first part of that apology, Elsie. The latter half you're not responsible for, and you need to remember that in the days to come. Understand?" Miss Gracie sat across from us in a chair next to Lizzie's, her posture as perfect as it had been more than forty years ago when she'd been my teacher.

"Yes, ma'am," Elsie responded.

"Good. I've never been one to hold a grudge, least till I met that scoundrel Wallace. God and I have been working on that issue these last two years."

She took a sip of her tea, then glanced at Lizzie. She placed her glass on the small table between them, reached out toward the girl, then withdrew her hand, placing it onto her lap with a sigh.

Watching these two petite women, similar in stature and weight, each possessing a natural poise, grace, and innate serenity, placed me in awe.

It also made me feel like Gulliver in the land of the Lilliputians.

"I know you were wanting to speak with Lizzie, but until she's finished praying, that won't be possible." Miss Gracie smiled softly. "When she's like this, she doesn't hear anything but His voice."

"Perhaps you—" A shake of the older woman's head stopped Elsie in mid-sentence.

"Her story is hers to share or not." Miss Gracie regarded us, her expression thoughtful. "The moment I saw the two of you in that house on Friday, I knew we'd be having this conversation." She turned to me. "I didn't figure any kind of warning from your gentleman friend would keep you out of this, Glory Adele Harper. But perhaps that's for the best. Someone has to put all of this together. Perhaps that someone is you."

"I was only there because Dr. Finley sent me to look for Wallace's grades." It was a feeble explanation, even if it was the truth.

"Um. And you didn't feel compelled to investigate the man's demise after your dog found his hand?"

"I was curious, of course."

"Of course." She held up her hand to halt any further protests or justifications I might have. "You're here for information, correct?"

"Yes, ma'am," Elsie and I answered.

"And you believe that since I've been Dr. Wallace's neighbor these last two years I might be able to enlighten you?"

Once again we agreed.

"I don't believe in gossip, girls. If I'm not mistaken, that's the root cause of this mess with Dr. Wallace in the first place."

Elsie shrank back against the sofa, her face red.

"I'm not trying to embarrass you, Elsie, or bring you more grief," Miss Gracie continued. "Proverbs warns against talebearers and how they bring strife. I'd say everyone in this room has witnessed this in action."

"We'd never ask you to repeat anything that didn't directly involve you, Miss Gracie. Glory and I are just trying to put together a picture—I'd like to say of who Zeke was, but we already have a pretty good idea about that. We—I—need to find out what happened to him."

"And you believe I know something because . . . ?"

"You were his neighbor," I said. "Neighbors notice things."

I certainly did. It's how I helped solve a crime three months ago.

"And," I rushed on, "we know something happened between you and Wallace that upset you enough to leave Kelly's in the middle of your shopping."

Elsie flashed me a curious look, reminding me this was information I hadn't shared. But I was more interested in Miss Gracie's reaction. A secret smile flitted across her lips, and her eyes brightened.

"It's no secret the man had a cadre of women in and out of that house these last two years," she finally said. "He seemed partial to blondes." Miss Gracie glanced over at Lizzie who remained in a trance. "The others were none of my business, but this little gal . . . "

Silence descended over the room, broken only by the constant tick, tick, tick, of an old mantel clock. While Miss Gracie determined what—or if—she would tell us, I became aware of the delicious scents wafting through the house; pot roast was a definite, but there was a tang of cinnamon and other spices too, and all of it made my stomach growl.

Miss Gracie released a heavy sigh and pulled herself up even straighter than before. "Olav asked me to keep an eye on Lizzie. You know she lives in my garage apartment, right? Well, I'm not one to pry, but in this instance, it was warranted. Zeke Wallace needed a comeuppance, and I was ready to see it happen.

"The weather was slightly cooler those last days in July, so I was outdoors a lot, seeing to my flowers and such. Folks had their windows open to enjoy a respite from air conditioning. He had his open too, else I wouldn't have heard a thing. A sudden wailing came from his property. It just went on and on. Scared me half to death just thinking what he might be doing over there."

I could feel Elsie tense next to me as Miss Gracie drew in a deep breath.

"That horrible wailing continued until I just knew I had to do something about it. There was no thought for myself, you understand, just for that poor woman. Here I was in my gardening clothes, still holding my trowel, stalking onto that man's porch and pounding on his door."

It wasn't hard for me to imagine this little seventy-eight year old woman, with her thin arms and cloud of white hair, prepared to stand up against Zeke Wallace. She may look frail, but she was one tough lady.

"It took him forever to answer the door, and that poor woman just kept crying out!" Miss Gracie shuddered. "I was surprised when the man came to the door fully clothed. Thankful too. I asked if he needed some assistance, that I'd heard his . . . companion crying and thought perhaps I could help. The bore laughed at me, called me a nosy old woman. And then he pushed me!" She drew up her shoulders, her fiery gaze locked on us. "I'm not one for violence, you understand, and don't condone its use, but I determined that bully wasn't getting away with treating me so roughly. So I decided it was time to practice S.I.N.G."

While Miss Gracie gave us a sly little smile, my brain was conducting a thorough search to answer why this sounded so familiar.

"Sing?" Elsie asked. "I don't understand."

"Solar plexus, instep, nose, and groin," Miss Gracie said proudly. "I saw it in a movie—"

"*Miss Congeniality!*" I snapped my fingers.

Gracie Kay Naner nodded. "It works too. I laid that sucker out in a flash, then marched into the house until I found that poor woman."

"What was happening?"

"Did you save her?"

Our rapid-fire questions were met with a grimace. "Oh, I found her all right. She was back in his bedroom." My fifth grade teacher lowered her eyes and blushed.

Elsie and I leaned forward, anxious to discover what happened next.

"There was Ashley Tanner hooked up to one of those miniature recording things, dusting the room and, well, I guess you'd call it singing. But till the day I die, I'll swear it sounded more like someone was trying to kill her."

Chapter 36

I don't know if it was the laughter that brought Lizzie out of her trance, but I noticed she was suddenly watching us, an amused expression on her pretty face. Though she didn't join in, I had the impression she approved of Miss Gracie's decision to share this particular story.

"So you see, there was a perfectly logical explanation for my behavior at the nursery. It had only been a couple days since my courageous, yet foolhardy, effort, and I didn't care to be reminded of how I'd brought Dr. Wallace to his knees in an attempt to save someone who didn't need saving—at least in the traditional sense of the word. I'm not certain if dear Ashley can be saved from being tone deaf." Miss Gracie glanced at Lizzie. "I see you've returned to us. Would you care for some tea?"

Lizzie shook her head, shining strands of hair falling across her shoulders. "I would like to speak with these ladies alone, though. If you don't mind."

"Not at all."

"I understand why you left Kelly's; I would've done the same," I said, hoping I might get Miss Gracie to stay a little longer. "Was that what Ollie and Wallace were fighting about?"

The older lady patted me on the back as she walked away. "You would need to ask Olav about that, dear."

Lizzie waited until Miss Gracie was gone before she spoke.

"I know how people look at me, that they believe I'm some kind of religious zealot or fanatic. I'm not saying either of you see me that way," she said quickly. "But others do. Even Gramps has questioned why I was so determined to share my faith with Zeke Wallace. And that was before Zeke had shown his, shall we say, true colors." A curtain of hair hid her face from view.

"We don't always have a choice who we are to witness to. We strain to hear that still small voice within us, then strive to honor what we feel has been spoken. In the case of Zeke, well, it wasn't an easy path. Family and friends didn't agree with my decision to follow through with it." Lizzie shifted slightly in her chair. "In honesty, they were adamantly opposed."

"Zeke was very attracted to you," Elsie commented. "So much so that it frightened me."

Lizzie tucked the glistening strands of hair behind her ears. Her crystal blue eyes looked in our direction, but I had the feeling she wasn't seeing Elsie and me.

"It sometimes frightened me as well," she said softly.

"But you continued to—associate with him." I studied the young girl across from me. "Why deliberately place yourself in danger if you didn't have to?"

"Haven't Christians done that since the beginning, sacrificing their lives to spread the Word? Of course they have. And I know I was making a difference; it was in the way his arguments changed, the way our discussions became more focused."

There was a strength radiating from her that I'd never noticed before. Lizzie Cawley was tiny in form but mighty in her belief.

"Yet he continued hurting people," Elsie said quietly.

"As did Saul until he saw the Light. Before that, he betrayed and murdered hundreds. But God still loved him in spite of his actions. No, Zeke Wallace was not, and never would have been a Saul/Paul, but I know our Lord still loved him."

Comparing the apostle Paul to Zeke Wallace was a stretch of the imagination that reached beyond the limits of good taste and common sense. While part of me understood what the girl was trying to get across to us, the other part saw past the surface talk to what she left unsaid. And it was that part, my intuition, that led me to a startling conclusion.

"You fell in love with him!" The words were out before I had an opportunity to check in with my brain to okay them.

Lizzie met my gaze without faltering. "Our hearts choose who they will. I know that sounds like romantic drivel, but it's the truth. We start out as friends—or enemies—and sometimes a seed will be planted and take root. Somewhat like the seeds of faith I was trying to plant within Zeke's heart and soul."

"Dear God in heaven!" Elsie's cry certainly came from the depths of her soul.

I was still trying to picture this beautiful waif with the swaggering, arrogant, yet handsome rogue. And rogue was really too kind a term to use for Wallace.

"Zeke wasn't stupid. He would have realized how you felt and tried to take advantage of it. Weren't you afraid he might force you, that he might—" Elsie lowered her eyes.

"Rape me? Zeke Wallace was a lot of things, but rapist wasn't among them. He already possessed power and control over others, and his anger was focused outward at what he considered crippling religious trappings. So no, I wasn't concerned about him forcing me. I was, however, concerned about my own resolve. Just because I'm a

Christian doesn't mean I'm not human." She gave us a sly smile. "Even when I was frustrated by his lack of faith and refusal to take Christ seriously, I found him attractive. Did he tempt me? Yes. But I remained strong in my resolve to win him over to the Lord—*and* equally strong in denying my baser self."

What was it about the proverbial bad boy that seemed to draw some women? I'd read and seen reports about how women would get involved with men in prison, going so far as to marry them. I didn't understand the mentality, the appeal this had for them.

"There are things you don't know about your half brother, Elsie, things he tried to keep hidden from everyone. But once in a while I would get a glimpse into the man he could be, *should* have been if he'd learned to forgive. Instead, he allowed resentment and jealousy to control his life. Not that he would have admitted these were behind his determination to destroy your friends and community."

Elsie blanched. "You're saying all of this, the blackmail schemes and trying to force Tarryton away from its religious base are because of me?"

"Not just you. Your father choosing you and your mother over Zeke and his mom obviously played an important part. And then you had this loving and supportive community and your faith to draw on; Zeke couldn't even count on his mother."

"I couldn't know that."

"Of course you couldn't. And you did try to befriend him. He showed me dozens of letters you wrote to him. He thought so highly of them that he kept them in his safe in a file called 'sis.' He said you'd given him inspiration."

I didn't think Elsie could get any paler, but she did. She'd already suspected the SIS file was about her; now she had confirmation.

Which meant that her gossipy letters had been used as a basis for Wallace's blackmail.

"Anyway," Lizzie went on, "I finally had to admit I was outmatched, that nothing I said would convince Zeke to convert from his evil ways. Especially after he started working with Renée Brent. He took to calling me a shy little trinket who needed a man to show her the facts of life, and seemed to enjoy hurting me whenever Brent was around."

A tear slid down her cheek. "So I refused to see him any more, stopped taking his calls. That infuriated him. He barged into my office at the church and demanded I meet him at his place that night. He said he had something that would change my mind. And he was right."

She sat quietly for a moment. I looked to Elsie for a possible explanation and noticed my companion had become as rigid as a statue.

"I think we sometimes get complacent, don't you?" Lizzie spoke softly, her gaze never wavering from us. "We believe our secrets will remain in that dark closet where we left them. As Christians, we know that when we confess our sins and ask for forgiveness, our slate is wiped clean. But as human beings, that doesn't usually happen."

Elsie clamped a hand over her mouth as I resisted the urge to throw my arms around this poor girl and the loss of her innocence.

"When I arrived at Zeke's that evening, July 31, Renée Brent was leaving. She spotted me coming across the street and waited for me. There was a smirk on her face, and the way she watched me gave me the creeps. I asked if she wanted something, and she told me she'd already delivered my gift to Zeke. That's when I knew she'd been digging into my life."

I was getting more confused by the second. What deep, dark secret could this sweet little thing have that should concern a hardcore like Brent? Had I missed something?

"So I was prepared for the worst when I saw Zeke."

Lizzie swallowed, looked toward the table where the pitcher of tea still sat, then noticed Miss Gracie's glass on the table next to her. Rather than get up to get her own drink, she picked up the nearly full glass Miss Gracie left behind, raised it to her lips, then paused. "I'd never seen Zeke any way other than in complete control. But that night he was agitated." She took a sip of tea, then held the glass in front of her.

"That's when he told me about the fight he'd had with Dr. Finley that afternoon and how she'd refused to accept his grades. But I could tell from the way he was acting there was more going on. I tried to get him to talk about it, figured it would delay the inevitable discussion about me. I knew he was concerned about Renée Brent's tactics. He'd often said she didn't play by the rules, that someone was going to get hurt. I've no idea what he meant by that, but it made him . . . nervous. And for Zeke to be nervous, something very dangerous had to be happening."

"They've matched Brent's prints to those left on Albert Donovan's car," Elsie volunteered. "Public Safety figures she left them when she sliced Albert's tires."

"That's good." Lizzie took another sip of tea. "But Zeke wouldn't have had this sort of reaction over slashed tires. No, it was something bigger, I could feel it." She shook her head. "Around the time I asked him what else was wrong, I heard the door off the kitchen close. Though we both went to check it out, it was obvious he already knew what was going on. He tried to pass it off as a gust of wind catching the door, but it was a lie. Someone else had been in the house."

A shiver of apprehension sneaked down my spine. The night she was describing was a little over a week after Jane's fire. Could Wallace's concern about Brent's tactics have anything to do with that?

"Once he'd locked the back door, he wasn't as keyed up. That's when he turned on me." Her hands trembled as she set the glass of tea on the table. "He said, here I was all pious and claiming innocence when he had it on good authority that I'd abused drugs and run wild in college."

Elsie nearly dropped the glass she'd just picked up. Her quick intake of breath brought on a case of the hiccups. I patted her on the back, hoping it would help, but was too wrapped up in what Lizzie was saying to really care as much as I should have.

"He knew about the abortion I'd had and threatened to tell my grandfather if I didn't cooperate with him. I had no idea what kind of cooperation he expected, but I guarantee it wasn't my turning the tables on him."

Lizzie Cawley lowered her gaze for just a second, then peered back up at us through the thick bangs covering her forehead.

"By this time, I knew enough about Zeke to protect myself from his threats. In the last two years I'd seen more than one open file lying about. He had no idea that all it took was a glance, and I could retain the information. I knew he had dirt on different people in town. I had a few names, a few details."

"Because of your photographic memory?" I asked.

Lizzie shrugged. "Some people call it that. I think it's more a case of paying close attention to details. Anyway, I knew it was wrong to ignore what he was doing, but I'd felt it more important to bring him to Christ and have the changes come from that rather than to . . . " Lizzie shook her head. "Don't you see, I'd been there—outside the will of God, chasing after all the wrong things and never being satisfied. That's why I believed I could get him to change." She closed her eyes so tightly, I was amazed when tears leaked through.

"I felt I had one last chance. And what could be more perfect than to blackmail the blackmailer? People would be disappointed in the life I'd led during college; my family would be hurt. But Zeke wouldn't be so fortunate if his secrets were revealed."

Lizzie opened her crystal blue eyes and shuddered. "I just hope the Lord can forgive me."

"I'm sure God understands, honey." I went to kneel in front of her, taking her small hands into mine.

"You don't understand, Glory," Lizzie answered slowly. "I tricked Zeke into marrying me."

Chapter 37

I was in shock. My mouth dropped open, and no matter what I did, it refused to close.

"*You married him?*" I finally managed to regain control of my mouth and jaw. "How, why, for goodness sake?"

"Did you know you can't be forced to testify against a spouse?" There was a slyness to Lizzie's smile that I hadn't noticed before. "Well, he knew. I dropped a few names, their connecting information, the codes on their files, and Zeke knew I had him. I wouldn't tell what I knew, but he had to pay my price. Marriage. He'd been trying to get me into bed for two years, so now was his chance—and it would keep me quiet at the same time."

"But where does the 'tricking' him come in?" Elsie stuttered.

"Gramps already knew my secret—so does Pastor Connor and his wife. That's how I got to where I am today. Convincing Zeke everyone was still in the dark perpetrated a lie. But I honestly believed it was for the best. I thought if we were married, I could finally convince him to change, to come to the Lord."

"And he agreed?" I moved like a sleepwalker back to my place on the sofa.

Lizzie nodded. "It was easier than it should have been. If I hadn't been so elated, I'd have realized that. Instead, I chalked up my success to his fight with Dr. Finley. Well, that, coupled with his unease about Renée Brent and whatever she was doing. She's far worse than Zeke ever was." A sudden thought seemed to occur to her. "You've kept her out of Zeke's safe haven't you?" She peered anxiously at Elsie.

"We caught her going through things earlier today. She managed to shred some files, but I had her arrested before she was able to take anything."

"That's good. I shudder to think what she might do . . ."

The tables being turned on Wallace was an interesting thought, but it was also confusing. He never seemed the type to allow anything to sneak up on him. I assumed that, like a Boy Scout, Zeke Wallace would be prepared for any contingency. With this in mind, it seemed out of character for him to cave under Lizzie's threats.

I studied the beautiful girl across from me, taking in the crystal blue of her eyes; her shining, white-blonde hair; and her tiny figure. She still looked as pure and wholesome as she always had—perhaps even more so now I knew what she'd overcome. She was everything Zeke could never be—and maybe everything he'd wanted.

"Did you know the marriage license offices in Las Vegas are open 24/7?" Lizzie asked with a smile. "It takes about fifteen minutes or so to fill out an application, then you're off to the chapel of your choice. I insisted on this sweet little place that looked like a miniature cathedral. Zeke wasn't feeling well, so we had a short service. I barely got him back to the motel room; he was so dizzy and out of it."

"When was this Lizzie? When did you get married?"

"Sunday, August second."

I had to check my notes, but I was sure someone claimed to see Wallace in town that day.

"We left for KCI late Saturday afternoon, shortly after Zeke arranged with Kelly's to have them take care of the yard while we were gone. He was on break, and I'd convinced

Pastor Connor I needed to take an immediate leave. We got into Vegas around midnight."

"And when did you come back?"

Lizzie regarded me thoughtfully. "I can see your mind spinning, Glory, trying to piece it all together."

"True. Though at this point Detective Spencer should be involved."

"He already has my statement. I spoke with him this morning."

"Then why are you talking with Elsie and me?"

"Elsie's my sister-in-law, and, well, Gramps has always said you have a way with solving puzzles. When Elsie asked if we could meet, I talked it over with Gramps and Miss Gracie. They both agreed that having you on the case couldn't hurt."

I was pretty sure Blue Eyes would disagree.

"It's getting late, and I'd like to finish my story, so you can head out. Besides, I'm sure your sweet puppy would like to get back home as well."

I'd totally forgotten about Misty. I hoped she hadn't ruined anything on their porch. Like boots and shoes and anything else she might latch onto.

"Anyway, Zeke continued to act like he had stomach flu. But when it didn't get better and all he wanted to do was sleep, I got him in to see a doctor." She wrung her hands. "The medicine just seemed to make him sicker. Because he's allergic to so many things, he thought maybe it was an allergic reaction of some kind. I didn't know what to do, so I got us reservations to return home, loaded him up on Benadryl, and we were back in Kansas City early August seventh. Zeke was so out of it, I had to leave him with a Skycap while I got his Mini Cooper from the lot.

"The drive back home was a nightmare. We kept having to stop, so he could get sick. When I got to St. Joe, I stopped at an Urgent Care facility. By this time, Zeke had taken so many Benadryl, he was barely cognizant—but he was aware enough to tell the doctor to go to hell and demand I get him out of there immediately."

Lizzie sat twisting her hands, tears flowing freely down her cheeks. "I knew he was sick when we set off for Vegas on Saturday. His hands were cold, and he just didn't look right. But he insisted we leave. Now, here we were just a few miles from home, and he was writhing in his seat. I detoured to Maryville and took him in to the emergency room. They pumped his stomach, saying he'd virtually overdosed on the other meds. His blood work seemed fine, so I got him back into the car and came home.

"He was angry about the emergency room incident, but too weak to make much of a protest. I got him tucked into bed, then took a look around the house. It didn't look the way we'd left it, and since Ashley was gone on vacation, that concerned me. But there were so many other things on my mind I didn't stop to figure it out. I did notice the refrigerator wasn't working, so I called Finley Appliance and ordered a new one. They said they'd bring it over about two. That gave me a couple hours to let Pastor Connor know I was back, break the news to Gramps, and run a few errands.

"I left Zeke's Mini in the drive and walked over to my apartment to talk with Miss Gracie and pick up my car for the errands. She wasn't around, so after giving Pastor Connor a quick call, I headed for the store. While I was shopping, I decided it was more important to get back to take care of Zeke than it was to tell people we were married. I was gone less than three hours.

"By the time I returned, the Mini was no longer in the driveway, the fridge had already been delivered, the rotten food shoved into the kitchen garbage can, and Zeke was gone. There was no message, nothing."

"You said he was so groggy he could hardly stand," I said, trying to wrap my mind around what she was saying.

"Exactly. And from what I'd seen in those last few hours, I'm positive he couldn't have driven anywhere. But I checked the hospital and left a message with his doctor's service. I put away the groceries, wondering what else I could do. I stayed a couple hours, but it just didn't feel right. I kept remembering the night before we left for Vegas, and how the back door had closed while Zeke and I were talking. I knew he had other women in his life and figured some of them might have keys. What would I do if one of them showed up? I certainly didn't want to face any of them, especially Lila Samson."

Lila? If Lizzie thought the wheels in my brain were spinning before, she should have seen them now!

"It was making me crazy," Lizzie continued. "I finally decided it would be best to wait in my apartment. He had my home and cell numbers. I was sure he'd call as soon as he got back.

"I didn't sleep that night. I was so worried about him, about his health, but I was also afraid he'd changed his mind about me, about us. And I was ashamed, so very ashamed at what I'd done in tricking him."

She lowered her eyes, fidgeting in her chair. "I finally packed a bag and came out here to stay with Gramps. I spilled my guts about the quickie wedding and a groom who couldn't keep his eyes open. Gramps was furious, but he kept a clear head. He said we should wait, that Zeke would call. But he didn't call, ladies. And by Monday night,

I was frantic. Despite Miss Gracie's and Gramps' advice, I drove over to the house. I didn't know what I'd find. Answers, I guess."

This time it was Elsie who moved to the distraught girl. She held Lizzie's hands, offering words of encouragement. I had begun to compile a timeline in my mind, and what I was seeing wasn't making a lot of sense. The moment I got home I'd have to get it down on paper before I forgot anything.

"What did you find, honey?" Elsie asked, her voice soft, encouraging.

"Not the house as I'd left it," Lizzie said, a kind of wonder tingeing her words. "Every blind in the house had been shut, the drapes and curtains closed. There was a single lamp on in the living room, next to the recliner Zeke used, and a newspaper on the arm of the chair—open to something about the K.C. Royals, I think. There was a coffee mug on the lamp table with what looked like dried coffee inside.

"In his bedroom, the bed had been neatly remade, no sign Zeke had been there, been sick. The rotten food in the trash permeated the kitchen, making it unbearable. I should have thrown it out, but . . .

"I was almost afraid to enter his office. It was too clean, too organized. There were no papers lying about waiting to be graded, no nefarious files to taunt me. Zeke's grade book was sitting near his computer, and when I moved the mouse, the screen awakened to reveal his grades. I hoped that maybe Zeke had decided to make peace with Dr. Finley, that he was in his office at the college. I called that number, but it went straight to voice mail."

"Just like his cell and home numbers were doing every time I called," I added.

Lizzie nodded.

"The way you described the house is exactly how it looked when I was there yesterday," Elsie said. "I walked through it knowing something wasn't quite right, but I couldn't put my finger on it."

"Ashley did," I volunteered.

Elsie and Lizzie turned to me.

"When Ashley Tanner thought Wallace was back in his office, she chided him for having the blinds and curtains shut on such a beautiful day. She also commented on the oddity of him having a sports page open to a story about the Royals."

"I remember," Elsie piped up. "But what makes that significant?"

"Along with being allergic to everything, Zeke was claustrophobic. He would never, ever have shut out the sun—or the moon for that matter. He wasn't afraid of much," Lizzie said, "but that sort of thing terrified him. And as for the Royals . . ."

I was about to say something when Ollie rushed in through the front door.

"Lizabeth, get on the phone to 911. Your uncle's just found something interesting in our pond."

Lizzie grabbed up the phone and dialed. "What do I tell them, Gramps?"

"Tell them we just found Zeke Wallace's car in our stock pond."

Chapter 38

Elsie and I managed to catch Lizzie as she collapsed. The phone tumbled from her hand, smacking the floor as the 911 operator picked up. Ollie grabbed the receiver, gave a terse explanation for the call, then shoved the phone at me. He lifted his granddaughter in one strong arm at the same time he prepared a comfortable place for her on the sofa.

The next few minutes became a blur of activity. While Miss Gracie and Ollie ministered to Lizzie, Gavin Cawley, Ollie's sixty-four-year-old son who helped with the farm, burst into the house. There were a few whispers, but most of the communication between father and son were in hand gestures, nods, and shakes of the head—all very mysterious to an outsider like me.

Elsie and I were edging our way toward the door when Gavin rushed by on his way out. About the same time, Ollie seemed to remember we were there. He left his granddaughter's side and escorted us to our car.

My curiosity was high, but Lizzie's story and the events I'd just witnessed tied my tongue. If it hadn't been for Miss Gracie bringing Misty out to us, I'd have left without her.

"I warned him to stay away from my Lizzie," Ollie muttered as he helped load the puppy into the backseat. "He took off with her that same day. Now look what it's come to."

He tapped Elsie on the shoulder, barely waiting for her to turn before he said, "You're not to breathe a word of what my girl's told you, you understand?" His voice harsh, threatening, he continued, "If'n I hear a thing about them bein' married, I'll know you done it, *and you will be sorry.*"

Elsie swallowed audibly. "Y-you've m-my word."

Ollie slammed the door and stood watch as she backed down the first leg of the driveway, her hands trembling on the wheel.

"You want me to drive?" I offered, not certain I'd be any steadier.

"If he wasn't still glaring at us, I'd be tempted. As it is, I don't want to stop."

I looked to where my long-time friend stood, his arms slightly bent, big hands knotted into fists. He didn't look so friendly now.

"Naw, I don't think you should stop either."

Elsie turned the car around the first chance she got. It wasn't really a turnout, but it got the job done, and we no longer had to see Ollie's crystal blue eyes drilling holes in us—though the feeling persisted until we rounded the last curve in his long drive.

Within seconds of when we pulled onto the county road, the sheriff drove by, followed by a tow truck and a Crown Vic belonging to Tarryton Public Safety. I got a glimpse of the officer at the wheel of the Crown Vic and shrank down in my seat.

"It's too late, Glory. He spotted us." Elsie glanced in the rearview mirror. "And he's turning around." She pulled onto the shoulder to wait for my favorite cop—though I wasn't certain I was his favorite citizen anymore.

"We're outside the city limits," I said, forcing myself to sit up straight and tall. "He really doesn't have any jurisdiction here."

"You want to tell him that?" She looked in the mirror again. "Now's your chance."

She rolled down her window as Rick came into view.

"Ladies." He leaned forward, his dark eyes skewering me. "You two staying out of trouble?"

"Is that a rhetorical question, or are you looking for information?" My attempt at being funny wasn't rewarded with a smile.

Misty whined in the backseat. She shoved her face between the side of the car and Elsie's head, her tongue lolling out as she tried to get to Blue Eyes. He patted her head, pointed to the seat, and the puppy immediately withdrew to the back and laid down.

"We were invited to the farm to visit Lizzie," Elsie said quickly, wiping dog slobber off the side of her head. "She was in need of prayer support and . . . "

"You two were her first choice." Rick's dark gaze remained on me.

"Save it. He's not buying." I turned in my seat and attempted to look bold and confident.

I'm pretty sure I failed. Miserably.

"You're messing with a murder investigation—"

"Then you've established a cause of death?"

"Nothing official, Elsie. Sorry."

He'd seemed about to say something more, but I think my presence changed his mind. He tapped the roof of the car.

"You two try to stay out of trouble. That's an order, not a suggestion. You've a date with Gus tonight, right?"

Elsie nodded. "I—if it's still on."

"I know he's looking forward to it." He grinned at my blushing companion before glancing over at me. "As for us, Glory, I'm going to be tied up for a while."

Reaching through the window, he lightly touched Elsie's shoulder, and she nodded. What was that all about?

"But everyone's got to eat," he went on. "I thought about running by Marcello's and picking up veal parmesan for two. Sound good?"

Was this a trick? Did he have something up his sleeve, or did he just want to make sure I didn't do any further sleuthing tonight?

"Great. 'Bout what time?" I glanced at the clock on the dash as he checked his watch.

"Eight?"

Two hours. What could I do in that time? What did I want to do? The timeline, a shower, visit with Jane about her day . . .

"See you then."

He thumped the side of the car, stood back, and waved us on.

"Why the tap on your shoulder?"

"Huh? What are you talking about?" Elsie swerved slightly, then straightened the car.

"Back there. Rick tapped your shoulder, and you nodded."

"Oh, well, maybe it was to reassure me about going out with Gus. I'm still new at this, you know."

She might be new at dating, but not telling the whole truth used to be her stock in trade. You'd never know it from the whopper she just tried to pass over on me.

I eyed her, trying to assess whether or not it was worth pursuing. When we passed Rick's grandparents' old home and the garden that filled the lot where I grew up, I sat back in my seat, locked inside old memories. We continued in silence until we reached Liquors Are Us at the city limit.

"Pull into the parking lot!" I shouted.

"You've got to be kidding. Can you imagine what people would say—"

"Do it, Elsie. That's Lila Samson."

Lila was struggling with a case of beer, the strap of her purse, and staying upright. It looked to me like the girl had already had one too many.

When she stopped alongside Lila, Elsie was still mumbling about the woes she was bound to suffer if anyone saw her in front of a liquor store.

"Stay put," I told her. "I'll be right back."

My open door set a temporary block in front of Lila. She threw me a filthy look as she maneuvered around it.

Misty's growls turned to high pitched barks as I slammed the door. I threw an apologetic glance at Elsie before going in pursuit of my prey.

"I'd like to ask you a few questions, Lila," I called as I marched toward her.

"I don't have to talk to you. What kind of moron do you think I am?"

Her unsteady gait proved she'd been drinking and, from the case in her arms, she didn't intend to stop anytime soon. She was impaired—but that wasn't an excuse for me to ignore the perfect opening.

I stepped in front of her. "Garden variety is my guess."

"Huh?"

I ignored the sound of Elsie's car easing away behind me. "You asked—never mind. I understand you were having an affair with Zeke Wallace."

She stopped and half turned to me. "What of it? 'S'free country. Might wanna tell that to your Gestapo sister."

"Excuse me?"

"The witch got me thrown outta Daily Mart for thirty days," she said loudly as she leaned into my face. "She told 'em I was shopliftin' 'cause I was eatin' some cookies in the store."

"That I had a receipt for." David Quinn suddenly appeared beside us. He took the case of beer from Lila in one arm and placed the other about her shoulders.

"Mrs. H."

"David. What's all this about?"

"Just what Lila said. I bought some cookies, and Lila was munching on them while we continued to shop. Your sister stuck her nose in where it didn't belong and caused a lot of trouble where there wasn't any."

"I . . . see. I apologize, and I'm certain Jane will too, once she knows the circumstances."

"Not Miss Holier Than Thou," Lila hiccupped. "She's 'most as bad as you an' your kid, always struttin' 'round like you're better'n everybody else."

I had no idea what she was referring to. And though I'd like those answers, we were beginning to gather a crowd. Elsie's nightmare come true. I hoped she hadn't driven off without me.

After advising David to take care of his less than sober companion, I went off in search of Elsie. I found her at the farthest end of the lot, hunched so far down in her seat it took her a full five minutes to resituate herself. By that time, David's Mazda had zoomed past us out onto the highway, going far faster than the speed limit.

"Did you know David Quinn and Lila Samson have been seeing each other?"

Elsie shook her head. "I recognize Quinn's name, but I don't know him. Why? Is it significant?"

"Not to the case. He's a nice young man, and I hate to see him involved with Lila. That's all."

There was still so much activity at Wallace's when Elsie dropped me off to get my car that I was reluctant to transfer Misty and risk her getting away from me. So rather than take that chance, Elsie agreed to let the puppy stay where she was and followed me home.

A few minutes later, as I was getting Misty out of the backseat, Elsie stopped me with a touch of her hand. "Please tell Jane he didn't do it," she said softly.

"Huh?"

"Just tell her. Promise?"

I nodded, confused, and more than a little curious.

It only took a slight tug on the puppy's leash for her to leap out after me. She loped happily at my side all the way up the sidewalk—even waited patiently while I unlocked the door.

Elsie remained in the driveway until I switched on an inside light.

"See you at church tomorrow," she called out with a wave.

Church. Tomorrow was Sunday.

I went inside, unhooked Misty's leash, and followed her to the back door. I let her out, then stood there watching her jump after lightning bugs.

Jane and I had found Wallace's hand on Thursday. Today was Saturday. Two days. That's all it had been.

But it seemed like a lifetime.

Chapter 39

D ates and times, people and events. Instead of a nice, relaxing bath, my mind was filled to bursting with things I needed to record before I forgot.

I dressed in a clean pair of jeans and a T-shirt before I was totally dry, tracing back through the interviews Elsie and I had with our suspects. Everything seemed to be on a collision course, crisscrossing one memory synapse, then another, spilling out of my Swiss cheese brain only to be sucked back in to start the process over again.

I ran a brush through my tangled hair, recalling someone commenting that Wallace seemed to prefer blondes. While there might be an element of truth to the statement, from what I'd learned in the last two days, the man considered every woman fair game.

Misty followed me from room to room as I gathered the necessary tools to draw my timeline. I spread everything out on the kitchen table, and with a ruler, a small posterboard, and colored pencils in hand, I designed a calendar that started with July 31 and ended on August 13, the day we discovered Zeke Wallace's hand. I filled in the dates with the pertinent information, then sat back to study my handiwork.

FRI., JULY 31—A. Tanner sees W before leaving for vacation.

Lizzie sees R. Brent leaving W's house as she goes in. W tries to blackmail Lizzie – she turns tables on him.

Someone leaves by back door while W and Lizzie are talking.

SAT., AUG. 1—Miss Gracie leaves Kelly's when W arrives.

W & O. Cawley fight about Lizzie.

W & Lizzie fly to Vegas.

SUN., AUG. 2—Lizzie & W marry in Vegas.

W. seems to be sick with flu.

R. Brent claims to see W in bed with Lizzie (not possible unless she flew to Vegas!).

MON., AUG. 2—W still sick, Lizzie takes him to doctor.

TUE., AUG. 3—Meds seem to make W even sicker – begins Benadryl.

FRI., AUG 7—Lizzie & W return to MO, W really sick.

ER pumps W's stomach—Possible OD on meds, blood work seems ok.

Lizzie tucks W in bed, orders new fridge, then leaves on errands.

M. Hobbs delivers payment to a groggy W.

H. Finley signs invoice for fridge delivery.

Lizzie returns & finds W & his car gone, no messages.

Uncomfortable in W's house, Lizzie goes to her apartment.

SAT. & SUN., AUG. 8 & 9—Lizzie repeatedly calls W's phones. No answer—voice mail—she goes out to stay with grandfather.

MON., AUG. 10—Lizzie returns to W's and finds it all shut up, blinds & curtains closed, not like W, who is claustrophobic.

Finds office too clean and neat, computer on—grade file open, grade book on desk.

THURS., AUG. 13—Misty finds W's hand at Fitness
  Park

W died late Aug. 9 or early Aug. 10.

When I was satisfied with what I'd recorded, I jotted
down Wallace's symptoms across the bottom of the chart:
cold hands, gastric distress, flu-like symptoms, lethargy.

Wallace wasn't feeling well before he and Lizzie left
for Vegas, and from what Lizzie told us, he seemed to get
sicker after he sought treatment. I didn't know what the
Las Vegas doctor had given him, but Lizzie said he'd taken
so much Benadryl later on that he was barely conscious.

Had there been an adverse reaction from the combination of drugs, or had he overdosed like the ER doctor
here in Missouri suspected? I didn't know enough about
medical issues to even hazard a guess—but maybe the Internet could point me in a possible direction.

The doorbell rang before I got to my office. Misty's excited yips and wagging tail were a pretty good indication
it was Blue Eyes. A thrill of excitement coursed through
me as it always did—at least on those occasions when we
weren't at odds because I was in investigative mode. Despite our differences on this issue, we'd managed to get
beyond these bumps in the road. The important thing to
remember was how we felt about each other.

I paused with my hand on the doorknob.

How *did* we feel about each other? It was a question
that needed an in-depth exploration—more than I had
time for right now, with him waiting to come inside.

I opened the door to the sweet smell of roses, luscious
marinara sauce . . . and Rick. I stared into his incredible
blue eyes and knew everything would be fine.

All we saw was each other.

Q Q Q

"I had a nicer evening in mind," Rick said as he helped to clear away the remains of our meal. "But at least I was able to get away for a little while."

He set the take-out dishes back on the table and caught me around the waist. "You smell like coconut shampoo and veal parmesan," he said, nuzzling my neck and giving me goose bumps. "A very exotic combination, Glory Harper."

Is it possible to remain coy, demure, when the man you . . . like a lot, is covering the back of your neck with warm, spine tingling kisses? He didn't play fair.

I closed my eyes and leaned against his chest only to be set firmly away from him. "What's this?" he said, reaching around me.

I shook my head in the hope of restarting my brain—from lust to dust in less than two seconds. Well, not lust, exactly, but it was headed in that direction.

I turned to find him examining the timeline I'd shoved to the opposite end of the table. Though I'd put the ruler and box of pencils on top of it, the bright colors denoting each date and event must have caught his eye.

"There was so much information, I decided to write it down."

I watched while he studied what I'd written. His face remained shuttered—except for that quirk he has of lifting an eyebrow. I knew I had his interest the moment the brow raised.

"May I have a copy of this?"

Leaving our dirty dishes on the table, we went to my office. I didn't take any chances with the printer this time; I didn't turn my back on it until the copy spit out.

I handed him the timeline. "Do you see something there that you didn't know before?"

"You know your fishing expeditions don't get you anywhere, so why do you keep trying?"

"Glutton for punishment, I guess."

His eyes narrowed, and his expression grew more serious. "I'm going to give you a warning you can pass along to Elsie. If you don't stop interfering in this case, I'll be forced to charge you with obstruction."

I followed in his wake as he strode from the office. "I don't see how you can say we've been interfering. Until this afternoon, we'd no idea you considered Wallace's death a murder—"

"Now you know."

"O-kay. But have you ever stopped to consider we might be able to help?"

"Leave it to trained professionals. We've enough to deal with; we don't need the added worry that one of you might become the killer's next victim."

"Hi, you two! I hope I'm not interrupting."

Jane entered through the front door, startling both of us—though the big, strong detective tried to act like he hadn't been surprised by her sudden appearance. He rushed to help her with the sacks she was carrying, while Misty pranced nearby, eager for her greeting.

Jane handed over the sacks, clearly grateful for Rick's assistance. "I think Suzanne's trying every recipe she owns." She slipped out of her shoes and shut the door. "If I'd realized they were so heavy, I would've had Steven help bring them in. I just hope we've room in the fridge for all of this."

Jane gave Misty a quick hug before heading for the kitchen. The rest of us followed close behind.

"We had a cookout—hamburgers and hotdogs for Becca, steaks for the adults—and the sheer quantity of everything—" She shook her head. "You'd think they were cooking for an army instead of four people. We've got a mountain of potato salad, baked beans, and I don't know what all."

Rick set the bags on the counter, eyeing Jane as he did so. She winked at him.

"I'll send some of this stuff with you as a reward, though I'm tempted to have you take the lot down to the station. I'm assuming you have a refrigerator."

"We do. But I couldn't ask you to do that."

"You didn't ask. Glory, put those things back in the sacks. I'll tuck in some paper plates and you're all set."

Though she still looked a little stressed, Jane's voice was strong. And taking charge of the situation like a drill sergeant was right in character.

"I see you've packed up more things," Rick said, watching my sister closely. "You still feel threatened?"

"Has the arsonist been caught?" Jane leveled her gaze on him. "It wasn't Wallace."

"You're sure about that?" His detective side made a subtle appearance.

He was never that subtle with me . . .

"I can feel it."

Rick's nod had me curious. "So the note—" His dirty look stopped me in mid-thought. "Hey, she wormed it out of me."

His harsh "um" wasn't reassuring, but he was too much of a gentleman to accuse me in front of Jane.

"In her defense, Glory's never been able to keep secrets from me," Jane told him. "I kept after her until she told me."

"Twisted my arm," I muttered.

"*Did* you find out anything about the note?" Jane put the paper plates in one of the sacks and tied it closed, her eyes never leaving Rick's face.

"I'm not at liberty to say at this time. However, I do have a question for you. Maybe you'd like to have a seat first."

"Is this a formal interrogation, detective?" Though there was a lilt in my sister's tone, I didn't get the feeling she was teasing.

"It's been reported that you threatened Zeke Wallace with a gun," he said evenly, his detective persona fully engaged. "You want to tell me about that?"

I'd been watching Blue Eyes so closely I hadn't noticed Jane was trying not to laugh. She finally lost her battle.

"I suppose you heard that from Renée Brent—or maybe Lila Samson." She giggled like a schoolgirl. "I'm sorry, but that's just too funny."

"So?" I prompted.

"Glory."

Between Jane's laughter and Rick's warning tone, I almost lost it. But since I didn't want to be sent from the room—in my own house, no less—I backed off.

"I told you about the day Wallace confronted me at the grocery store, then went to my house. Well, I didn't tell you what happened after I slapped him."

"I'm listening."

So was I, but I knew better than to say anything.

"I followed him out to his car and told him I was calling Public Safety to report his harassment. To show him I was serious, I took out my cell phone and shook it at him." Jane covered her mouth with a hand as a chuckle bubbled out. "All of a sudden I heard someone scream 'Look out, she's got a gun!' That's when I noticed Brent in the car. She was yelling and carrying on so much that I was ready to duck for cover. Then I realized that the little antenna on my phone was pointing toward Wallace."

Jane and I were laughing so hard I thought Blue Eyes would join in. I think he wanted to, but decorum forbade it.

"Then what happened?" he asked.

"Wallace and I started laughing. Then he left. I couldn't believe her reaction. I had the impression Wallace was surprised by it as well." Jane leaned against the counter. "I didn't think too much about it—until Lila accosted me in Daily Mart later."

"Was this the same day?" I was glad he'd asked because I was dying to know.

Jane nodded. "She followed me through the store, eating from a bag of cookies, practically shouting—or so it seemed—about me pulling a gun on Wallace. By the time I got to the register, I was angry. And embarrassed."

"So you turned her in for shoplifting." It was out before I knew it.

"How'd you—" Jane shook her head. "Silly question. And yes, I turned her in."

"Anything else?"

Jane looked away from Blue Eyes and reached for the open sack of food. Her fingers shook as she tied it off.

"I know now I was overreacting, that Lila wasn't really shouting in the store, and it wasn't a big deal. I mean, Glory never heard the rumor so . . . "

I should have felt insulted but was too caught up in my sister's actions to care. Jane untied the sack, poked around inside it, then re-knotted the handles.

Rick placed a hand on top of hers, and she looked up. "The more I thought about the incident with Lila, the more upset I became. I couldn't sleep that night, then couldn't concentrate on a thing the next morning. By lunchtime I was ready to confront Wallace."

Jane removed her hands from beneath Rick's. She pulled out one of the counter stools and sank onto it.

"He answered his door still zipping his pants. I was outraged by his audacity. He laughed at me, then made some snide remarks that I refuse to repeat. I was turning to leave when I heard a woman crying."

"Ashley Tanner trying to sing?" They both looked at me like I was crazy.

"I pushed past him. I don't know why I did it, but . . ." She shook her head. "A woman dashed into the closet before I got anything more than the impression of blonde hair."

Rick stood back from the counter, his eyes never leaving my sister's face. "Who did you think it was?"

"I—I haven't wanted to believe it, and couldn't swear to it, but I think it was Lizzie. Lizzie Cawley."

Chapter 40

The cool night air held a false promise of an early fall—but the middle of August in the Midwest is not the time to believe the back of summer has been broken. The heat would return. Guaranteed.

I stood on the porch, Rick one step below me, which put me at eye level with the six-foot-two detective. My heart skipped a beat as I looked into his beautiful eyes, marveling again how much he reminded me of Harrison Ford in *Indiana Jones and The Last Crusade*. All he needed was a worn leather jacket, a fedora—and a whip.

"I don't want this to go to your head, but your time-line's given me a few ideas." Blue Eyes transferred the sacks of food to one hand, then reached up and brushed a curl from my forehead. "That's not an invitation—"

"Did you have to go and ruin it? Here I was, basking in the glow of your compliment—"

He silenced me with a kiss. A very nice one too, considering he only had one arm with which to hold me.

"I have to go," he said, releasing me. "I'm afraid I won't make it to church, but I'll try to give you a call later in the afternoon."

He gave me another peck on the cheek before heading for his car.

"Did you know your garage door is open?"

I joined him at the edge of the driveway. "I've been meaning to have it looked at. The silly thing gets about a foot and a half off the ground like that and just stops. I'll have to go inside and release the lever to close it the old fashioned way."

"Make sure it's locked afterward, okay?"

I assured him I would, then waited until he'd pulled out of the driveway before punching in the code to raise the garage door. It rumbled and protested but finally engaged and started to rise.

Once inside, I had to find a footstool, so I could reach the release lever. That was the easy part. It seemed to take forever to lower the door by hand, but after a lot of huffing and puffing, I finally got it closed.

Rather than lock it, I reengaged the lever so we'd be able to use it in auto mode. It was safer than Jane and me forgetting and backing into the door tomorrow morning.

Jane was on the sofa in the living room. Though she was flipping through TV channels, her attention wasn't on the set. Misty lay in front of the sofa near her. The puppy lifted her head and stared at me with big brown eyes that seemed too heavy to hold open.

"The garage door was up again. We'll have to get someone out to look at it."

"You probably need a new system or kit—whatever it's called. I'll check into it first thing Monday morning." Jane turned off the TV, then tossed the remote onto the coffee table. "You and Elsie get squared away with the new job?"

"Not exactly. She wanted help going through Wallace's things. It didn't take us long to determine that Public Safety needed to get involved." I told her a little about what happened, Renée Brent's arrest and Albert Donovan's heart attack, but I knew she wasn't really listening.

I sat on the other end of the sofa, angled toward her, waiting for her to open up to me. Knowing my sister, that might take a while. Misty yawned and got up, licked Jane's knee, then settled back down for a nap. That seemed to wake Jane up.

"How am I going to do it, Glory? I'm fifty-five, too old to be the mother of an eight-year-old." There was a helplessness to her voice that tugged at my heart.

"Who says?"

That was brilliant. *Dear Lord grant me wisdom.*

"I do." She drew her feet up onto the cushion, knees tight to her body. "It's not that Becca isn't adorable, she is. She was really sweet this evening. We talked about my teaching, the students, all kinds of things. She's already in love with Andi and Seth, and she thinks you're hilarious."

"Bright kid."

"Yes, well, despite that, she seems to like the idea of having this extended family. She even wanted me to read to her before bedtime." Jane placed her chin on her knees. "Steven says Becca tries very hard not to cry, even though he's encouraged her to grieve. His mother believes she's adjusting quite well, which is all the more reason not to throw something else at the poor kid."

"Like a stepmother?"

"She needs time to get used to having a father. That's the most important thing right now."

I scooted closer, so I could see her better in the dim light. "What's Dr. Dreamboat think about all this?"

"He—he thinks I'm being silly. He pointed out that I'm the same age he is, that I'm not thinking clearly because of all that's happened, and that I'm being too hasty."

"I'd have to agree with him." I caught my sister's hand and gave it a gentle squeeze. "I know I'm a little flighty at times—"

"A little?"

"Be that as it may, sister dear, right now one of us has a clear head, and believe it or not, that would be me."

"Glory—"

"You love Steven, Janie, and he loves you and always has. Always," I repeated at her protest. "Look, I don't know what's going to happen down the road, what the future has in store for any of us. But God does. And I think I can state with absolute assurance that He put you and Steven back together for a purpose. Not just because you still love each other after all these years, but also because He knew Becca was going to need a family. That she'd need both of you. So before you start thinking about giving back that engagement ring because you're afraid of an eight-year-old, remember all those years, all those prayers, begging God for a child."

"Like Sarah," she said quietly.

"Yeah, right. Abraham and Sarah were a lot older than you when Isaac was born. Think about that when you get discouraged. And pray, Janie. Don't make a decision without praying first."

I didn't know if what I'd said made any sense, but it must have gotten through to her in some small way because she reached over and wrapped me in her arms.

"Thanks, little sister. You've given me a lot to think about. Who'd have thought I'd be getting advice from you?" She softened the words with a gentle laugh. "You're a lot wiser than you think you are, Glory Adele Harper."

"I'm holding you to that statement, Janie. But right now, I've gotta get to bed. I'm beat."

I followed her to the kitchen and waited with her while Misty went out one last time. It wasn't until I spotted the drawing equipment on the table that I remembered Elsie's strange message for Jane. I knew bringing up Elsie could upset my sister's hard-fought-for serenity, but I'd made a promise.

"Elsie asked me to give you a message."

Jane rolled her eyes, then turned back toward the screen to watch the puppy.

"She said to tell you he didn't do it."

"What did you say?" She whipped around to face me.

"He didn't do it," I repeated.

Jane clutched my shoulder for support, her breathing far too shallow. Worried she might collapse, I led her to one of the dinette chairs.

"In light of all that's happened, it shouldn't matter. But . . . she really said that?" When I nodded, Jane closed her eyes as shivers seemed to overtake her body. "Remember the year we went to Pennsylvania for Grandpa's funeral?"

"When I was a freshman and you were a senior. Wasn't it in February? I remember it being cold."

She nodded. "After we got back, I started hearing rumors about a wild party at Elsie's while we were gone. Steven said the evening was a blur. He remembered a lot of loud music and feeling out of it but not much else. He guessed someone had spiked the punch.

"Anyway, a few weeks later, Elsie missed a lot of school. It got to the point that we all wondered if she might be really sick, maybe dying. That sounds melodramatic, but she'd changed so much that year, it seemed a likely explanation. We'd always been best friends, then suddenly she acted like I was her worst enemy."

"That's the year she found out about Zeke and his mother."

"Ah, that explains a lot. I wish she'd told me. Maybe . . ."

"What happened? What does her message mean?"

Misty barked, letting us know she was ready to come in. I urged Jane to stay seated while I let Misty inside and locked up. The puppy went obediently into her kennel and curled up with her favorite stuffed animal.

Back in the living room, Jane perched on the edge of an overstuffed chair. "Elsie claimed she was pregnant with Steven's child."

Stunned by this bombshell I sank into a chair across from my sister.

"When I heard the news, I was even more shocked than you are now. We'd planned a life together—marriage after I'd gotten my elementary ed degree so I could work while he finished medical school. It was a little naïve, but I never doubted our future together.

"I finally got the story out of Steven, how he'd passed out at the party and awakened the next morning on the couch in Elsie's basement. He was so embarrassed about the whole thing that he hadn't told a soul. And even though he didn't remember anything, he was ready to take Elsie at her word, ready to do the honorable thing and marry her. When it turned out she wasn't pregnant, she dumped him and went running back to Rex Stout. After-ward a wild story went around about Rex breaking it off with her because she wasn't good enough for him."

"She told me Rex wanted you."

"Like that would ever happen." Jane rolled her eyes. "I always wondered if Rex walked out on her because she was pregnant."

"So she chose Steven."

"His family had a little money, and he was a good, re-sponsible young man. A perfect candidate. Anyway, after Elsie was back with Rex, Steven and I tried to pick up where we'd left off. I still loved him, but I didn't feel like I could trust him anymore. It took a long time for me to come to terms with what happened, and by that time, I'd met Don." Jane flashed me a sad smile. "I always felt Don was God's special gift to me. I still feel that way."

"But you never forget that first love," I said softly.

"You never do."

Chapter 41

Sunday, August 16

There's something very comforting about going to church after a long, hard week. Coming together with like-minded individuals is part of it, as is seeing friends and neighbors you don't see other times. But for me, the most important thing of all is the total acceptance I feel when I come before the Lord in His house.

Coincidence wasn't involved with the timing and poignancy of the day's theme. The necessity to have a forgiving heart was brought home to everyone when Elsie Wilkes entered our Sunday school room a few minutes late.

People who normally greeted Elsie with warm smiles averted their eyes or turned their heads with a sudden urgency to visit with their neighbor. Jane rose from her seat between Steven and me and led a red-faced Elsie to sit next to us. Those who'd grown up with the two women, who knew their history, looked on in amazement, suddenly convicted of their judgmental attitudes. A quiet descended throughout the room as our Sunday school leader read from the book of Luke.

"Judge not, and you shall not be judged. Condemn not, and you shall not be condemned. Forgive, and you will be forgiven."

The message of forgiveness continued later in the worship service. Pastor Grant gazed out across the sanctuary, noting the absence of many members, and praying for their health and safety.

Anyone familiar with our congregation would immediately have noticed that the Cawley family and Miss Gracie were missing. Ollie, his son, Lizzie, and Miss Gracie always sat in the third pew on the right side—the same pew Ollie's parents had occupied Sunday after Sunday from the day the church was built.

Another notable absence was Marla Hobbs. Marla made sure she was in attendance at every church function whether her husband could be there or not. But neither Marla nor Gordon were there today.

My eyes sought out little Becca Eberling where she sat near the front between her new friends, Kelsey Grant and Chloe Henderson, Seth's number one girlfriend. Before the start of the service, the girls had their heads together, whispering and giggling like they'd been friends forever. Now, under Madison Grant's watchful eyes, they sat straight and tall, trying hard to pay attention.

When the Praise and Prayer segment began, I noticed the girls had their heads together once again. Madison didn't correct them, which seemed curious to me, but the answer soon became apparent.

The girls stood as one unit, holding hands. When Pastor Connor finally nodded in their direction, Kelsey leaned over and whispered in Becca's ear. The little girl nodded, appeared to grip her friends' hands even tighter, and cleared her throat.

"I want to thank God for my new family and ask if everyone would pray about my Mommy and G-ma. She was my grandma. They died." Becca's voice shook, but it was loud and clear. "Kelsey and Chloe said you'd pray for me not to be sad anymore, and for me not to be afraid when I ride in cars." She drew in a deep breath. "I'm ascared of drunk drivers 'cause one hit my Mommy's car. I don't want to be ascared anymore."

There wasn't a dry eye in the church.

After the service, everyone wanted to meet and greet the brave little girl and her new dad. Becca held fast to Steven's hand, trying to hide behind him each time some-one new approached.

"Look at her eyes, Janie. She's scared to death."

My sister excused herself from her future mother-in-law and intercepted the next person bent on greeting Becca and her father. I don't know what she said, but the woman nodded, then stood her ground until Jane was able to whisk the child out of the sanctuary.

"Good," Suzanne Acklin said, patting me on the back. "Keep encouraging her, Glory, and they'll be a family in no time at all."

She and her husband strode over to the crowd surrounding their son. I took the opportunity to find Andi and Seth.

On my way out of the church, I saw Elsie and Gus Bradley speaking with Pastor Connor. Though it was likely about the funeral tomorrow, there was always the chance it was for a more personal reason.

Officer Bradley smiled down at Elsie as he put his arm around her shoulders. Her look of surprise and pleasure was a thing to behold. Of course, so was Bradley smiling. I just might have to find a new nickname for him if this kept up.

Elsie too, for that matter.

I found Andi in the parking lot, talking with several other women whose husbands had been deployed with Jared. Seth and the children played near the circle of women, who I now realized were praying. Seth caught my eye and ran over to me.

"Hey, Bouncy, Bouncy, are we still having our campout tonight?" He tugged on my hand, batting his long lashes, and giving me his best pleading expression.

"I'll have to think about it, buddy. I'm starting a new job tomorrow."

"Oh please, please, please! School starts in a week, Gramma, an' I wanna chance to use my new tent before that."

"I think that's an excellent idea," said a voice behind me. "I always loved sleepovers at my grandmother's house."

I turned to find Elsie grinning like the proverbial Cheshire cat. "Go ahead, Glory. I'm planning to close the office tomorrow for the funer—the day. I've worked you pretty hard these last two days as it is. Enjoy your family."

"I—thanks, Elsie."

"I've appreciated your support," she smiled, "and expect to see you at nine a.m. sharp on Tuesday."

"You've got it."

Officer Bradley came up behind her and slipped his arm around Elsie's waist. She gave me a little wave, then went off with her beau.

"Is she nice now?" How like my grandson to get down to the nitty gritty.

"She's trying."

"Who's trying what?" Andi asked, joining us. "And why the big grin, slugger?"

"Gramma said yes to spending the night in the tent." Seth bounded over to his mother and gave her a gentle hug. "Hi in there, baby," he said, his lips as close as possible to his mother's tummy. "Sometimes when I do that she kicks me."

"She, huh? You're that positive?"

Jane seemed to appear out of nowhere, Becca at her side.

"Goofy here has decided we're having a girl." Andi poked her son in the ribs.

Giggling, he squirmed away to stand behind me. "Hey, Becca, you wanna spend the night in my tent?"

The little girl's smile lit her entire face. "I'll have to ask." She gazed up at Jane. "Do you think Daddy will let me?"

"I'm sure he will, but why don't we make certain." Jane pulled her car keys from her purse and handed them to me. "I'll meet you back at the house. We're going to go make arrangements for Becca to sleep over."

The kids shouted "Yay!" then waved at each other as they parted.

Andi laughed. "Looks like you're going to have your hands full."

"And love every minute of it," I agreed—and meant it.

Chapter 42

We decided to have lunch on the patio—not just to enjoy the beautiful day, but also because it was the only place we could all sit in relative proximity to one another. Since my dining room set was locked up in a storage unit, all that was left was the dinette in the kitchen. And there was no way it could seat eight people comfortably.

Jane's scrumptious pot roast was accompanied by Andi's special orange Jello/tapioca salad with mandarin oranges and a large green bean casserole contributed by Suzanne Acklin. Mrs. Acklin also brought along one of Randi's Dandies' specialties: a triple layer, double chocolate cake with mint chocolate frosting—guaranteed to satisfy any chocoholic's craving.

After we'd stuffed ourselves till we could barely breathe, Steven and his father kept an eye on the kids and Misty while we women cleaned up. A little old fashioned, perhaps, but since we outnumbered the men two to one, it seemed fair.

I watched the camaraderie between Jane and her future mother-in-law, happy to see how well they got along. There seemed to be a genuine affection between the two, which was a definite plus. Jane didn't need any more speed bumps between her and Dr. Dreamboat.

The Acklins left soon after the dishes were done, off to visit a relative in a nearby nursing home. Though Steven and a reluctant Becca went along, Jane remained behind, saying she had a headache and needed to lie down for a while.

Andi and I returned to the patio and stretched out on the lounges. An occasional feathery cloud accented the rich azure of the afternoon sky. A mild northerly breeze rustled the leaves on the silver maple, making it glisten in the sunlight. The giant oak, Seth's favorite climbing tree, whispered its secrets as its branches swayed in the gentle wind.

Seth lay in the grass beneath the jungle gym, his head on Misty's tummy. They were both so still, I wondered if they'd gone to sleep.

"You think they wore each other out?" I nodded in my grandson's direction.

"You'd better hope not, or he'll be up all night." Andi laughed. "Then again, with Becca here too, it's hard to tell if they'll sleep anyway."

"Not a problem. Elsie's given me tomorrow off. I do want to attend Wallace's funeral, though, as a show of support."

"Have they figured out how he died?"

I shook my head. "I have it on very good authority that he was ill when he took a trip to Nevada."

"Nevada? Did he decide to make one of his bevy of blondes an honest woman?" Andi's snort reminded me briefly of Ashley Tanner's unusual laugh.

Ashley's highlighted brown hair could be mistaken for blonde in the right light.

"Bevy of blondes, huh?" I eyed my daughter. "Do you know something I should know?"

"Maybe." Andi lowered the back of the chaise a little more and put her hands behind her head. "Mindy saw Rick Spencer loading you and the others into the squad car Friday. From the way she tells it, you guys had quite an audience."

Mindy Allen, who lives next door to Gracie Naner—right across the street from Wallace—has been Andi's best friend for years. They've spent even more time together these last few months with both their husbands deployed in the Middle East.

"Terrific." I tried to keep my expression innocent. "She ever say anything to you about those blondes?"

Andi giggled. "You are so transparent, Mama. Do me a favor and never take up poker; you haven't got the face for it."

"You're about the fifth person in the last few days to say that to me—the transparent part. I'm starting to get a complex." I rolled onto my side, facing my daughter. "I'm not going to deny I'd like some answers. I don't know how many clues I've handed over to Rick without any reciprocation. It's more than a little frustrating."

"You thought he'd just turn evidence over to you?"

"Not evidence, exactly. Answers to a few questions, a few leads. I found a note that looked like a how-to list to set Jane's house on fire. Does he let me know if it's a forgery? No. I found out that Wallace and Brent were supposed to meet someone over at Mount Pleasant Church after the service on August 2. Instead, he was getting married in Las Vegas."

I slapped my hand across my mouth and rolled over onto my back to avoid looking at my daughter.

"I *knew* it!" Andi clapped her hands. "Lizzie, right?"

I tried to remain perfectly still, figuring any movement of my 'transparent' body would give it away.

"You don't have to answer, Mama. Mindy and I have been betting on Lizzie for the last six months. Besides, his other main squeeze was still in town."

I decided to hazard a guess. "Lila Samson?"

"Very good. Mindy said that between the women going in the front and others running out the back, the man should have put in revolving doors. It's pretty disgusting if you ask me. I'm still trying to picture Marla Hobbs and Hannah Finley being involved with him when they've got perfectly wonderful men at home."

"Which would give the men a motive to kill him. Though I can't see Joe Finley or Gordon Hobbs as a murderer. Hannah, however, would be ruthless enough. Renée Brent, too." I threw up my hands. "There are too many suspects to narrow it down."

"Then why don't you just leave it to Public Safety and let it go?" Jane came out onto the patio followed by David Quinn. "I found this young man wandering around out front. He said you and he talked about him mowing the yard."

"We did—a couple weeks ago. When you didn't mention it again, I thought you weren't interested." I got out of my chaise and offered David a glass of lemonade.

"No thanks, Mrs. H. I can't stay long. I just thought I'd come over and check things out, so I could quote you a price. I'd been kind of tied up lately, but I quit the trash job since I'll be working more hours at the school—oh, hey, I'm sorry. I didn't mean—"

"Don't worry about it. I'm glad you have the position. As for the mowing, we'll probably need it once a week through the end of September. And I can't offer you much—"

"Hey, no problem. I like working outside, and I'd do anything to help you out." He pushed his glasses back on his nose, flashing a smile at the three of us. "Why don't you show me your equipment, so I can get a feel for things."

I pointed him to the door that led directly into the garage. He headed toward it.

Before I could follow, Jane waylaid me. "Since when do you need someone to take care of this yard? I've been fine with mowing."

"You're starting back to school in three days. I thought it would free up some time for you and Steven. And now that Becca's in the picture . . ."

"Yeah, yeah, okay. You'd better get in there before he trips over something and ends up suing you."

I found David checking out the gas trimmer.

"I got that from Sears about three years ago. It's a little heavy but works really well. The mower is a bit older. Ike bought it a few years before he died, but it still runs like a charm."

"I'm sure they're fine, Mrs. H. You have a gas can or do I need to bring my own?"

"No need for that." I led him to the back right corner of the garage—the farthest from the house. "Ike always said it was best to keep it over here on its own, away from where we store the other things."

David picked up the large plastic container. "It's full. Good." With his other hand on his hips, he looked about the small two car garage and nodded.

I offered him what friends said was the going rate for a yard my size. "So what do you think? Are you interested?"

"It's a deal." He set down the gas can and pulled a business card from his wallet with his cell phone number. "Just in case you don't want to call the college."

He was turning to leave when his eyes caught something on the narrow work bench that stretched across part of the rear wall. He shoved an old space heater out of the way and pulled up a small electric trimmer.

"This work? If it does, it will do a great job around your flowers. The other one's got too much power and could tear them up."

I'd had that happen more than once.

"I think it works. You want to try it out?"

He shook his head. "Nah. I'll just put it over here with the big one."

When he tugged on the heavy electrical cord still attached to the trimmer, the space heater tumbled to the floor. Every time he set the thing back on the bench, it wobbled and eventually fell. He was so embarrassed by the incident that I finally told him to just leave it on the floor.

We arranged for him to mow on Thursdays, the one night Jane and I were usually home. With that settled, I led him through the house to the front door. On our way, he noticed the crate he'd brought me from the college, right where he'd left it yesterday afternoon.

"You might want to go through that, Mrs. H. I know the faculty took up a donation for a farewell gift."

"Thanks for the reminder. Things have been a little hectic around here." I opened the front door and thanked him again for coming by.

"No problemo. I've been meaning to do it, and today seemed like a good time."

"Well I appreciate it." I wanted to ask him about last night, about Lila and their drinking, but it just didn't seem important at the moment.

After reaffirming the mow date, he was gone. And I was ready to get back to lounging in my chaise.

Chapter 43

I looked around my living room, praying Jane would overcome her fears so I could retrieve my things from storage. There was something about all the empty spaces—on the walls and surfaces—that was unsettling. Without the photos and knickknacks, the place just didn't have that homey, comfortable feel. The absence of so many items made me sad in a way I couldn't quite explain.

Misty was carrying on outside. Her barking continued until I could no longer hear the rumble of David's car as it drove out of the cul-de-sac. I wondered if she'd been reacting to his presence or if something else—like my grandson—had gotten her wound up.

I picked up the crate, spotted the set of keys David had mentioned, and tried them on the front door. They worked. I'd have liked to put them in the drawer of the entryway table—but it was another in the long list of things Jane had put into storage.

With a heavy sigh, I carted the crate—keys in hand—into the kitchen. I removed my fanny pack from a hook just inside the door that led to the garage, replacing it with the key ring. I grabbed the greeting card, set the crate aside, then aimed for the back door and my comfy chaise lounge.

Just then the doorbell rang. Jane rushed into the house, nearly colliding with me.

"It's probably Steven and Becca," she said, scooting past.

"I'm sure you're right." I lifted the flap on the card but was distracted when Misty flew across the patio, barking her head off.

The doorbell rang again. It had no sooner finished chiming, when it rang one more time. Curious, I set the card and fanny pack on the counter, then headed for the living room.

Jane stood at the front door, blocking Renée Brent's entry. The CCR rep tossed her head, flipping a length of blue-black hair over her shoulder. Her smoldering look bore into my sister, but Jane was having none of it.

"If you think you can come to my house and intimidate me—"

"Your house? I was under the impression this was your sister's place. Isn't yours a pile of rubble?" Brent gripped the door frame, striking a pose worthy of Madonna's song "Vogue."

"You're not welcome here," Jane said evenly. She tried to close the door, but one of Brent's size nine Nikes stopped her.

"I can't wait for you to be charged with murdering Zeke Wallace."

"With a cell phone?" Jane laughed. "I'd think you'd have more reason to want him dead than anyone else, Ms. Brent."

"You're going to fry, you self-righteous, sanctimonious—"

"Just a point of fact, Ms. Brent. Missouri uses lethal injections, not the electric chair." I went to stand by my sister. "And as for the wonderfully expressive terms you're spouting, it seems to me they'd be more accurate if used to describe your belief system. Or would that be lack of belief?"

Brent pulled up sharply, and brought her hand dramatically to her chest. "You have no idea who you're dealing with," she seethed. Misty's barking and growling seemed to punctuate her words.

"So you're not just the petty lackey of an extremist group that espouses vandalism, harassment, and felonious assault against innocent people who don't happen to support your policies?" I smiled when her mouth dropped open. "State your business, Ms. Brent, before I summon law enforcement and have your skinny butt charged with trespassing on private property."

Jane stared at me like I'd lost my mind. Which was strange, since I felt particularly proud of myself at that moment.

"I want access to my files—"

"Wallace's files? They're in police custody, I'm afraid. And I'm pretty sure that's where they're going to stay."

The woman swallowed audibly. "You and Wilkes turned everything over to what you laughingly refer to as cops?"

"And to whom you mistakenly referred to as morons. That got you a long way yesterday, as I recall." I waved Jane aside and took point. "You have a problem with authority, Brent, and from the various charges they've already got against you, I really don't think you want to add to them any time soon."

"You've no idea what you're talking about," she said through clenched teeth. "Our lawyers—"

"Will likely keep you out of jail like all highly paid shysters manage to do for obvious criminal offenders. You see, I may not know who I'm dealing with or what I'm talking about, but I understand a few things very well. Now if there's nothing else I can do for you, I suggest you remove your foot from the door, or I'll have my sister grab one of her nice, sharp knitting needles from that little bag over there. It's not a gun, but I know how to use it."

I don't know if it was the threat of the knitting needle or if she'd decided she'd had enough, but she took her foot off the door.

"You haven't seen the last of me." Her narrowed eyes shot daggers in Jane's direction, but she just gave me a look of dismissal. "CCR will bring this town to its knees—you wait and see."

"Great. And until that time, *goodbye.*" I slammed and locked the door.

"What the devil was that all about?" Jane had turned pale, and her hands were shaking.

"Remember I told you about Elsie and me going through Wallace's things yesterday? Well, there's something in there Brent wants really bad. She was shredding papers when we got there and wasn't too happy about being forced to stop. I have a source that stated Wallace was uneasy with the way Brent was behaving, that he might have been a little afraid of her."

"Do you think she killed him?"

"I don't know, Janie. It's possible. I know she lied about the last time she saw Wallace. She claimed she caught him and Lizzie in bed together on the second, when I know for a fact neither of them were in town."

"They were in Nevada getting married, right?"

"Wha—where?"

"Andi told me a few minutes ago. Relax. I won't say anything."

"You'd better not. Ollie would have both our heads on a platter." I thought about the fierceness of Ollie's expression as we'd driven away yesterday. Maybe he . . .

The image in my mind was not a pretty one.

"Glory? Something wrong?"

I shook my head, erasing the thoughts on my mental blackboard. Olav Cawley couldn't have killed Wallace. If he had, he wouldn't have ditched the man's car in his stock pond or 'accidentally' run over the body with his tractor mower—which I assumed is how Wallace's hand was severed.

He hated the man, hated Lizzie's relationship with Wallace, but he wasn't a murderer.

"No, I'm fine. What do you think about turning off the air and opening up the house?"

My rapid change of subjects received a roll of the eyes and a laugh from my sister.

"Don't want to share your thoughts on this case?"

"Nope. I just want to enjoy the rest of the day. So how about it? Open it up?"

"They're expecting the heat and humidity to go back up tomorrow, so it hardly seems worth it."

The doorbell rang. A quick peek out the small window in the top of the door revealed Dr. Dreamboat and Becca on the other side, both with their hands full.

I let them inside, and Jane and I relieved them of their burdens.

"Daddy stopped at Wal-Mart and got me a new sleeping bag." Becca nearly danced in her excitement. "We brought over UNO Attack too. It's a really fun game we can all play."

Jane's expression brightened as she watched the little girl. My sister hadn't said anything about a change of heart, but from the looks of things, I believed it wasn't far in coming.

"Did you know your garage door is open about two feet? I tried to get it shut, but it's stuck fast."

"Daddy got a splinter from the door, Aunt Jane. You gonna get it out?" Becca wrinkled her nose. "I don't like needles," she whispered to me.

"Me neither," I whispered back. "Why don't you and I go out back while Jane doctors the doctor."

Becca giggled, grabbed my hand, and tugged. I gave the two lovebirds a jaunty wave then happily followed the newest member of my family.

Chapter 44

"Lila Samson?" Andi looked confused. "I don't think I've talked to her since she graduated from high school—except when she answered your phone at the college."

"So you've no idea why she'd have something against you?" I waved at the kids who were both hanging upside down on the jungle gym.

"No, I . . . wait a second." She clicked a thumbnail against her teeth, a sure sign she was trying to figure something out. Her eyes suddenly brightened, and I knew she'd hit on an idea.

"You know, Lila was always getting into trouble. I don't have the details, of course, but I know she got suspended a lot. The last time was pretty close to her graduation. She was tossed for smoking in the girls' restroom."

"What's that got to do with you?"

"She always blamed me for turning her in since I was the last one to leave after she lit up. I tried to tell her it wasn't true, but she wouldn't listen."

"Sounds a lot like her big sister. Hannah doesn't listen to reason either."

"I can't believe she still holds a grudge. How lame is that? I mean, it's been what, almost fifteen years?"

Andi could never stay angry for more than a few minutes; she was always ready to make up and put the incident behind her. It's too bad Lila hadn't learned to do the same. If she had, she might not have gotten mixed up with a man like Zeke Wallace.

I didn't approve of Lila's relationship with David Quinn, but there might be an up side. Maybe David could help her change her life for the better.

Dr. Dreamboat and Jane came out onto the patio. It looked like Dr. Jane had done a thorough job on his hands; he had small BAND-AIDs on several fingers.

"I tried to pull your garage door down from the inside, and it only moved about six inches before it stuck fast."

"You have to release the lever—"

"We did." Jane took a seat at the table. "Steven tried it both ways, and it's stuck. It's a good thing we don't have to go to work tomorrow—there's no way to get the cars out."

"Don't worry about the kids, Mama. I can pick up both of them in the morning and take Becca to the Acklins'."

"Or she could stay here," Dr. Dreamboat said, a hopeful gleam in his eyes.

There was only a slight hesitation before Jane smiled and nodded. "That would be fine."

Misty settled down at my feet while we gathered around the table for a rousing game of UNO Attack. Every time a breeze picked up one of the cards or the game spit out more than a couple cards, Seth and Becca giggled like crazy.

After two games to five hundred, the adults were tired and the kids were ready to eat. Andi and I left Jane and Dr. Dreamboat to finish an improvised game of kickball—it was more the kids kicking the ball, then Steven and Jane fighting to get it before Misty did. It added a special flavor to the contest.

Andi and I put together a platter of cold cuts, cheese, bread, and crackers. We carted out pickles and other condiments, placing them on the table alongside the platter. Lemonade and ice water with lemon slices, and the leftover cake from Randi's Dandies, completed our dinner offerings. And from the way everyone dug in, we'd chosen well.

Andi and Steven said their goodnights as the first lightning bugs made their nightly appearance. The kids passed out hugs and kisses before running off to join Misty in the pursuit of the magical little creatures. While Jane walked Dr. Dreamboat to his car, I stood on the porch with Andi, promising to watch out for the kids.

"You're sure that platform is safe?" my daughter questioned for the tenth time.

"You read the specs when we ordered it, sweetie. I could be up there with them, and it would still hold. Of course, there'd be no room for them to sleep . . . "

"I'm being serious, Mama. We brought Seth's two-man tent if they aren't comfortable with the other one. It's easy to erect and has a nice floor lining."

"Go home, honey. Take a long, relaxing bath, then curl up with a good book." I kissed her on the forehead.

"I'm not used to being . . . alone. It's not the same with Jared gone. We used to have a date night whenever Seth stayed over with you."

I wrapped her in a bear hug. "Maybe you could call one of your friends, see if any of them want a girl's night out. Or you could stay here if you want."

Andi shook her head, her long blonde curls dancing across her slender shoulders. "Seth wouldn't understand . . . and it might scare him if he realized I was afraid of being alone. I can't do that. It's hard enough on him with his daddy gone." She gave me a quick peck on the cheek before skipping down the porch steps. "See you in the morning, Mama. You guys have fun."

Jane joined me on the porch. We waved goodbye to our loved ones, then went back inside.

"I think I'll set up a bed for myself on the patio," I said after making certain the front door was locked. "Just to be close if either of the kids need something. I've got an old sleeping bag—"

"Sounds good. Would you happen to have two bags?"

A search of Andi's old bedroom closet yielded two tightly wound sleeping bags. We collected enough pillows for all of us, then carried everything outside.

"Hey, Bouncy, Bouncy, you have some jars we can use to catch lightning bugs?"

"Fireflies," Becca corrected with a giggle.

"Yeah, fireflies," Seth agreed. He examined the items Jane and I were unloading. "Where's our sleeping bags and backpacks?"

"Still in the living room. Why don't you and Becca go get them while I look for those jars?"

Jane followed the duo into the house via the back door; I went in through the garage entrance. I was pretty sure there were at least two small coffee cans on the work bench that Seth had used before to catch bugs.

The murky light from the single window in the door wasn't enough to keep me from running into things on my way to the light switch near the kitchen entrance. I banged into the electric weed trimmer, knocking it over, and catching my foot in a tangle of the orange extension cord. It was still wrapped around my ankle when I finally got the light on, which made the first order of business removing the cord and wrapping it up so it wouldn't attack anyone else.

When I tucked the trimmer next to the larger one and the lawn mower, the tangy smell of old grass and gasoline seemed a little stronger than usual. Just to be on the safe side, I felt around the fuel tanks for a leak, but they appeared fine.

After nearly tripping over the old space heater, still where it had fallen while David Quinn was here, I finally found Seth's bug cans. Desiccated lettuce and other unidentifiable things were in both containers, meaning I got the wonderful job of cleaning them out for the new occupants.

When I entered the kitchen, Jane and the kids were at the dinette eating ice cream bars.

"You found them!" Seth said around a bite of gooey fudge.

"Yep, and they'll be ready for your fireflies in just a few minutes." I dumped the contents of both cans, making a face as the stuff plopped into the garbage can. Seth elbowed Becca to look at me, and soon they were laughing so hard it's a wonder ice cream didn't come out their noses.

It wasn't long till they were outside with their freshly washed cans, chasing after lightning bugs, with Misty running and jumping at their sides.

"I don't know about you," Jane yawned, "but just watching them makes me tired. I'm ready to curl up on that chaise and conk out."

"They won't be ready to settle down until they catch a few bugs." I checked my watch. "It's almost nine."

I glanced at the wall phone, wondering why I hadn't heard from Blue Eyes. He had said he would call today.

"Thinking about Rick. Or should I say *Blue Eyes*?" My sister gave me a sly grin. "Still want to tell me there's nothing going on between you two?"

My answer was short and sweet—I stuck out my tongue—before I dashed into the living room and grabbed the cordless phone. With it in hand, I turned on the light to the half bath in the hall, then went through the house switching off other lights. On my way out the back door, I swung my fanny pack over my shoulder and picked up the greeting card from my former faculty members.

Jane had lit a citronella lamp on the patio table to help keep away unwanted visitors. She'd also brought out the two small camp lanterns I kept on hand for power outages. One lantern was sitting between our lounge chairs; she was taking the other out to the platform tent. I set my things on the table, then picked up the kids' sleeping bags and followed my sister.

While we spread out their bags, Seth and Becca grew tired of catching bugs. They popped up now and again to check on our progress, then went back to seeing who could swing the highest. Misty's occasional yips and their giggles had Jane and me stopping to watch their newest game. Every time they swung forward, Misty tried to capture their toes.

Once the sleeping bags and pillows were comfortably arranged, we managed to convince the kids to check out our handiwork. They liked it so much they decided to bed down—as long as one of us read them a story.

To my surprise and delight, Becca chose Jane as the storyteller. A wink from me kept Seth from protesting and allowed Jane to bask in the glow of Becca's smile. I was sent to retrieve their backpacks with their books and sleeping companions from the patio. After hugs and kisses from both kids, I returned to my chaise while Jane read.

After checking my cell phone to make certain I hadn't missed any calls, I hovered over the small lantern to read my card. Summer school meant about half the faculty was gone, but those who'd heard of my dismissal had gathered nearly seventy dollars as a farewell gift. Only two people hadn't signed the card: Dr. Finley and her sister, Lila.

Misty had followed me to the patio and sat alongside my chair. I reached down to pat her and could feel the sudden bristling of her usually soft fur. A low growl rumbled in her throat, then she was off across the yard in a flash. She didn't bark, but the growling continued as she paced back and forth in front of the fence that separated my property from the old Stout place next door. She was still stalking the area a half hour later when Jane left the kids. No matter what we did, we couldn't entice her to join us on the patio.

It didn't take long for Jane to fall asleep. I stayed awake until the whispers and giggles from the platform tent finally stopped and Misty returned to the patio to bed down between Jane's and my chairs.

With no moon, the cloudless night was lit by a zillion stars. I stared up into the heavens, thanking God for the beautiful day and the hope I'd seen in my sister's eyes as she'd watched Becca play.

"Please help Becca through this difficult and confusing time, dear Father, and grant her peace."

That was something we could all use.

Chapter 45

I batted at the hand on my shoulder, too weary to speak or open my eyes. I felt someone shake me again, a little more forcefully this time.

"I think someone's in the house," Jane whispered, her mouth close to my ear.

"Not possible," I mumbled. "It's all locked up."

"Did you put the security chain on the front door? Glory?" She shook me again.

"The chain?" I opened my eyes to find her hovering over me with a sky full of stars as a backdrop.

"Are you awake?" she demanded.

"My eyes are open, and I'm talking to you, so that's a good indication."

Misty growled nearby. I prayed she wouldn't start barking and wake the kids.

"Should we call 911?"

"For a noise that could have come from anywhere? You know how sound gets distorted here in the cul-de-sac."

I felt around in the chair for the cordless phone I'd brought outside in the hope Blue Eyes would call. I didn't find it, but I did discover my fanny pack stuffed in a little pocket created by the way the sleeping bag draped across the chaise. I retrieved my cell phone, then joined my sister at the back door.

"I can't see a thing," she said, peering inside the darkened house.

"Why don't you grab the lantern, and we'll check it out."

Even though Jane didn't look thrilled with the idea, she did as I suggested. When she switched on the lantern, I noticed a garden trowel lying next to a planter of wilted geraniums. I snatched it up, almost laughing at the memory of Miss Gracie confronting Wallace with her trowel in hand.

"What's that for?"

"A weapon," I said, gripping it tightly in my hand.

Jane shook her head. "Why don't we just have Public Safety check things out?"

"Don't be silly. We're fine."

I felt a little odd, sneaking into my own house. But if it made Jane feel safe and kept her from putting the rest of my belongings in storage, it would be worth it.

We opened the door and were assaulted by the smell of the trash I'd forgotten to empty. Jane pinched her nose and gave me a disapproving glance before we continued into the dining room.

The light from the lantern sent ghostly shadows out in front of us that bobbed and weaved as we walked. Jane stayed behind me, one hand on my shoulder, the other holding the lantern high and out to the side.

"Check the front door," she whispered, her hot breath tickling my ear.

The security chain wasn't hooked, but both the deadbolt and the lock on the knob were engaged. Jane fastened the chain as I headed down the hallway. The light spilling out from the half bath illuminated my office enough that I could see no one lurked inside. When Jane finally joined me, we proceeded to check the three bedrooms and all the closets.

"There's no one here but us chickens," I said as we finished up in her room. "Now aren't you glad we didn't call 911?"

"I could've sworn I heard something. And the way Misty was acting . . . "

"She was likely reacting to you, Janie. If she'd been really upset, she'd have been barking her head off."

"You're right, of course. It's just . . . " She shivered. "My nerves have been so raw since my fire. I have to get past this, stop allowing my fear to control me."

I draped an arm over my sister's shoulders as we made our way back to the kitchen.

"It really does smell in here." I lifted the lid on the trash can and quickly tied off the bag.

"It's not just that." Jane sniffed. "It smells . . . hot."

Even though there were no indicator lights on the stove, Jane checked all the burners, then opened the oven and felt the element.

"I don't know." She sniffed again. "Maybe it's something coming in from outside."

"Since we've searched everywhere else, I might as well check the garage. Why don't you go on to bed. I'll just be a moment."

I had my hand on the doorknob when she stopped me. "Let's both go to bed. I've already allowed my fear to steal enough of our night. Look at Misty." She nodded to the screen, where the puppy sat waiting for us. "If she's not worrying, why should I?"

"Excellent point."

I was grateful to return to my chaise. After tucking the cell phone in my fanny pack, I settled down into the chair, pulling the sleeping bag across my legs. But no matter how hard I tried, I couldn't get my mind to shut off.

There were flashes of Marla, defiant in her biker babe outfit, then later, contrite and afraid of going to jail. Hannah Finley took center stage, ordering me to go to Wallace's home to search for his grades, then handing me the key. Haughty Hannah morphed into Angry Hannah as she stared at the delivery receipt from her husband's store.

My mind refused to go blank, to blot out thoughts of Lizzie's distress and Ollie's fury. I pictured a field of wild flowers that suddenly changed to a cow pasture with a stock pond tainted by Wallace's Mini Cooper. Nothing I did seemed to work.

Renée Brent's taunting voice echoed through my brain, accompanied by a gum-smacking Lila Samson, toting a six pack, and calling my family names.

Frustrated, I opened my eyes and stared up at the beauty of the stars in the night sky. Misty must have noticed my restlessness, for she left Jane's side and sat with her head on my knees. I wound my fingers in her silky hair, drew in a deep breath, and closed my eyes.

Misty jumped into my lap and licked my face until I swatted her away. She'd yanked me from a peaceful dream of blue skies and children's laughter to a reality of deep guttural growls.

She hopped off me and onto Jane, her growls and persistent barking quickly bringing us both to full consciousness. Once she was sure she had our attention, she darted out across the yard to the jungle gym, barking frantically.

Jane flew out of the chaise and was partway to the anxious puppy when Seth and Becca peered out of the tent. I grabbed the lantern, switching it on as I joined my family.

"Are you two all right?" Jane asked, climbing the ladder to the platform.

"Why's she barking like that, Aunt Jane? She woke us up." Seth rubbed his eyes, looking around until he spotted me. He'd never admit to being afraid, especially in front of Becca, but I could tell he was.

"It's going to be all right, honey," I told him. "She probably saw a rabbit or something."

My grandson nodded, doubt filling his big blue eyes.

"Can you sleep up here with us, Miss Jane?" Becca's voice shook with uncertainty. "I don't think I like it by ourselves."

"Well, I—"

"Stay with the kids, Janie. I've gotta get Misty to settle down before she wakes the entire neighborhood."

One of the kids switched on the lantern in the tent, then Jane climbed inside.

I turned to find Misty running back and forth across the width of the yard. When she wasn't barking, she was growling so fiercely I was actually afraid to approach her.

"It's okay, girl, it's okay. Come on, Misty, come here." I knelt down, patting my leg.

The puppy ran to me, whining and crying like she was in pain. I set the lantern down and did my best to check her over to make sure she was all right. Though she wagged her tail and licked my hands, her entire body was one quivering mass. She didn't appear to be in any physical pain that I could see, but something had her scared.

"Is everything all right?" Jane called from the tent.

"I think so. You guys try to get back to sleep."

Misty continued to shiver even though I was holding her. I lifted my lantern, turning it from side to side, trying to search the darkness for what might have frightened her.

I turned toward a sound behind me, my heart thudding. Jane was climbing down the ladder, while behind her the kids waited their turn to follow.

"What's up?"

"We've decided to spend the rest of the night inside. We're going to spread the sleeping bags on the living room floor."

The moment Jane's feet hit the ground, Misty broke away from me. She ran to Jane and resumed her frantic barking. No matter which way Jane turned, the puppy refused to allow her to pass.

"Glory, what the devil is going on?"

"Looks like she wants you to stay there. I don't know—just stay put for a moment, and let me look around."

As I headed back toward the house, I saw a light flicker in the window of the garage door. I knew it hadn't been there before.

I ran to the patio with Misty going crazy behind me. I slipped into my sandals while I searched the sleeping bag for my fanny pack, keeping my eyes trained on the window. Instead of wasting precious time to hunt for my cell phone, I flung the purse over my shoulder, then cautiously approached the back door of the garage. The closer I got, the more certain I was that the orange glow wasn't a light but a fire.

"Glory?"

I turned and started to run when I smelled the gas.

Chapter 46

Frantic voices and hands touched my face, lifting me out of an unfamiliar blackness. The closer I came to consciousness, the more aware I became of the pain that seemed to cover my entire body.

My chest ached like the air had been knocked out of me. Just as I managed to open my eyes, I was seized by a fit of coughing.

"Her eyes are open, Aunt Jane!" Seth's anxious face peered into mine. "You're gonna be okay now, Gramma. Can you hear it? An ambulance is coming."

I tried to speak, but another spasm overwhelmed me, taking my breath away.

What was going on? Why did Seth look so frightened? And why was it so dark?

The sound of crying caught my attention. Turning my head slightly, I saw Becca clutching Jane around the waist, her little face smashed against my sister's chest. My eyes strayed to the night sky and the strange light that seemed to flutter at the edges of my vision.

My olfactory senses returned at the same time memories washed over me—Becca and Seth's sleepover, Jane's fear someone was in the house, Misty's frantic barking. There was something else . . .

The smell of smoke in the air filled my heart with dread, bringing to life the haunting suspicion: a fire in the garage.

I flew up from the ground, startling my grandson and the puppy he held so tightly. Jane reached out to steady me as a wave of dizziness threatened to send me back into that strange darkness. She led me to a swing on the jungle gym and eased me onto it, all the while talking on a cell phone.

"Put your head between your knees," she ordered. "And be still. Help is on the way."

Multiple sirens filled the night air, blaring their discordant tones to a brain that was still trying to comprehend what was going on.

I followed Jane's directions, lowering my head, while my grandson patted my back and offered reassuring words. Misty sat at my feet, licking my hands, my knees, anything she could reach. When it finally felt like my head wouldn't fly from my shoulders, I raised it and looked at the flames that were engulfing my garage.

"Was there an . . . explosion?"

Seth nodded, his eyes wide. "It went boom, and you flew." His voice shook. "I tried not to cry, Gramma, but I was so scared. I love you so much . . . "

I wrapped Seth in my arms, trying to soothe away his fears. His narrow shoulders shook as tears coursed down his cheeks.

Becca peered out around Jane, her tear-stained face showing relief when our eyes met.

"Are you—are you okay?"

"I'm fine, honey. A little shook up, but fine."

"You flew," she said, obviously astounded.

"God gave me wings to keep me safe."

I smiled, holding a hand out to her. She latched onto me, leaving the safety of Jane's side to wrap me in a hug.

"I was ascared of you dying," she whispered.

The backyard suddenly seemed filled with people. Someone threw a blanket around my shoulders and helped me out of the swing. A man dressed in firefighter gear lifted Becca in one arm, Seth in the other. Another captured my confused puppy, threw a blanket over her head, and took off across the yard.

"It's okay, sweetheart. Everything's going to be okay."

I'd never seen Blue Eyes in his fire gear, could barely see him now as dark as it was, but I knew his voice. He lifted me in his arms and rushed along the end of the house away from the fire.

The entire cul-de-sac was filled to overflowing with emergency vehicles. Both of Tarryton's fire trucks were present, as were police cars, and Tarryton Valley Hospital's ambulance. Blue Eyes deposited me with the ambulance personnel, then turned to go. I fought the hands pawing at me to run after him. I ended up running *into* him, but at least he stopped.

"What are you doing?" he said, righting me in the growing crowd of looky loos.

"Jane was right. Whoever set her fire did this."

"Go back to the paramedics. Let them check you over." He tried to turn me in their direction, but I wanted none of that.

"Don't you see? This all has to be related, the fires and Wallace's death. Firebugs like to watch their handiwork, Rick. He's out there right now. Watching. All we have to do is look for someone who doesn't belong here. We have to keep an eye on the crowd."

"The only thing you have to do is let the paramedics examine you." He scooped me up and, despite my protests, returned me to the ambulance, setting me inside. "Keep hold of her until you've checked her out. If she tries to get away before that, give her a sedative."

"I'll take care of her." Dr. Dreamboat appeared at the side of the vehicle, carrying his daughter. My sister, Andi, and Seth stood next to him, the shock on their faces quieting my retort.

Andi rushed over and wrapped me in her arms. "Are you okay, Mama? I can't believe this is happening."

"I'm fine, honey, don't worry; it's not good for the baby." I touched her tummy, then patted her cheek. "What about Seth, sweetie. Did he get hurt?"

"We're all going to be checked out," Jane said, coming forward. "We were far enough away when the—when you . . . were hit, that we're okay. Physically, anyway."

Blue Eyes disappeared in the crowd while the two paramedics went to work examining my family and me. Jane and the kids were pronounced injury free by one paramedic before the other had finished his painstaking examination of me.

When he realized I was cooperating, Steven returned to stand with the others. He lifted his daughter back into his arms, facing her away from the fire.

As the EMT poked and prodded my aching body, I evaluated our location. From the street lamp overhead, and the angle the ambulance was parked, I calculated we were in front of the Devlins' home—directly across the street from my place. The apex of the cul-de-sac, the old Stout property, was off to my right. Behind that property and mine was an empty field—and a perfect escape route for whoever set the fire.

"You've got cuts on the back of your head and arms from glass and debris, and a possible concussion, Mrs. Harper. We need to get you to the hospital to have—"

"Is it life-threatening?"

"Excuse me?" The young man stared at me.

"Right now, is it life threatening?" I glanced out at my family's worried faces staring back at me. "Because if it's not immediately life threatening, I want to stay."

"Head injuries are nothing to fool around with, Mrs. Harper. We can have you at the hospital in minutes. The

ER doctor has been apprised of your injuries and will want to take a closer look to ascertain the degree of head trauma and whether or not you have internal bleeding."

"Fine, but not now."

"Ma'am—"

"I feel perfectly all right, Mr., er . . . " I searched his chest for a name tag, thankful the letters didn't swim when I found it. "Mr. Banks. You've done a wonderful job, and I'll take your advice into consideration, but right now I need to stay here."

A loud boom filled the night air, the concussion so strong it felt like the ambulance rocked. Everyone's attention was drawn toward my house, giving me the perfect opportunity to slip away. I ducked into the crowd, crouching low as I passed my family.

"Where's Mama?" Andi's voice was barely audible, but Jane's sounded loud and clear.

"When I find her, I'm gonna kill her myself!"

I kept my head down, refusing to look toward the fire that was consuming my home, and counting on the growing crowd and all the excitement to keep me hidden. A sharp bark off to my left along with a sudden flurry of activity told me Misty was loose—and she'd spotted someone she didn't like.

The puppy flew by me a moment later, disrupting the crowd and giving me the perfect opportunity to stand up straight and look in the direction she was heading. Lila Samson stood outside the main glow of the lamplight in the Stout's yard. Even with her blonde hair covered by a hoodie, I was able to make a positive ID.

I ducked back down and pushed my way through the crowd, following the sound of my puppy's barks. When I finally broke free of the people watching my house burn,

Lila was nowhere in sight. But it wasn't going to be difficult to find her with Misty leading the way.

Around the side of the old mansion, between the house and detached garage, the backyard fence stood open. Only the light from the fire lit my way, and even that was greatly diminished behind the house. I walked carefully across the uneven ground, hoping I wouldn't fall into a hole the city had failed to fill.

A yelp and cry up ahead ended Misty's barking, then the sound of feet running over firmly packed ground continued, going away from me. I started to run as well but stumbled and fell to my knees, my hands stretched out in front of me. A whimper just to my left led me in that direction, still on my hands and knees, searching for my puppy.

By the time I found her, she was no longer crying. Fear gripped me as I lay my head on her chest; she was still breathing.

A spotlight of some kind briefly lit the area. It was enough for me to see the piece of two-by-four that had probably been used as a weapon. I picked it up, weighing it in my hands before deciding it would work as well against a human as it had against my puppy. Before getting up, I lay my head back on Misty's chest and gently patted her. I'd no idea where Lila had struck her and didn't want to risk hurting her more.

"You'll be okay, Misty-girl," I whispered. "She won't get away with this."

With the bat-length of two-by-four in hand, I rose. The sound of singing up ahead stopped me momentarily. I didn't recognize the tune, even the voice was so distorted I began to wonder if I'd been right about my ID of Lila. But whether it was her or—Ashley—it gave me a general direction.

But only if the echo effect in the area wasn't playing tricks on my hearing.

My heartbeat throbbed in my head as I continued my pursuit over the rough terrain of the Stout's backyard. Gravel beneath my feet told me I'd reached the alleyway behind the houses; the open field was next. And right now, there was a lone figure in the field, singing at the top of her lungs.

The singing stopped when a shadow separated from the trees up ahead. I sank to my hands and knees, hoping the darkness and high grass would cover me.

"*What the hell was that?* I told you there were kids around." The man's voice caused bile to rise in my throat.

"It was glorious, stupendous, my best performance ever!" Lila Samson shouted. "Why do you have to be such a wimp, David? They'll never figure it out. They never have."

That's what she thought.

I started to rise, only to be knocked to the ground in a tackle worthy of an NFL linebacker. A hand clamped roughly over my mouth.

"If you utter a sound, I'll throw you in jail."

I fought the urge to bite his hand, deciding it was better to acquiesce.

"Stay put," Rick ordered in a hoarse whisper as he rose into a crouch.

"They hurt Misty." Before the sentence was completed he'd already disappeared.

The voices gradually receded. Either they'd stopped talking or moved too far away. I waited for what seemed like an hour or more but was probably less than fifteen minutes.

Finally I turned around, using the fire licking the sky as my marker. Before I'd reached the alley, Misty bounded out of the dark, yipping in pleasure at finding me. Tears streamed from my eyes as I bent to hug her.

"Thank you, Father." I took hold of Misty's collar and headed toward the mayhem in front of my house.

With every step, I uttered another prayer: praise that Jane and the kids were all right, a plea for angels to surround and protect Rick in his pursuit of David Quinn and Lila Samson, another praise that Misty hadn't been killed, and a big thank you that I'd survived.

At least until my family got hold of me.

A few minutes later I joined Jane and Andi where they stood next to the ambulance. Seth and Becca, who were sitting on the bumper, spotted me first.

"Gramma!" Seth ran to me, enveloping both Misty and me in a hug.

"Oh, Mama! Thank you, Father!" Andi threw her arms around all of us, tears of relief flooding her eyes. "How could you—why did you—"

"Have you forgotten who you're talking to, Andi?" Jane's voice was harsh, but her quivering chin told a different story.

When Steven came around the side of the ambulance, Becca jumped from the bumper and latched onto his hand. He gave her a quick hug as he sized up the situation. After removing his belt, he fastened it into a makeshift leash around Misty's collar.

"She's been hurt," I told him. "She should see a doctor."

"I'll make you a deal. You go with the EMTs, and I'll get her to a vet."

Another explosion rocked the cul-de-sac, scattering ashes and debris all around us. I looked helplessly at the place that had been my home for more than twenty years, wondering if there would be anything left when they finally got the fire extinguished.

"I'll go," I said, still watching the bright red-orange flames as they leaped toward the stars.

"Oh, my. Look!"

Jane pointed to the Stout's driveway where Rick and two other officers were leading Lila Samson and David Quinn toward the street. A squad car parted the crowd and pulled alongside the suspects, neither of whom seemed to comprehend what was going on.

I'd worked alongside David for three years, with Lila for two. The thought of their betrayal deflated me. As the two were assisted into the squad car, blackness seeped into the edge of my vision. I turned to my sister and daughter, reaching for someone to hold onto.

"Please catch me," was all I managed to say before the darkness descended.

Chapter 47

Saturday, August 22

The police found evidence in Lila Samson's apartment that connected her not only to the fires at Jane's and my houses, but also to the rash of fires ten years earlier. Tarryton had found their firebug, but had they found their murderer?

Chemical analysis of Zeke Wallace's hair showed he'd been given small doses of arsenic over the last several months. Whether a final, larger dose had killed him wasn't determined—at least it wasn't common knowledge. As with most criminal cases, specifics were kept from the press— even when they were as nosy and persistent as Will Garrett.

No matter how Wallace had died, Public Safety appeared to have compiled enough evidence to charge both Lila Samson and David Quinn with the murder. David had admitted to helping Lila set up the false clues in Wallace's house. The note I'd found with Jane's name on it had, indeed, been a forgery as Elsie suspected. And while David swore he had no idea what had happened to the professor, Lila swore he'd been in on it from the beginning— even to using Wallace's house as a love nest when he was away. From what I understood, the two were so busy pointing fingers at each other that the authorities might never sort the whole thing out.

Motives for the fire and murder were mostly speculation—at least on the part of those outside the law enforcement community. As for the fires, a long-held grudge against my family, fueled by Jane accusing Lila of shoplifting, likely sealed my sister's fate. And after I confronted Lila outside the liquor store, she probably figured she could take out both Jane and me with a single blow.

But what about the poisoning and eventual murder of Zeke Wallace?

Jane now believed it was Lila, not Lizzie, she'd seen ducking into the closet that day at Wallace's—two days before the fire that destroyed Jane's home. Perhaps Wallace had decided to break it off with Lila. That would account for the crying Jane heard. Lila had to know about Lizzie Cawley and the draw she had for the professor. Jealousy could have been the fuel behind the poisoning and eventual murder.

Or maybe there was a simpler motive. After all, the victim was into blackmail . . .

Though everyone in town would have liked to include Renée Brent in the indictment, it appeared she was innocent—at least of murder and arson. Realizing she might be linked to the arsonist, Brent admitted to shredding the file Wallace had put together on Lila's penchant for setting fires. She'd only agreed to shred it after Lila promised to reveal where Wallace kept his 'special' files, including the investigation he'd begun on Brent.

The day we'd caught Brent at the house, she'd expected Lila to show up and keep her side of the bargain. Being caught with her hand in the cookie jar, so to speak, and charged with trespassing had not been on her agenda.

Or that of the CCR. Scuttlebutt had it that the CCR had threatened to withdraw Brent's lawyer if Brent didn't fully cooperate in the murder investigation. I was still waiting to find out what all that entailed—and if we'd finally seen the last of the woman. With all the charges leveled against her, maybe the CCR lawyer wouldn't be able to keep her out of jail.

Even Hannah Finley stepped up to do the right thing, going to Public Safety with the information that her sister had forged her name on the refrigerator delivery receipt. She and her parents—the people Wallace and Brent had intended to meet at Pleasant Valley Church—had been protecting Lila all her life. But the possibility that her sister was a murderer was outside Hannah's comfort zone.

It was Hannah's last-minute decision to go to the police that tied Blue Eyes up Sunday afternoon—the reason he hadn't called me. Who could have guessed Hannah Finley's action would throw us a lifeline—the phones I'd held onto waiting for Rick to call?

When the college decided to give Hannah another chance as department chair, she offered to rehire me. But ready to try something different, I turned her down.

Lizzie Cawley attended Zeke Wallace's funeral as his wife, admitting before the curious crowd that gathered her devotion to a man everyone hated. It was reported that Ollie stood by his granddaughter's side like a statue. Probably because Miss Gracie stayed close by to keep him in line.

I spent two days in the hospital with a concussion. They said it was necessary for observational purposes. I figured it was because no one wanted me to know how badly the fire damaged my house.

Either that or they didn't want me wandering off, trying to find something else to investigate.

As more information trickled in, I learned there had been a cell phone and extra batteries connected to a small amount of gunpowder beneath a false bottom in the crate David Quinn had delivered. When this makeshift bomb failed to work, it was speculated that David was sent to check out my garage. Since we'd talked about him helping out with the mowing, it gave him a perfect excuse.

I was also told we were lucky the garage door had stuck open. Had it been closed, the explosion that tossed me into the air might have killed me. Lila's pièce de résistance was using the old space heater. After fraying the cord to cause a short, she'd set the unit on high, cut the fuel lines in both cars, and emptied the can of gasoline on everything that could help fuel the fire.

It had been a harrowing experience for everyone involved—especially for Seth and Becca. Though they had occasional nightmares, they both fully believed they'd seen an angel lift me off the ground during the explosion. Their unconditional love for their Savior gave them the best explanation of all.

Jane and Steven had grown even closer these last few days. Though my sister still wondered about her ability to be a mother at fifty-five, her love for Becca was quickly winning her over. Each time I saw them together, I knew this was how it was meant to be . . . God's perfect plan.

Misty was also doing well. According to the vet, she'd received a glancing blow. And while it fractured a rib, there wasn't any permanent damage. She was currently being shuttled back and forth between Andi's house and the Acklins'. She couldn't seem to make up her mind which of the kids she wanted to stay with. As much as I loved the puppy and her heroics, I was voting for Becca as her permanent mistress. They seemed to be a match made in heaven.

Without a car and with almost half my house destroyed, I was dependant on Andi for a place to live, and on Elsie to get me to and from work. Sally Hawkins was working with the insurance company to get me back on my feet, but I knew it wouldn't happen any time soon.

As I sat in Rick's car in front of my ruined home, I thanked God none of us had been badly hurt.

"Janie really knew what she was doing," I said, thinking about everything she'd insisted go into storage.

Rick stroked my cheek. "Going with your gut is sometimes the best thing you can do."

I leaned into his hand, accepting the comfort it offered. "I think it was more God instinct than gut instinct."

"You're probably right. Are you ready to go?"

I took one last look at the house, hoping the enormous tarps the construction company had put up wouldn't blow away in a sudden storm. For some reason, the thought made me laugh.

"As ready as I'll ever be. Are you sure a blindfold is necessary?"

"Absolutely."

I turned around so he could tie the scarf Jane had loaned him across my eyes.

"Can you see?"

"I'm as blind as a bat."

We drove for about fifteen minutes before he stopped the car. When I reached up to remove the scarf, he pushed my hands away.

"Just a few more minutes."

Taking both my hands—most likely to keep me from removing the scarf—he helped me out of the car and led me forward. "There are three steps here. One, two—"

"You've blinded me, not taken away my ability to count."

I was so busy talking, I missed the third step and nearly went down.

"That's why we were counting," he said in a way that told me he was smirking. "We're almost there."

I heard the sound of a screen door opening, then he gently pulled me over the threshold and shut the door behind us. The smell of vanilla filled the air.

"Candles?"

"Take off your blindfold and see."

Candles of all shapes and sizes were spread throughout the open floor plan of a house I recognized as his grandparents', though I hadn't been inside for more than forty years. From the entryway you could see the spacious living room on the left and the large dining room on the right. An island bar separated the dining room from the kitchen beyond, and everywhere I looked there were more candles. The sparkling light was reflected in the beautiful oak flooring, which had been polished to a high gloss shine.

"It's . . . breathtaking."

"Just like you, Glory."

Blushing at the compliment, I turned to face him. But he wasn't standing—he was kneeling right behind me.

"I had this planned for last Saturday," said my big, strong cop, his voice sounding a little hoarse.

"The tap on Elsie's shoulder!" I clapped my hands. "I knew you two were up to something. That explains why she was acting so funny at work yesterday—"

"Glory?"

"Oh, sorry. I tend to ramble when I'm nervous or upset, or—"

Blue Eyes stood. "Glory Harper will you shut up for just one minute? Can't you see I'm trying to ask you to marry me?"

He looked stunned that the cat was out of the bag. It was enough to give me a fit of the giggles.

"Well?" He asked, his lips nearly touching mine.

"When you put it like that . . . "

And then he kissed me.

Mirrored Image

A. K. Arenz

A new mystery coming October 2010

Prologue

A dull ache near the center of her back accompanied the gradual return of consciousness. What had begun as a hot, searing pain was now a nondescript thudding, like an overactive pulse point.

Was this death—when the brain failed to send proper messages throughout the body? She tried to focus on her surroundings, to move, but her limbs remained frozen to the floor where she had fallen.

Memory shot through her, causing her to relive the shock and horror of the cold steel blade plunging into her flesh.

She closed her eyes and fought the vomit rising in her throat. She refused to be sick, would not allow such an indignity.

She knew she was dying, could feel her life force drain from her as the blood oozed from the wound in her back. Death held no fear for her; it would be a welcome release into the arms of friends waiting on the other side—friends who had not betrayed her.

Betrayal, treachery, and deceit. Ugly words for an even uglier deed that conjured images of the man who accepted thirty pieces of silver to deliver his Lord into the hands of His enemies.

Tears stung her eyes. Would heaven reject her because of the course she had chosen?

Anger and resentment flooded her. The rage grew, a primal instinct for survival urging her to take control and resist the darkness that threatened to descend. She had to make certain the person who had done this was punished.

She struggled to draw herself onto her elbows, refusing to acknowledge the increased pain and nausea accompanying the effort. She bit her lip, the coppery taste of blood filling her mouth and gagging her. Still she fought to maintain control, to hold herself upright.

Arms shaking, the pounding in her head nearly unbearable, she locked her weakened shoulders and elbows into place. If she could slide her body across the bare floor onto the carpet in the adjoining room, she could make it the rest of the way and reach the desk phone.

The unexpected sound of water running in the kitchen sent a shockwave of horror through her. Her elbows collapsed, and her face smashed against the tile with an explosion of pain.

"Dear God, no!"

Did she cry that aloud, or just plead it in silence?

The thought of that—that Judas in her house, in her kitchen, produced a previously unknown fury. Rallying, she again made the effort to rise, determined to conquer the threat of death.

The resolution was destroyed by the sound of footfalls reverberating against the tile floor. Gripped with terror, she quickly closed her eyes.

Let me die in peace.

As the footfalls halted a few feet from her head, she held her breath—how foolish that seemed when she would soon have no need to breathe. Lying motionless, she willed her heart to stop beating so loudly, her limbs and eyelids not to twitch. She felt "Judas" watching her, looking for telltale signs that she was alive.

Surely the spreading stain of blood would make it obvious her death was imminent.

After what seemed like hours, the sound of muffled footfalls on the carpet told her the Judas had moved to another part of the house. She opened her eyes and exhaled slowly, found that exhaling slowly was no longer so easy.

Somehow she had been separated, detached from the normal bounds of reality. In this strange state of consciousness, she could observe herself, yet *feel* nothing. A film descended over her eyes, a haze similar to looking through water.

This is it. No turning back, no second chances.

A gentle smile played about her full lips as a brilliant light seemed to cleave the darkness in two.

"Call me, child."

Was it possible? Was there still a chance?

"Father, forgive me!" came the cry from her heart.

The unmistakable sound of a vacuum cleaner was the last sound she heard. And, as her body pulled into a tight little ball, the intruder, like some deranged maid, mopped up the blood around her.

Monday 6:45 a.m.

The photo on the front page of the *Lakewood Journal's* morning edition was remarkably clear despite smudges left by the paper carrier. The woman's eyes were bright, her smile infectious. Her proud bearing, the tilt of her head, and small, squared-off chin gave the impression of stubbornness, while her short, curly hair and the way it fell about her face added an ethereal quality.

Dave Watson, editor-in-chief of the *Journal,* stared, mesmerized, at the picture, his freshly poured cup of coffee falling from his hand. He sank onto a nearby kitchen chair, oblivious of the mess he'd just made.

"Lynette Sandler."

He gulped, nearly choking, as he scanned the story beneath the banner headline.

CITY'S FIRST HOMOCIDE IN TWO YEARS—POLICE SEARCH FOR CLUES

"Thirty-seven year old Lynette Sandler was found murdered in her Lakewood Estates home early this morning after a neighbor reported seeing the front door of the home wide open. Mrs. Sandler—"

Watson dropped the newspaper onto the edge of the table. He became aware of the damp patch on his pants, but the sting of the hot coffee on the skin beneath hardly registered.

He grabbed his jacket and bolted out the door to his car. Pulling out of his driveway, he turned on the radio and switched from station to station to pick up all the news he could on the murder. He spotted a phone booth in an empty parking lot and started to pull over, then changed his mind. There would be plenty of time when he got to the office.

***

When Watson burst through the front doors of the *Journal,* Heidi Branscom watched him brush past the receptionist without a word. He scanned the spacious room that accommodated eight journalists and other personnel until his eyes came to rest on the small desk near the back of the room.

"She's not in yet."

Frowning, Watson transferred his gaze to Heidi. "Have you called?"

"I doubt she's back from that convention in Kansas City."

Watson grunted and strode into his office. Heidi fetched him a cup of coffee and joined him. She watched him load a cassette into the VCR as she placed the mug on his desk. The television screen reflected his stern expression.

"Gather all the information on Lynette Sandler you can find and have it ready for Cassie the moment she arrives."

"Very well." She was thankful he didn't seem to notice her slight hesitation.

"She can handle this story." He turned to her, expecting her agreement.

"She doesn't have the experience, but if you believe she's capable, that's all that matters."

As always, she told him what he wanted to hear. It didn't matter whether she agreed or not.

He switched on the TV, nodding in satisfaction as the mid-morning news came on. "This is the kind of serious journalism we've always wanted for her. Something to get her feet wet, to be proud of." He leaned forward, his eyes glued to the set. "Her columns are all right, but this will challenge her. We've been carrying her far too long; it's time she took responsibility for her future."

Though Heidi had heard this many times, she was certain he'd never shared his opinion with Cassie.

His face impassive, Watson drew his chair closer to the screen as the camera zoomed in for a close-up of the crime scene. "This is the biggest story to hit town in several years, and we're going to make the most of it."

He placed his elbows on his knees, chin in his hands. Without raising his eyes from the TV, he added, "You'd better get started. And tell Cassie I want to see her ASAP."

Heidi left the room, closing the door behind her. She knew it was useless to argue with him—especially when it came to Cassie. He always got what he wanted.

With one exception. The thing he wanted most was something he would never have.

With a look of satisfaction, she grabbed a new file folder and typed the name of the dead woman on the folder's tab. On its front she wrote in large black letters:

CASSANDRA CHASE

Chapter 1

"How do you pass the time while the highway patrol and wreckers clear the remains of a four car pile-up? Put on some music, turn up the volume, and relax the best you can in the space available in your car. And if the music is good enough, and you're lucky, time will fly by. It helps, of course, when the songs fit your mood. Attire is optional.

"In case your eyes wandered down the page and you started reading without looking at the column title, welcome to 'Cassie's Capers' where being retro is in and nostalgia the rage. My name is Cassandra Chase and, if you buckle those seat belts and batten down your hatches, I'll take you on an adventure bound to tickle your funny bone.

"Enough with the clichés. Let's get down to business!"

Cassie paused the tape, rolled down the window, and adjusted the outside mirror. Noticing the driver's expression in the car next to her, she grinned and received a peace sign in return. She examined herself in the rearview mirror, laughed, and rolled the window back up as she depressed the pause button on the tape recorder.

"I want to assure you that you weren't seeing things if you were stuck on the expressway at eight a.m. on Monday, April 21. You really did see a blonde in a lime-green Nehru jacket, a peace sign drawn on her left cheek, driving a crazy blue Bug. It wasn't your imagination.

"And why, you may ask, was I wearing those threads and sporting bona fide artwork on my face? Well, my friends, how else do you throw yourself into the 60's revolution? And what a way to prepare for a summer of concerts that your teeny bopper heart will flip over even if you're way past your teens! Prepare yourselves, dear readers, for a summer of love—a summer filled with stories on the resurgence of the era that changed the world. Prepare yourselves for the Monkees, Herman's Hermits, Rob Grill and The Grass Roots, and Gary Puckett!"

Pausing the tape once again, Cassie glanced down at her white bell-bottomed, hip-hugger pants accompanying black leather "go-go" boots, and the crowning glory, a necklace of "authentic" love beads that hung to her navel. Laughing again, she adjusted her blonde wig, then dabbed a little powder onto the peace sign.

"We won't be talking about Civil Rights marches or violent protests against the Vietnam War . . . not in my column, folks. We're going to take a lighter look at rock 'n' roll, and who better to star in this but the guys who were brought together for a TV show and turned into a cult classic that never died.

"Everyone knows about the Fab Four. They are legends. This columnist is going to take you on a summer journey with the Prefab Four—that's prefabricated for those of you who aren't hip. And if I'm very lucky, maybe I'll get the inside scoop on our faves Davy Jones, Peter Tork, and Micky Dolenz. Michael Nesmith has not yet committed to join the tour. And just for the record, folks—they really do play their own instruments."

Cassie punched the off button, rewound the tape, and listened to her column. Pushing the seat all the way back, she stretched her legs as far as the floorboard of her '73 Super Beetle allowed.

Satisfied, she shut off the recorder. "Maybe I'll run off and become a groupie."

Or try to make it to every one of the reunion shows playing in the tri-state region.

With the brilliant April sun baking the car as it sat motionless, the Bug had become hot and stuffy. She rolled down the window and drew in a deep breath. Coughing from a lungful of exhaust fumes, she hastily pulled her head back inside the car.

The Monkees' "Shades of Gray" ended and Gary Puckett's deep voice began "Woman." Cassie smiled at the thought of seeing all of them at the reunion concert.

"But I won't be wearing these threads."

She fiddled with the wide belt that dug into her hips. She couldn't wait to chuck the clothes in her locker and pull on a pair of jeans.

The traffic began to inch forward as the bottleneck cleared and traffic again flowed smoothly. She turned onto the State Avenue exit with relief and within fifteen minutes pulled her battered VW into her parking place outside the *Journal*. Grabbing the fringed leather shoulder bag she'd gotten from a fellow conventioneer, she checked her face paint, then hurried inside.

"Hi, Jill." She greeted the receptionist with a wink, twirling her love beads as she headed to her desk. An uncomfortable silence followed her as she made her way down the aisle.

"Do I look that bad?" she asked nobody in particular, scanning her co-workers' faces. Everyone deliberately avoided her gaze. She glanced down at her outfit.

"Come on, guys. Frank? Susan?" When the only response she received was shuffling papers, she focused on Martin Abrams, the sports editor. He'd always been attentive. A jock past his prime by a good ten years and thirty pounds, he was a nice man; easy prey for one of Cassie's smiles. She maneuvered across the room to his desk.

"Martin," she cooed, "is there something you'd like to tell me?"

Abrams cleared his throat and looked toward the Plexiglas windows of Watson's office. "Have you seen this morning's paper?" His voice rose barely above a whisper.

"I've only—"

The hairs on the back of her neck stood on end, and her smile tightened. She turned around to face Heidi.

"I see you're not wearing my present yet." Cassie saw Abrams hide a laugh behind his hand, suddenly entranced by whatever was on his terminal.

"What in heaven's name are you wearing?" Heidi scowled, her thin brows drawn together to form a straight line across her forehead. "Will you ever grow up, Cassandra?"

"I hope not." Cassie walked past the other woman and over to her desk. She threw her purse into an open drawer.

"Dave wants to see you," Heidi said with an exaggerated sigh. "Perhaps you should change fir—"

"Change? You've got to be kidding!" Cassie smoothed her jacket and, with a gleam in her eyes, brushed past Heidi and breezed into Watson's office.

Sinking into a chair, she placed a hand to her forehead. "It's a conspiracy. I've been sabotaged!"

"A little melodramatic, don't you think?" Watson gave her a weak smile. "That's some get-up. What happened to your hair?"

"It's a wig." She twisted a strand around her index finger. "Wanna tell me what's going on, David? Have I interrupted something clandestine, or has everyone suddenly gone crazy?"

"Cute." He swallowed a laugh. "Have you heard the local news?"

"Sure. I listened to the news on the way in. What's that got to do with my reception, or the fact someone's been in my desk?"

Settling back into the chair, she noted Watson's rumpled clothing. It wasn't like him to come to work looking as if he'd slept in his clothes.

"You okay?"

Ignoring her question, he turned to the television and popped a tape in the VCR. "I don't know anything about your desk. Anything missing?"

"Don't know. I just got here, remember?"

He nodded. "I'll check into it. Now, I want you to take a look at this."

Cassie watched the Newswatch team from the local station relate the latest information on the Lynette Sandler murder. The details of the gruesome crime shocked her.

"I want you to take particular note of this," Watson said as the camera zoomed in on a photo of the murder victim. He froze the tape on the close-up, then adjusted it frame by frame until the victim's features came into focus.

"There," he said, turning to Cassie.

She glanced at the screen, then back to Watson. "All right. What am I supposed to see—exactly?"

"You're kidding, right? That woman is the spitting image of you!"

"Well . . . " Cassie narrowed her eyes. "She's blonde and has blue eyes. There's a superficial resemblance, I suppose. Nothing out of the ordinary."

He shook his head, glaring at her. "So how was the convention?"

The swift change of subject made Cassie's head spin. "Um . . . great. Fantastic. Wonderful turn out." She eased back into the chair, studying him warily. "The interest in the reruns of the old Monkees' episodes is phenomenal. They've introduced a whole new generation to the Prefab Four." She grinned.

"And the outfit?"

"As much for your benefit as mine. What do you think?" She got up to model for him, slowly turning to allow him to get the full effect.

"It looks about as good today as it did twenty years ago."

"You don't have to be so sarcastic."

"Yeah, well, I was under the impression it was a Monkees convention, not a hippie reunion."

Cassie wrinkled her nose. "Ah, come on, David! I wanted to get into the mood, get a real feel for the time when all this was in fashion."

She wandered around the small office, picking up items, and then replacing them. As always, her eyes came to rest on the photos behind Watson's desk.

There was Harry, smiling out at her along with younger versions of Watson, her brother Danny, and Danny's wife, Galena. The pictures ranged from playful to serious to sad, all showing a part of the past that sometimes seemed too close to the present.

"It was a great weekend," she said.

"I'm glad you had a good time. Just make sure to check your dates when you get around to writing it up. In the meantime—"

"What do you mean 'when'?" Cassie eyed him with suspicion. "From the moment I came in here, I could tell something was up. Come on, David, spill it."

"You're right. I won't deny it."

The way he watched her made her skin crawl. By the time he turned back to the TV, her nerves were frazzled by the intensity of his stare. It didn't take a genius to see where all this was heading.

"Not only is this the first murder Lakewood has had in years, the victim happens to look remarkably like one of the city's most celebrated columnists. Which is why you're going to be the one to write about it."